A COLLECTION

OF BEAUTIES

AT THE

HEIGHT OF

THEIR

POPULARITY

RANDOM HOUSE | NEW YORK

whitney otto

a COLLECTION

OF *beauties*

AT THE

height OF

THEIR

popularity

a novel

All rights reserved under International and Pan-American Copyright Conventions. Published in the United States by Random House, Inc., New York, and simultaneously in Canada by Random House of Canada Limited, Toronto.

RANDOM HOUSE and colophon are registered trademarks of Random House, Inc.

Grateful acknowledgment is made to Farrar, Straus and Giroux, LLC, for permission to reprint "One Art," from *The Complete Poems, 1927–1979*, by Elizabeth Bishop. Copyright © 1979, 1983 by Alice Helen Methfessel. Reprinted by permission of Farrar, Straus and Giroux, LLC.

LIBRARY OF CONGRESS CATALOGING-IN-PUBLICATION DATA

Otto, Whitney.
A collection of beauties at the height of their popularity : a novel / Whitney Otto.
p. cm.
ISBN 0-375-50545-8 (acid-free paper)
1. Young adults—Fiction. 2. San Francisco (Calif.)—Fiction. 3. Bars (Drinking establishments)—Fiction. I. Title.

PS3565.T795 C65 2002
813'.54—dc21   2001041908

Random House website address: www.atrandom.com

Printed in the United States of America on acid-free paper

9 8 7 6 5 4 3 2

FIRST EDITION

Book design by Barbara M. Bachman

For Sam

Living only for the moment, turning our full attention to the pleasures of the moon, sun, the cherry blossoms and the maple leaves, singing songs, drinking wine, and diverting ourselves just in floating, floating, caring not a whit for the pauperism staring us in the face, refusing to be disheartened, like a gourd floating along with the river current: this is what we call the Floating World (ukiyo).

—ASAI RYOI, TALES OF THE FLOATING WORLD
   (Osaka writer, seventeenth century)

February 12, 1951

[On her novel *The Wicked Pavilion*]
It is vital that this place—the Pavilion, where people wait for some solution—is actually set in 1947, when people waited. The war was over, but nothing was settled. This is a novel of the desperation and ruthlessness of peace.

—DAWN POWELL, THE DIARIES OF DAWN POWELL
   (American writer, twentieth century)

an eighteenth-century table of contents

::

A COLLECTION

OF BEAUTIES

AT THE

HEIGHT OF

THEIR

POPULARITY

. . . entrance . . .

By four-thirty the young woman with pilfered stationery, a thick, inexpensive notebook, and a fountain pen has seated herself at the table that affords the best view of the comings and goings of the patrons of the Youki Singe Tea Room. The place is fairly empty now, in these languorous moments that fall between the end of the workday and the beginning of nightlife. This is fine; she needs to orient herself between the two worlds—the working world and the leisure world—with a further adjustment regarding her life as an observer as well as that of participant. There are two forms of writing before her (letters to a lover on the stolen stationery, a pillow book in the guise of a note-book). What someone once called "the daylight mind and the night mind."

The Youki Singe Tea Room in San Francisco has been a North Beach fixture "for about a million years," as Coco said. It had entertained Italian immigrants in the teens and rich, slumming girls in the twenties, nearly folded in the thirties, revived in the forties, and, upon an American victory in two theaters of a single war, become populated with Beats by the fifties. Closely followed by the Love Generation, it was shunned by the Disco Generation since the place lacked any aspect that was slick or shiny, sparkling or loud. It was during that period that the Youki Singe Tea Room came dangerously close to metamorphosing into a bar bar. A barfly bar. A place with longshoremen and bold women, a place that, in truth, was more or less a return to its slightly rough and oddly adorned beginnings.

Its decor is an eccentric combination of Japanese (*youki*, meaning snow) and French (*singe*, meaning monkey), with no one mistaking the entire effect as anything close to *japonais*. This jumble of styles was actually the result of the taste of a single individual, someone who appeared to delight in things Japanese and French, without a coherent idea of what either meant.

These kitsch clichés and genuinely lovely elements, as the young woman had written in her pillow book notebook, included gorgeous mahogany walls, worn and burnished like the walls of an elegant men's club in some colonial city; Japanese paper lanterns that strung together myriad reproductions of Edo (old Tokyo), Osaka, Nagasaki, Mount Fuji, Nijo Castle in Kyoto, a dry landscape garden, and Tokaido, one of the main roads that led out of Edo.

Then there were Eiffel Towers that lit up, or were situated in little snow globes, or made of brass. Some of these were clustered like a shrine on shelves, while others sat on random tables. Sock monkeys wore berets and sat near a very beautifully written quote etched on glass that read *Monkeys are only three hairs from being human.* An old Japanese saying.

The stretch of wall above the paneling but below the portrait molding was covered in expensive, honey-colored grass paper, with an occasional picture of Lautrec's Jane Avril hastily tacked over it. An element of the famous Lapin Agile made an appearance in the form of painted mirrors that were improved by the marks of age, placed behind the bar. And obis were randomly strung like streamers from the ceiling. A little Art Nouveau accent to the tables harmonized with the faintly Asian black lacquer chairs and their now discolored silk cushions.

Now if you went to the back, you would find a sign pointing up toward the top of a narrow stairway. The sign says CITÉ FALGUIÈRE, though it has nothing to do with what you will find on the landing. (The young woman casually looked up the meaning of the words on the sign and discovered that they referred to the place the artist Tsuguharu Foujita lived in Paris.) What you will find is a sign pointing to the unisex bathroom as well as a wall of heavy velvet curtains, falling from a remnant of an iron Métro entrance.

A man sits to the right of the curtains, his eyes meet yours, then he draws the drapes aside to reveal a small theater that stages very spare, live sex shows. Man to woman, girl on girl. Once, the young woman stopped on her way to the bathroom and was shown another young woman clad in nothing but a cowboy hat, holster, and boots high-kicking to an Elton John song. Then, as always, the man drops the curtain, tells you the price of admission.

Downstairs is an archway of enameled cherry blossoms, beautifully arrayed and polished, forming an informal arch above the front door. The cherry blossoms are repeated, in unexpected ways, throughout the café, sometimes carved into wood, sandblasted onto glass, or rendered in silk and artlessly arranged in a bottle.

Perhaps the most remarkable feature of the place is a small, enclosed room in one corner of the café. It is scarcely larger than a walk-in closet, with a low opening that one has to crawl through. A sign that reads THE WAY OF TEA sits propped up beside the room. And painted over the opening, rubbed off here and there, are the words *Leave your sword outside with your worldly concerns.* The original owner of the Youki Singe had been impressed by the rough elegance of a modest sixteenth-century teahouse (little more than a hut, really) that he had once read about. He liked the part that said with such limited space, intimacy follows and one's actions become, involuntarily, the actions of all within.

Of course, the only tea that ever made its way into this teahouse was grass. Everyone loved the joke and few realized that it wasn't the intention of the little private room. Even fewer cared.

So, the eighties arrived and the Youki Singe Tea Room continued its life of improvement and decay, its clientele as transitional as the bar itself, prompting talk among those in power that it should be either declared a historic landmark (in effect, rescued) or razed to the ground.

::

NOW THE YOUNG WOMAN, whose name is Elodie Parker, jots down a title heading, *When I Make Myself Imagine,* on a fresh page in her pillow book, a distinctly Japanese construction of informal literature over a thousand years old. Pillow books were often filled with the miscellany of daily life in the ancient imperial courts of Japan. Elodie models her diary on a famous tenth-century pillow book penned by a lady-in-waiting: She borrows the lady's titles and quotes, incorporating them into her own record of the vignettes, the lives that intersect her life.

Elodie lights another cigarette. The ink from her fountain pen stains her fingers as she writes:

When I Make Myself Imagine

MY CURRENT POSITION ON LOVE could best be illustrated by the temporary tattoo on the inside of my upper thigh. It is tiny, with the first initial of my sweetheart placed on top of a Japanese *inochi* ideograph. *Inochi* means life. In seventeenth-century Japan it was the tattoo of a lover, it meant that you loved that person longer than life, or more than life. The length of the tail of the symbol represented the length of that love.

I read that it was not uncommon for some priests and acolytes to mark themselves with the same lover tattoo, *inochi*. Not surprisingly, since all these impulses of love seem the same to me, really.

⠶

ELODIE'S TATTOO HAD a tail long and slender, the width of thread. Her flesh the color of the moon.

This perfect mark, limned in ink, but not yet beneath the skin. This drawing, this word, this statement of intent, this prelude to a kiss.

Distressing Things

THE BEAUTY OF A BOOK is that if you are patient and thoughtful, it will come to you. Something can seem so remote at one point in your life, and so close and clear at another. When I was sixteen, someone gave me a novel called *The Wicked Pavilion* that I did not much care for. It began with a writer walking into a café where the bartender kept his unfinished manuscript in a space behind the bar. The writer wrote about the people he knew and the time in which he lived, things like

It was an old man's decade.

In the city the elements themselves were money: air was money, fire was money, water was money, the need of, the quest for, the greed for. Love was money. There was money or death.

and

There must be someplace along the route, a halfway house in time where the runners may pause and ask themselves why they run, what is the prize and is it the prize they really want?

Now I find myself well into my twenties, living the way I live (that is to say, on the social outskirts) in San Francisco, in the early 1980s, never realizing at sixteen how well I would come to know this story: witnessing the race, understanding completely the way in which air can be money.

Things That Are Not Easily Evident

BETWEEN THE EXTREMES of street poverty and riches, there are people like me. In the margins. Drifting, drifting, living, as Asai Ryoi says, "only for the moment; turning our full attention to the pleasures of the moon . . . diverting ourselves in floating, floating . . . refusing to be disheartened."

I discovered that you can refuse something and still it stays with you.

The Patrons of the Youki Singe Tea Room

THE YOUKI SINGE TEA ROOM is frequented by those of us out of college by a handful of years, not yet settled, who live in studio apartments so small that even a modest dinner party is out of the question. The Youki Singe, then, becomes an extension of our homes. It is a place to see friends, to laugh, to drink, to smoke, to change partners. To live in the moment.

::

ELODIE GAZES AROUND the room, growing soft with the shadows of the coming night. She catches the eye of Jelly, who sits with Coco and a man Elodie doesn't recognize. There is something wonderful, she believes, about apartments that push their tenants into places like the Youki Singe. She likes places where people play out their lives in public, leaving Elodie to speculate, or to hear quiet accounts, of their lives in private; people seldom realize that the line between public and personal is fine and frequently crossed, but only if someone (someone like Elodie, for example) is paying attention.

She continues:

Elegant Things

A GIRL NAMED JELLY, whose given name is Gillian, though no one calls her that since Jelly suits her absolutely. She is with a revolving group of men, or in the company of very pretty girls.

Surprising and Distressing Things

UNLIKELY PEOPLE INVOLVED WITH pot or cocaine, provided by Roy, a purveyor of "artificial paradises," who is neither sinister nor extraordinary in any way. Odd to think he is such a sunny fellow with smart girlfriends.

Pleasing Things

"SOMEONE HAS TORN UP a letter and thrown it away. Picking up the pieces one finds that many of them can be fitted together." This was in the lady's pillow book, but I would say it describes the love between Lucy and Sal.

People Who Have Changed as Much as If They Are Reborn

SUZANNE, BY WAY OF HER INVOLVEMENT with Micha, though she cannot yet see it. And Micha had begun his own transformation prior to meeting Suzanne.

Also, the lucky in love.

Outstandingly Splendid Things

RAPHAELLA'S VOICE.

::

ELODIE CHECKS HER WATCH, stubs out the cigarette, begins to gather her things to leave. She has someone to meet, someplace else. She hands her stationery and her pillow book with its impressions of things around her, tied in a folder, to the man behind the bar. He keeps her papers for her until the next time she comes in.

As she passes through the front door, she brushes up against two young women, Theo Adagio and Gracie Maruyama, who say hello but are clearly preoccupied; they do not stop to talk though all the girls know one another. This causes Elodie to turn and look back through the window as they make their way to a table where a third young woman sits.

a story of love on the veranda

SUZUKI HARUNOBU
(1767–1768)

::

*This is a story of entangled love. The figure on the
right is a young man, and the woman whispering in
his ear is the go-between or emissary for her mistress,
who is as young as the man. The mistress watches
from a crack in the screen behind the couple on the
veranda. However, it is the way in which the whispering woman wraps her hand around the wrist of
the young man (the young man who does not draw
away) that suggests she may want him for herself.*

T HAT'S THE THING ABOUT THE YOUKI SINGE: YOU CAN ALMOST always count on running into someone you know. Why just this evening Theo Adagio and Gracie Maruyama literally bumped into Elodie Parker as she was leaving the café.

They have known Elodie for about three years, but their own friendship goes all the way back to kindergarten. It then flourished for the rest of elementary school, weathered time spent in separate middle schools, became revitalized when they found themselves attending the same high school. They went on to different universities on opposite ends of California, from which they graduated, and discovered they each longed to live in San Francisco. Currently they are happily settled as roommates in a moderately run-down, generously proportioned flat in the avenues.

So many nights begin this way, with Theo and Gracie walking quickly up Columbus Avenue after another uninspired day at their Financial District office jobs. While it is not their intention to stay at the Youki Singe for dinner, chances are they will end up dining on doughy gyoza and bland onion soup as the evening quietly slips away unnoticed. The limited menu also offers a truly terrible Welsh rarebit.

"Why do you even sell it?" Theo once asked the bartender.

"Because the owner read that it was a favorite of American expatriates in Paris who used to dine at La Coupole in the twenties."

"Can it still be considered an expatriate dish if it is served here? I mean, we're all pretty well patriated here. Unfortunately." Theo suffers from daydreams of a life in foreign places.

The bartender cleared away some glasses. "No one ever orders it anyway. Would you?"

Of course not. No one would. Not with all the aerobic hours required to counter a single serving of the stuff. Such is the romance of Paris.

It was never the food that brought customers into the Youki Singe Tea Room: it was the alcohol and the permissive atmosphere and the way it did not try to be anything other than what it was. It was the expensive studios that were too small for the social life the Youki Singe offered; it was the absence of family. It was the promise that each evening held. Though tonight they are here to see a German woman named Margot Mueller.

::

"YOU KNOW, GRACE, I don't really need to be here. I barely know Margot. We don't mean anything to each other," complains Theo. "She's really Roy's friend."

Roy and Gracie have known each other since college; Theo is acquainted with him by way of Gracie. Margot is Roy's latest flame.

"That is why I appreciate your company," says Gracie, firmly taking hold of Theo's elbow as if she might bolt before they arrive at Margot's table.

Margot Mueller's clothes are a tragic combination of current fashion favoring denim and lace. Her slightly dirty hair is tied back with what appears to be a kneesock. One hand grips her black-rimmed eyeglasses while the other holds a wet clump that used to be a cocktail napkin. But more striking than Margot's clothes is her facial expression: brokenhearted, baffled, lost. Her face makes Theo want to pull back.

"I hate this," whispers Theo. "I'm the wrong person for this."

"Sweetie," says Gracie when they arrive at Margot's table; Margot already on her unsteady feet and collapsing, crying into Gracie's arms.

::

"I KNOW HE'S NOT MY LIFE or anything like that," Margot Mueller says in a slight German accent that is altogether sexier than the girl herself.

Margot blows her nose into the useless napkin. Without interrupting her, Gracie slides the napkin from under her own glass, deftly exchanging it for the sopping mess in Margot's fist. "But he *felt* like my life. You know? He felt—he feels so—*fundamental*," she says.

"What exactly did he say?" asks Gracie. Her hand upon Margot's shoulder rests as lightly as a breath.

Margot ignores her question. "He's not worth this—" She throws her arms wide as if to gather up the growing crowd in the Youki Singe in her empty embrace. "He's really not. My God, it is so embarrassing. To behave this way publicly." Margot turns to Theo, demanding, "How could I stay in that apartment, *our* apartment? How? Oh, let them stare." She fumbles for her bag on the floor, extracts a pack of cigarettes with matches tucked into the cellophane, lights the cigarette.

Of course, no one is watching. This is such an old, old story that even if the people in the Youki Singe knew the particulars of Margot's misery, it wouldn't cause so much as a brief interruption in their own thoughts or conversations.

Theo thinks how usual all this is: the defeated posture, the unfocused, red eyes, the preoccupation, the dazed aspect, the general brokenness. The shift of love. The failure of love. Then watches Gracie in all her kindness, thinking, She is so good. Theo's thoughts work themselves to Roy. Then Theo is again considering Margot, surprised to find that what she does feel is guilt.

"Everyone's been through this, right?" asks Margot. "Right, Theo?"

::

IT WAS LONG AGO when Theo won the heart of Gracie's first boyfriend. They were fourteen; Gracie was crazy about him; Theo didn't consider him one way or the other. Then, without warning, he withdrew his affections from Gracie, leaving her bereft.

Theo, with the conviction of a crusader fighting for the meek, confronted the boy. Why, she demanded, did he walk away from Gracie? What did he want anyway?

"Well," he said thoughtfully, "I like someone with cool clothes."

His answer was so unexpected that it immediately disarmed Theo. As his unabashed, sincere shallowness brought her up short, curiosity overtook righteousness.

"Oh," she said, "like who, for example?"

"Debbie Dean dresses cool."

Debbie Dean's indisputable homeliness drove her mother to spend irrational sums on her daughter's wardrobe in an effort to correct nature. Because her mother had such disregard toward reality, not to mention a predilection for snobbery, and Debbie's personality left much to be desired as well, Theo had supposed this was all evident to the boy.

"And she can't be taller than me," he continued.

"Anything else?" asked Theo.

"I like someone who makes me laugh," he said. "Someone like you."

Theo could feel her face warm to the unexpected thrill of attention. "I make you laugh?"

"I like you."

"But you can't," she said. "You really can't."

::

IT HAD NOT BEEN EASY to tell Gracie that the boy now liked Theo and that Theo (she was sorry) liked him back. Theo could barely tolerate the sound of her own words as they came hurriedly from her mouth. Still she was powerless to reverse these events. Gracie tried solemnly to follow what Theo was telling her, could see her trying to sort out loyalties. Theo unable to explain that her inexperience was so complete she could knowingly do a wrong thing because the magnetism of this boy—or maybe it was the compelling quality of the situation—overrode everything.

This boy, Theo wanted to say, held out a sense of possibility to her. Surely you can see that, said Theo, you of all people.

And, much later in her life, when Theo thought back on this conversation, she would add what she could not then articulate: You of all people, who fell as easily for him as I am falling now . . .

::

MARGOT IS AGAIN curled up in Gracie's arms. Gracie soothing *there there* as she leans her cheek into Margot's undone hair. Theo knows that she would not be as comforting, as natural, as warm. No closeness. No intimacy. There was a time when Theo had been jilted by someone she thought she loved and ended up following Gracie around for three days. When Gracie went to work, Theo called in sick and then went to Gracie's office. If Gracie went to the dry cleaner's, so did Theo. They spoke very little during this episode; the nearness of Gracie was comfort enough. Even at night, Theo crawled into bed with her.

Theo is wondering what it is like to be Gracie. Now, though she is not the brokenhearted one, Theo still responds to Gracie's whispered promise that everything will be all right. It will be all right.

::

"LAST MONTH," SAYS MARGOT, "for my birthday, Roy decorated the entire apartment with blue balloons. Everywhere. On the ceiling and blinds and our coats hung on their hooks. Even the dog had one attached to her collar. The cat was obviously less willing to participate since her collar balloon was a ripped piece of rubber hanging from her neck. And he made a blue dinner and a blue cake. He played blues on the stereo."

"What would constitute a blue dinner?" asks Theo.

Margot continues, "And I thought, What a funny guy. Does he plan this stuff or does it occur to him as he walks home from work?"

"Does it matter?" asks Gracie, pushing back strands of Margot's hair that have worked themselves free of the sock. She tucks them behind Margot's ears, which are a little large and jutting.

"It matters," says Margot emphatically, "because it changes everything if he planned it. It tells me who he does it for."

"Who else would he be doing it for if he's not doing it for you?" asks Theo, confused.

"Himself," says Margot.

::

ROY, IT TURNED OUT, was seeing someone else. That is what Margot says the following night at a Chinese restaurant so cavernous that polite conversation was close to impossible.

"Is that what he told you?" asks Gracie.

"It is what I know," says Margot, playing with her food using a pair of chopsticks until she tosses them on her plate, shoving everything away.

Ah, the Heartbreak Diet, observes Theo. It leaves you looking lousy in every respect except for your weight. And you feel as awful as you look; if you look starved, you also look starved for affection.

"Is this intuition or something more concrete than that?" asks Theo. This conversation is rendering her a little breathless.

"It's definite."

"Are you sure?" asks Theo.

"Yes. I'm awfully, horribly fucking sure." Margot's hand goes to her mouth. "I don't know what to do," she says softly.

"You still keep your studio, don't you?" asks Theo slowly. "You have another place."

"Oh, what difference does that make?" cries Margot.

"Listen," says Gracie, "I've known Roy practically half my life. Things will work out. He's just confused right now. That's all. It happens, you know."

"Have you talked to him? What did he say?"

"Actually, I didn't talk to him," says Gracie. "He called the other night and Theo"—Gracie gestures toward her—"he was talking to you, wasn't he?"

Margot turns to Theo.

"He really didn't say much of anything," mumbles Theo, but it doesn't seem to matter because Gracie continues, "No, look, I'm simply saying that this sounds exactly like Roy. I'm sure he'll come around. He gets restless and distracted, that's all." Gracie scratches her chair back to face Margot, pulling Margot's chair toward her. Margot's expression is unsettled, as if turning over what Gracie has just said.

Theo can imagine Margot's thoughts:

1. Is Gracie saying that this is how Roy treats his girls, thereby placing her as one of many, indistinguishable from all who came before?

2. Does he confide in Gracie (or is it Theo) things he will not say to her, his beloved?
3. Considering the first two things, what does it mean to be Roy's beloved?

Now Gracie is saying, "I think the three of us—you, me, and Theo—should embark on a little camping trip. Why not? We can go up around Mendocino, say. Or wherever we like. The gold country? We can play it by ear."

Margot is listening without listening. Theo cuts in. "Gracie, I'm not sure I can—"

Gracie cuts her off. "Wherever we want. You can get a clear head about all of this and, maybe, by the time we return, Roy will have come to his senses." Gracie's hands hold Margot's. "You might not even want him anymore."

"Why don't you two go wi—" Theo says, with Gracie silencing her with a glance.

"What do you think? Maybe things will be different."

Margot laughs ruefully. "Oh, like Roy will remember that he loves me?"

Gracie laughs. "Yeah. Something like that."

::

"WHY DO YOU INVOLVE ME?" asks Theo of Gracie as they walk toward the bus stop, illuminated by the summer moonlight.

::

SOMEHOW, THEO INHERITS MARGOT. She sits beside her at the movies (Margot's love-scattered mind is incapable of following any plot, and she often asks Theo to explain it, irritating Theo and everyone around them); sharing meals that only Theo eats; dancing in clubs (though neither is a particularly good dancer). All the while Theo is spinning endless theories regarding Roy's behavior (though Margot still sees him every morning across the kitchen table).

Gracie, busy planning their camping trip, presses Theo to keep company with Margot, saying, You be my emissary.

::

THE SUMMER DAY IS SO RARE in its beauty that when Theo climbs the inside stairs of the second-floor flat she shares with Gracie, she does not think to call out to her. Who could remain inside on such a day? When Theo reaches the landing, she notices a man's jacket casually tossed over the banister. In the kitchen are two empty cups and a tea bag, wet and crushed near one of the saucers. Cigarette butts mingle with the roachlike remains of a pair of joints. And still Theo does not call out Gracie's name.

Instead, she walks over to the bay window in the dining room, searching up and down their street until she finds what she is seeking: a 1959 black Hillman Minx. No one owned a Hillman Minx except Roy. The car was as distinctive as a fingerprint.

She turns to walk down the hallway to her bedroom, only to see that Gracie's bedroom door is closed. Without taking another step, Theo collects her thoughts, then turns around, walks back down the stairs, leaving as silently as she entered, out onto the street lit by the exquisite day. She tells herself that Roy and Gracie, old friends, are at the movies, strolling the Japanese Garden and the arboretum. Taking a carriage ride, renting a paddleboat at Stow Lake. Trying to lure the buffalo that live in a paddock in the park to come a little closer.

Then Margot comes to mind and the impending camping trip. Thinking of all the time Theo has unwillingly (ungraciously also comes to mind) spent with her. As Gracie edges back into Theo's thoughts, she thinks, *How could she?* then wonders if she means Gracie's treatment of Margot or Gracie's treatment of *her*. And Margot being Gracie's friend. Although it is really Roy who is Gracie's friend and Margot simply came along by way of Roy, so what does that make Margot with regard to Gracie?

Now Theo's distance from Margot is considerably decreased and she feels the discomfort of conflicted loyalties. They weren't even friends until Gracie thoughtlessly pushed Margot toward Theo these past couple of weeks.

Unless it wasn't thoughtless.

She remembers saying good night to Margot the other night on the phone and Margot saying, with all the faith of friendship, "Theo, you have been so good to me."

Theo closes her eyes.

::

IT IS MUCH LATER when Theo returns. She bangs the front door shut, steps heavily on the stairs. She can hear Gracie on the phone. All traces of Roy have now vanished. Gracie catches Theo's eye, mouths "Margot," agrees with something said on the other end of the line, nods, then says, "It'll be fun. Promise." She hangs up.

"I told Margot we'll leave on Friday, after work."

"For what?" asks Theo.

"The camping trip."

"Oh. The camping trip."

Gracie heads for the kitchen, with Theo behind her. Gracie takes leftovers from the fridge, pans from the bottom drawer of the old stove, and begins dumping the contents from various containers.

Gracie stops to light a cigarette.

"You know," says Theo, "you two could go without me."

"What would I say to Margot? You're just as much her friend as I am." Gracie adjusts the temperature on the oven. "I thought I'd make some biscuits. They don't really belong with anything else we're having tonight, but I'm in the mood."

"That sounds fine."

"Margot will be all right."

Theo says nothing. She lights a cigarette of her own, stubs it out by the second puff. "So, what did you do today?" she asks, trying to control the tone and cadence of the question.

Gracie, engrossed in measuring and mixing the biscuit batter, as well as stirring the heating leftovers, says, "I had a real lazy day. I didn't do a damn thing."

"Were you by yourself?"

"As a matter of fact, I was."

Gracie looks up at Theo. And that is how they end the day: with Theo watching Gracie watching her.

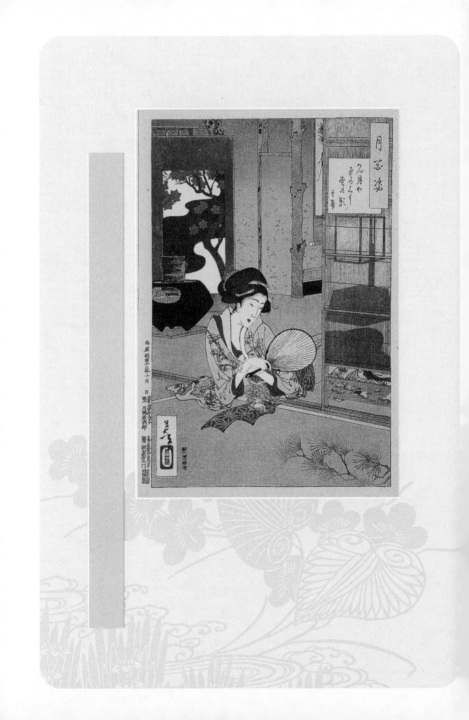

twelve hours in the yoshiwara

(A SERIES BY KITAGAWA UTAMARO)

From roughly 1615 to 1868 was a period in Japan
known as Tokugawa (named for fifteen generations
of shoguns), or Edo, the city from which the sho-
gunate ruled. These two hundred and fifty years
were a time of national isolation, and peace, and
a flourishing of the arts, and of pleasure.

Each large city in Japan had Kabuki theaters
and pleasure quarters, attracting patrons and artists
alike. In Edo, each direction offered pleasure quarters
with their own sexual distinctions, but it was the
Yoshiwara, to the north, near Nihonbashi Bridge and
not too far from Edo Castle, that proved most popular
with the city's elite. Often referred to as the Nightless
Castle, it housed geishas and courtesans—it was a
place where "money and taste mattered more than
social status and the government's efforts to enforce
a linear culture was most seriously compromised"
(Christine Guth, Art of Edo Japan).

It burned to the ground in 1657 but was quickly rebuilt as Shin (New) Yoshiwara.

Since not everyone could afford the entertainments of Shin Yoshiwara, there rose a demand for pictures, books, and prints of the fashionable life within its gates, the women in particular.

The eighteenth-century artist Kitagawa Utamaro devoted himself to the portrayal of the bijinga ("beautiful women") who lived and worked in these places: he captured them bathing, combing their hair, working in the kitchen, primping, smoking, reading, writing letters, flirting, resting, playing music. They behave shamelessly, wantonly, drunkenly. They wait.

What he did not show (what no one wants to see or know in this floating world of pleasure) were the tough realities of labor in such a glittering, glamourous place; these working girls.

This picture is by the nineteenth-century artist Yoshitoshi and is part of a series titled "One Hundred Aspects of the Moon." The moon is present in each of the one hundred prints, which are in no other way connected. Here, a woman holds a moon-shaped fan; the woman's beauty will fade as the moon fades.

The poem on the picture was written by the seventeenth-century poet Basho, who was once asked by a man so rich he bought all of Yoshiwara's brothels, twice, for an entire night, to compose a poem "so touching that heaven will be moved to send rain," ending a drought.

The woman's eighteenth-century hairstyle and posture are said to be an homage to Kitagawa Utamaro.

MORNING—AND ROY'S "mornings" can begin when it is no longer morning—is not Roy's best time of day. His movements are a little slow, a little tentative, as if he has somehow turned fragile in the course of his dreams. His nights find him electrified and rambunctious, talking so continuously that his throat feels raw when he awakens. He spends his days exhausted, worn, challenged by the need to concentrate. It is well that he seldom drives his 1959 Hillman Minx during the day.

"Why don't we just drag Roy's lazy ass out of bed," says Theo, stubbing out her cigarette.

The girls have been waiting on Roy for the better part of the day; by now they should be at a party—a barbecue—at a friend's house, though considering the guests that will attend, it is quite possible the party began last night.

Gracie and Theo have already been to lunch at the Vietnamese place on Clement Street, where they dined on spring rolls, licking the grease from their fingers; bought a pair of earrings made from antique Japanese buttons called *satsuma* (Theo); cigarettes (Gracie); and are now sitting in the kitchen of their Ninth Avenue flat, located next to Golden Gate Park.

Gracie Maruyama has been Roy's girlfriend for the past month, following a lengthy prologue of friendship (and a woman named Margot Mueller), and so is accustomed to his daytime lethargy. Familiarity has also made her immune to his questionable hygiene habits, such as infrequent bathing, spitting in the shower in the morning (whether she is in there with him or not), or tossing his discarded pieces of clothing in the air, inhaling their scent as they flutter down and settle on his face.

She was used to his tasteless trinkets of love: dull pearls that had belonged to his mother, an acceptable blouse ruined by cheap fabric, a sawdust-filled bear, an inexpensive ruby ring, plastic hair clips set with rhinestones. He simply didn't know the difference between the quality of one thing or the other. He wrapped each treasure carefully, handing them to Gracie with a sweet shyness that never failed to touch her. As the gifts accumulated on her dresser, they came to resemble a makeshift shrine of articles that were almost the right things.

To please him, she wore the pearls when they went out and, occasionally, the ruby ring, but drew the line at the blouse, which, she said, didn't fit her properly.

She and Theo often speculated on the origins of these gifts ("Do you think he really doesn't know?" asked Theo), yet during the course of her love affair with Roy, Gracie always held them dear.

As for the affair itself, Gracie was entertained by Roy's social and drug-influenced energy, his perpetual good spirits. The downside was his hungover mornings.

::

THE PHONE RINGS. "Save me!" says Coco, laughing. She is calling from the party, wondering when Gracie and Theo are arriving. Theo explains the Roy situation, then says, "Hold on a minute," as she watches Gracie drag her inefficient and ridiculously loud vacuum cleaner into her bedroom.

Theo hears her vacuuming the hardwood floor around the bed with still, sleeping Roy, the plastic wheels scratching along the planks, along with a variety of suction sounds. "I'm hanging up now," Coco yells into the phone as Gracie turns the vacuum cleaner off.

Gracie laughs as she drops into a chair at the kitchen table, says, "Oh my God, he didn't even stir. I can't believe I'm seeing this guy."

"Maybe he's dead," offers Theo.

"No," says Gracie, lighting a cigarette.

"How can you tell?"

"Well," says Gracie, exhaling the smoke, "he just performed a certain body function—"

"Stop!" cries Theo. "This is the sort of information you must keep between yourselves."

"In any case, we can conclude he is among the living."

On the word *living* Roy appears in the kitchen doorway, clothes and flesh rumpled, with his thinning hair neatly combed, and his face breaking into a smile of such pure delight at the sight of Gracie. Gracie smiles back, says lovingly, "You do make your very skin looked slept in."

"It's a gift," he replies. "Are we ready?"

Second Hour

THE HOUSE IS a forgettable multilevel affair that, if you were blind-folded while driving to it and had the blindfold removed upon arrival, you would never know was located in San Francisco, just a few miles from downtown. Even more surprising than its bland, contemporary architecture is the fact that it is one of a number of nearly identical structures in a housing tract. None of that picturesque painted-ladies Victorian style here; this just looks like anywhere.

The interior (four bdrm, two FB, garage, family room) reflects the personality and recent events of the owner—a newly separated man in his mid-thirties who was left with unwanted furniture, one or two pictures on the wall, all of it rather shabby and ignored. It is the home of a bachelor, but one who is unused to this state of being.

He says wistfully of his wife, "She was my high school sweet-heart." They had married young, had a daughter, then found them-selves in a marital limbo that made him silent in the evenings and his wife inspired to return to college for a double major in business and psychology. "The clearest manifestation of her intention to leave me" is how he tells it. This is not said with the least trace of wistfulness.

There is a deck with an uncared-for hot tub, along with a partial, almost accidentally romantic view of the city.

All in all, it is the perfect place for the parties that occur here, week after week. Month after month.

::

IT IS CLOSE TO six when Gracie, Theo, and Roy let themselves into the always unlocked door. Gracie has dated a fair number of the male guests; all of them are well-disposed toward her, for she is unfail-ingly generous toward them, though it is known that she is Roy's girl these days. That said, the truth is no one pines for anyone. All arrangements and previous arrangements are far too casual to pro-voke unhappiness or longing. When it is accepted that all things have a course to run, then it is very easy to like each other tremen-dously.

As the three wander out onto the deck, a palpable thrill runs a swift, excited circuit through the other guests. Roy is the procurer of "product," and no party fully swings until he shows up with his pock-ets of drugs. One by one, each man will arise from where he sits to follow Roy to a back bedroom where Roy will lay out his wares. Money will be exchanged, joints rolled and lit, cocaine sniffed.

This is no teenage experimentation; these men are in their very late twenties, early thirties (Roy is almost thirty-four), with profes-sions that pay reasonably well and job responsibilities. They have university educations. But their homes are modest, often rented and unkempt; their clothes are plain; their cars, once wonderful and new, are now a little sorry and eccentric, like Roy's Hillman Minx or someone else's Morris Minor. On the surface they can still give the impression of being on their way, not in a hurry, but still headed somewhere.

Roy has one more item in yet another pocket; something a few of the men will request later. They will smoke small amounts of the heroin on bits of tinfoil; little quantities used with regularity, not every day, yet with a consistency that alarms none of them. Maybe it is the lack of needles, or the amount, or the nondaily use, though all of them, without exception, will one day find themselves in ruin over this drug. Not now, not today, but later, in the not-too-distant future.

Today there is the wonderful aroma of Thai stick and sugary streaks of coke, cut and snorted from the glass that protects a photograph of the host's twelve-year-old daughter.

As each guest returns from his visit with Roy, the party grows louder and friendlier, less guarded. No one is actually having a conversation as much as he is waiting for his turn to speak, happily and without connection to anything preceding his turn. As Coco observes the men, animated by chemicals, she is reminded of the flock of wild parrots that circle her airy North Beach apartment; the way they line up and chatter, talking and talking without listening.

THIRD HOUR

"DO YOU FIND this troubling?" asks Coco of Gracie and Theo as they kneel beside the hot tub. "I don't think treated water is meant to be this shade of green."

"I don't think it is meant to be green at all," says Theo.

The three girls ponder. Gaze into the small pool.

Gracie squints, stares, moves her face closer to the surface of the water. Her glasses are still in her bag inside the house. "Look," she says, tapping Coco on the arm, "what is that? Along the bottom there? Is that . . . is it . . . dirt?"

Coco's face is almost touching the surface as well. All three girls wear baggy, Colonial Africa–style shorts, exposing only the upper halves of their one-piece swimsuits, worn with the intention of sitting in the hot tub. Now Theo shakes her head. "It's like, I think, maybe some kind of fungus."

They are interrupted by the voice of a man saying softly, "Nice," prompting the three of them to turn around and see their friend Jelly walking toward the hot tub, stepping out of her sandals, dropping her light cotton dress ("white trash dresses" is the girls' description of the style: flour-sack print, loosely fitted, very Tobacco Road. Jelly wears hers with an offhandedness that serves her beauty well), revealing a bathing suit, and quickly entering the strangely colored water. All this in one clean sequence of motion.

Jelly gasps. "Christ, it's cold."

Coco says to Gracie, "Where is the hot in the hot tub?"

"Where is the good in good-bye?" answers Gracie.

"Can moss exist without bacteria?" asks Theo.

"I don't think moss and bacteria are the same thing," says Gracie.

"Oh."

Gracie says with a nod toward Jelly, newly emerged from the water, smooth and shivering, "I know bacteria like wet surfaces, but this water is freezing, which I think would indicate an inhospitable environment."

Jelly's teeth chatter.

FOURTH HOUR

ONE OF THE MEN has lit the grill and is charring a variety of meat. Jelly is wrapped in a towel that has long since dried and is now sitting on the host's lap. Some of the other men steal glances at her, for Jelly is widely acknowledged to be something of a spectacular beauty. With her perfect, slim figure, her perfect breasts, her honey-colored hair, cropped and parted on the side and sleek, the heavy-lidded gray-green eyes, the perfect teeth, the perfect height. Perfect. Perfect. They all agree. Someone once told her that she looked like she could be Lee Miller's sister, leaving Jelly surprised that the speaker had ever heard of Man Ray's model.

Now the host is asking her where her other friends are today since she can occasionally be found in the company of other beautiful girls in cafés and at parties. They dance together; hold hands; create something of a stir, which is an effect that Jelly finds amusing—more amusing than the beautiful girls themselves. The host is saying how attractive he finds her, to which she laughs—Tell me something I don't know. She bites into the hamburger she is holding that has everything on it except hamburger.

Gracie and Coco have returned to the hot tub with beer, and a soda for Theo, and are dangling their feet into the cool, iridescent water. "You know," says Coco, sipping the beer, "I can't take my eyes off this water. I think I'm in its thrall." Her feet are making small, swirling circles of green.

Some of the other guests are eating the overcooked food in a rather disinterested manner, since their appetites have been monkeyed with by weed, or cocaine, or both. Their behavior is not the impulsive, indiscriminate dining of the pot smoker, or the coke sniffer's nervous inability to eat. And who knows if alcohol makes you hungry or averse to food.

Jelly eats because she only smokes pot, claiming that anything else brings her up but drops her down too hard. Once, when she took speed, she said that her house was spotless but she was too cranky to tolerate guests, so it seemed to her that the purpose was, more or less, defeated.

Almost all the young working women Jelly knows take drugs, primarily pills. They don't like their jobs and they don't like their bodies. Even though their husbands and boyfriends indulge with a greater robustness and, eventually, more dramatic consequences, they still don't realize that the energetic thinness of their women is artificial.

Just like Jelly, Coco, and Gracie, these women have university educations that are never used in their jobs. They are bored. Restless. They are unmistakable on the street, in cafés where they read voraciously, converse, and shop (almost reflexively) for the next pretty thing.

All these girls have been imprinted with a life of the mind, having worked toward college when younger, and so cannot forget the wonder of words: written, spoken, heard. They miss ideas. And so the reading and the talking seems almost a compulsion, the desire for words in direct proportion to the mindlessness of their jobs. It is ironic that these smart, skinny women exude a kind of American work ethic of control while falling apart in ways that do not show.

The people at this party (secretary, contractor, computer programmer, bookkeeper) languish at their jobs like crows on a wire—overeducated, underemployed—and, in an almost genteel manner, spend their nights and weekends with each other, alighting in someone's flat, or at a party like this, mostly locating each other at the

Youki Singe Tea Room, inhaling, drinking, smoking, sniffing, swallowing, injecting, ingesting whatever is around.

FIFTH HOUR

GRACIE AND COCO go into the house, looking for Roy, making their own pilgrimage to the back bedroom. This place of procurement is largely the domain of the men, and its location is not fixed. For example, it can be someone's apartment or flat, car, the park, a café, the street, an office. Today it is the bedroom, but it can be anyplace where pleasure and downfall will eventually blend.

Theo declines altogether, and Jelly is nowhere to be found.

::

WHEN THEO CATCHES UP with Gracie and Coco, they are sitting on the dated harvest gold shag carpet in the hallway. The two of them have just come from Roy—who has such a high tolerance for cocaine that he forgets the effect the same amount might have on others—so the girls are experiencing a great deal of teeth grinding, fidgeting, and ceaseless, animated conversation.

"You know," Coco is saying, smoking still another cigarette when she has barely put out the last one, "this isn't really a conversation as much as a side effect—"

Gracie takes the cigarette from Coco's mouth, inhales, exhales, says, "—we don't even require a subject—"

"—isn't this the best party?—"

"—you know what we should do sometime—"

"—open an exotic spice store—"

"—I was thinking about sweaters—"

"—Mélange, we could call it—"

"—yeah, but we should sell something else, too, like sweaters—"

"—that we make ourselves!—"

"—except, what happens when the place gets too successful?—"

Theo finally says, "I'm looking for Jelly."

"Have you tried looking under the host?" says Coco. "You know, 'One more drink and I'll be under the host'?"

They laugh, while Theo just watches them. She says, "I can't stand it when you guys are like this," and leaves.

JELLY IS, IN FACT, off with the host. They are lying, side by side, on top of the madras cover of his daughter's bed. She thinks back to the photograph of the girl and realizes it must be a couple of years old, since she would guess that the girl who inhabits this room is about fourteen.

There are Mardi Gras beads hung in colorful disarray on a doorknob, stuffed animals (one wearing a hat with *Evie* stitched across the brim), vials of scent and lip gloss, a telephone. There is a diary, left out and unlocked, that no parent would bother reading.

There are pictures on the walls of beautiful boys (to love, Jelly thinks) as well as pictures of beautiful girls (to be, Jelly thinks). (Unless she has gotten that reversed.)

The host steered Jelly toward this room because he is hiding from two new guests: girls he apparently invited today and, even more apparently from the shy, kittenish behavior of one of them, has slept with.

"I could use your help," he is saying.

"Who are those girls?" Jelly asks.

"I have no idea."

Jelly props herself up on her elbow beside him. "But one of them knows you."

"And I know her. I just don't know her name."

"Isn't that romantic."

He says so softly Jelly isn't sure she is hearing him correctly, "Save me."

Jelly slowly slides to the bed and rolls onto her back. "You have mistaken me for someone else."

"Oh," says the host, "not you." He sighs. "It's my wife." His arm rests across his eyes. "I want her to come home, but when I tell her that she answers, 'I am home,' and I say, 'I mean our home.'

"You know I have these parties all the time, hoping she'll come. I never lock my door, ever, thinking maybe she'll just walk inside."

"Like Gatsby?" offers Jelly.

"Like Gatsby without the beautiful shirts."

All is quiet, then Jelly leans over and kisses him, very lightly, on the mouth.

He moves his arm, looks at her, and says, "Why don't you stay with me, Jell?" to which she answers, "As if that is what you want."

SIXTH HOUR

"I HAVE TO STOP at Ned's. Five minutes," says Roy to Theo, who is driving Roy's Hillman Minx with Jelly next to her. Coco sits in back with Roy, Gracie close beside him. He watches out the window, as if he is uninterested in Gracie's attentions, while his body language suggests otherwise. His arm is around her, there's a relaxed, content expression on his face. "I need to make a delivery."

None of the girls knows Ned's last name (no one that Roy knows seems to have a last name), so Coco often refers to him as Ned Nickerson, the boyfriend of Nancy Drew, Girl Detective. This never fails to crack Coco up, to which Roy inevitably says, "You do amuse yourself."

But Theo and Gracie laugh too. Sometimes, when Roy mentions Ned, Coco asks if Nancy Drew will be stopping by. And, once, at Ned's, Coco introduced herself as George and Gracie as "my cousin Bess." Neither Ned nor his friends offered the slightest smile.

Theo circles the block in the Marina before Roy directs her to park in a red zone. They all tumble out into the summer night, the air moist and fragrant with the bay. Jelly inhales deeply as she pulls the man's suit jacket she wears tighter over her thin summer dress.

::

"IT'S ME," says Roy when Ned's voice comes over the intercom. He buzzes them into a very nice, very well-appointed and preserved building. Roy, Gracie, Theo, Coco, and Jelly take a perfectly restored brass cage elevator to the fourth floor, where they step out onto a hall carpet patterned with green-on-green palm fronds.

Ned slouches in the open door of his place. He briefly speaks to someone over his shoulder.

Just to the right of Ned's door sits a young, boyishly built woman with her back against the wall; unacknowledged by Ned, in a posture of waiting. She is attractive in a party girl way, with her dyed black hair, short and jagged, eyes heavily smudged with kohl, plummy mouth, and snug white tank shirt tucked into very expensive men's trousers. Circling her upper left arm is a constellation of diamonds that, Jelly is positive, are genuine.

Ned invites them inside with a wave of his hand.

"Hello," says Jelly to the girl with the diamonds.

The girl glances up, then away, as she continues her vigil.

"Are you coming inside?" asks Jelly (the others have already followed Ned). The girl shakes her head no.

::

OVER A DOZEN guests sit and stand around Ned's tidy living room. Coco recognizes two Eames chairs with ottomans. There is an elegant chocolate suede sofa, and a coffee table with its glass surface held aloft by two perfectly sculpted reproductions of Michelangelo's *David* and Botticelli's *Venus*. Nearby is a Venetian floor lamp made of hand-painted silk and pleated velvet that Coco had recently seen featured in a glossy magazine for two thousand dollars. Ned's stereo system is a sleek and slender stack of components, unmarked by any brand name, looking very much like a collection of silver serving trays.

The guests are as expensively attired as the room. Expensively hip, is what Jelly would say. Coco seldom covets the belongings of others—the rich, she feels, can keep their stuff, she doesn't want it—but there are occasions, like this one, when someone, say one of the women reclining on the chocolate suede sofa, is wearing the most supple Italian leather boots and Coco finds herself wondering what it would feel like to wear luxury so casually.

Another woman has a necklace of blue, canary, rose, and white diamonds on a platinum chain so thin the jewels appear unmoored and floating.

Sometimes, Coco thinks, she cannot imagine what having these things would be like. Then she hears one of the guests say to another, "I always say it isn't a party until Roy arrives."

Another man turns to Coco and says, "You must be Gracie," and she says, awakened from her money reverie, "No, I'm George."

He laughs and Coco laughs because she knows this man has no idea what he is laughing at.

This time there is no line of retreat to a back bedroom; Roy's inventory is spread out across the glass held aloft by *David* and

Venus. The guests aren't much interested in reefer; they are a coke crowd. They are Roy's crowd in a much higher income bracket.

The woman with the Italian boots pulls from her pocket a tiny sterling silver spoon with a crescent-moon-shaped bowl. She dips the moon-bowl into the pile of sparkling cocaine, fastidiously holds it to one nostril, then the other.

Coco accepts a line, as does Gracie, and Theo. Jelly, as usual, declines.

The best thing about drugs, Coco thinks, is the rituals attached: the procurement, the taste, the etiquette of the sale, the rules of consumption, the paraphernalia. It is almost tribal; it can almost make you feel like you belong.

::

JELLY LOUNGES ON one of the Eames chairs, knees bent, her feet on the ottoman, slowly smoking a pin joint. Ned glances over at her from time to time.

Coco sees Jelly studying everyone in the room, but she cannot quite read her. That's sometimes how it is with Jelly, who can be mysterious, observant without judgment, beautifully still; she is one of the least judgmental people Coco has ever met, and Coco wonders if it has something to do with the sense that Jelly primarily exists in some state of uninterrupted solitude, regardless of her social surroundings. This solitary aspect makes Jelly compelling to both sexes because it gives the impression that if she keeps your company it is a choice and a pleasure, untainted by obligation or other motives—advancement, loneliness, guilt—and so her attention carries an unavoidable flattery. Unless you misunderstand her.

Jelly's mind seems elsewhere, not in this room, so that when Coco sees her push back the ottoman, rise, and quietly leave Ned's apartment, she is not surprised.

SEVENTH HOUR

WHEN JELLY RETURNS, a friend of Ned's walks straight up to her and announces, "I have to say that when I first met you I thought you unpleasant." He is wearing a hat that is sort of a shallow-brimmed Panama in an attempt to obscure the sight of his thinning hair, which everyone knows but doesn't care about.

And though he is just under six feet tall, he appears shorter because he is on his way to being portly; this extra weight tends to give him a soft, almost feminine air. He speaks with a studied affectation, and everything he says he says with tremendous gravity, for he is, he feels, the champion of sensitivity and honesty for all people.

"But now," he says, "I like you."

"I like you too," says Jelly in a voice that commits to nothing.

He hesitates. "Yes, the first time we were introduced, I didn't care much for you at all."

Jelly nods.

"But I feel differently now." He smiles in what is meant to be a beguiling manner.

"That's nice," says Jelly patiently.

The guests, despite the drugs, are remarkably silent, engaged by this unexpected entertainment—the man in the hat tossing handfuls of Honest Words in Jelly's direction, as she effortlessly catches them without offering anything in return.

Now the man's voice changes, threaded with the emotion of confession, as if he is working up to something rather profound. Possibly moving. Something that cannot, must not go unsaid. "Yes," he says, "in our first encounter I thought you were a real bitch."

The audience holds its collective breath.

The man steps closer to Jelly, offers her his open hands as if to take her to him. "But now"—inhaling a deep, mournful breath, finally relieved of his burden of truth—"now I think you're just wonderful. Yes. I do. I really, really, really"—pause—"just love you." Smiles.

All eyes slide toward Jelly, who says nothing at first, then, in a serious voice, "I"—and begins to laugh that kind of uncontrollable church laughter in which you know you shouldn't, you mustn't, but all you do is laugh harder. "I'm sorry," she squeaks. "I . . . understand"—then surrenders.

The man's mouth loses its shape as his eyes begin to scan the room, weighing the humiliation at this reception, after he has just publicly bared his heart. But then everyone knows this man bares his heart regularly, though he would claim each time is unique.

One of the men jumps up, races out of the room, and returns with paper and pens. "Okay," he instructs, "here's what we do." As he explains he hands each guest a pen and a torn piece of paper. "Everyone, attention please, we are going to take a vote: Is Jelly a bitch or not a bitch? Please, we need to settle this thing."

The guests pick up on the game, scribbling on the bits of paper. "May we borrow your hat?" asks the man, reaching for the shallow-brimmed Panama, whose owner slowly hands it over, as if in a daze.

Jelly has returned to her Eames chair, still looking entertained; Gracie is saying, "I don't believe this," and Theo and Coco pretend to be conflicted over their votes.

"Go with your hearts," Jelly advises.

"Well, all right," says Theo, throwing her vote into the hat.

The hatless man finally says quietly, "I don't think this is funny at all. I think it is cruel." But everyone ignores him (no one for a minute supposes he means it is cruel toward Jelly) as the man taking the vote dumps the results on the floor and begins to read aloud: No. No. No. Sometimes. Maybe. No. Yes. Yes. I want to date her—the man looks up, "That's a big disqualification"—No. No. And so on, despite the fact that almost no one there had previously met Jelly.

As the man tallies the votes he says, with exaggerated relief, "Jelly's okay."

The hatless man fights back tears, insisting that everyone is "awful, awful," as he stands like an angry child.

Roy says, "We really should be going," though Coco tells him she thinks she'll stay a little longer.

Eɪɢʜᴛʜ Hᴏᴜʀ

"ᴍʏ ʜᴇᴀʀᴛ ɪs ʀᴀᴄɪɴɢ," says Gracie as they unlock the doors of the Hillman Minx.

"Is it the nearness of me?" asks Roy, half-speaking, half-singing.

"I'm serious. Listen, can we just walk around for a minute?"

"Hey, are you okay?" asks Theo.

Gracie shakes her head, says softly, "Maybe. I think so. I don't know." It seems what little conversation there is is making over-whelming demands on her system. "I want some water and I want to walk."

They lock up the Hillman. A liquor store on Chestnut Street is open. Roy buys four bottles of water and some rolling papers. He twists the cap on one of the bottles and hands it to Gracie. "Here, honey." His concern coming through his casual tone.

Gracie takes a long drink.

The four of them walk toward the bay, then over to the Palace of Fine Arts, the sole remaining structure of the Panama-Pacific Expo-sition of 1915.

THEY WANDER IN CIRCLES. Gracie is conducting an inner monologue, reassuring herself that everything is okay, telling herself that
she is too young for a heart attack; that her friends (God, how she
loves them!) would not let her have a heart attack (though, for a
fleeting moment, she imagines herself dropping in the street like
Dr. Zhivago during his pursuit of Lara, with no one noticing; imagines her own friends, the ones of whom she is currently so enamored, hurrying off); wondering how she can trust anyone, really.

All of which has the effect of creating a terrible panic until Gracie isn't sure if her heart is running at such a wild clip because of the
drugs or because of her heart attack fantasies.

Maybe she should've eaten something? Although she does feel as
though she wants to throw up—isn't that a sign of a heart attack?—no,
she will not humiliate herself with a display of public puking. Even in
the face of a possible health crisis, Gracie clings to propriety.

Periodically, Roy asks how she is doing, to which she responds,
"Can we walk a little longer?"

"Sure, honey," he says, while Gracie scrutinizes his expression
for signs that she is going into recognizable physical distress.

When the troops were coming home from Vietnam, Roy and Ned
Nickerson were drug counselors at Letterman Hospital. It was how
they met, actually—Ned a year older than Roy, neither much older
than the men they counseled. Of course, they neglected to mention
their own regular drug use. "No one ever asked" is what they say
when asked how they managed to be both counselors and users.

It is the functioning drug users that surprise Gracie, and she
seems to know a fair number. They hold jobs, carry on love affairs,
make it home for Thanksgiving. They, well, *function*. She thinks of
what Jelly says about them, "Yes, they function like walking PDR vol-

umes," which leads Gracie to believe that if anything were seriously wrong with her, Roy would see it.

On the other hand, her panicked monkey-mind tells her, The man is on drugs himself, so what can he possibly know about anything?

Gracie walks over to the columns at the Palace of Fine Arts, standing in the midst of their half-moon formation. She leans against a column for support, then feels herself sliding down, down to the dirty ground. It is late and quite deserted.

Jelly stands over her. "Very unhygienic."

Gracie closes her eyes, then opens them again.

"I wish I could join you," says Jelly, "but I'm not as high as you, which makes me a shade envious."

But Theo stretches out beside Gracie ("So you won't be alone"), and Roy sits down, positioning himself so Gracie can rest her head on his lap.

Gracie concentrates on calming her fast-beating heart, then becomes distracted, looking up at the weeping women who are perched on the crowns of the columns, their faces hidden, their tears meant to express the "melancholy of a life without art."

As Gracie gazes up at the sad nymphs and the brilliant stars, her heart begins to slow down. Her breathing becomes less labored, allowing her a sense of contentment, lying here with Roy and Theo, and watching the women and the stars. Already she is making promises to whatever god will listen, while simultaneously experiencing guilt, for she knows they will be inevitably and quickly broken.

NINTH HOUR

ANOTHER STOP.

This time it is a party in Bernal Heights, a district lacking a cool cache though the house in which the party is held is spectacular—freestanding, generously proportioned, and painstakingly renovated. Theo thinks, If this were my home I would never allow this sort of free-for-all. It seems that the house, as spacious as it is, still has a bit of trouble comfortably containing all the guests that mill about.

Gracie, Theo, Jelly, and Roy have already run into other friends, including a beautiful young man named Max, Elodie Parker, and a handful of members of Jelly's beautiful girl coterie.

::

THEO IS TALKING to her friend Max, a man so handsome that she is always slightly shocked with each encounter. His attractiveness is the result of a mixture of Japanese, Spanish, and North African blood; his slate-colored eyes; his complexion that looks as if it contains roses. Dust and roses. None of this feminizes his masculinity as much as it transcends it, causing women to sigh over him as often as men. Though he is, as someone once commented, nicely made, there is also an elusive, unknown quality that is not physical and that cannot be separated from the equation.

Max is telling Theo about a misunderstanding he has had with his boyfriend, James. What he is saying is that he, Max, has a hard time saying no to the men who are drawn to him, and that James has grown tired of all this divided loyalty. "It would be much simpler if no one loved anyone," he says.

They have been standing in the kitchen, where someone had replaced the walls with enormous, multipaned windows. The view (one of the few in the district) is truly breathtaking: water, bridges, city lights that resemble the fistfuls of glittering diamonds that a dragon and a little girl, in a children's story, once tossed into a night sky. The lights are a necklace, a thousand fireflies, a fairy story with twelve dancing princesses.

Max turns to look out the window, says, "It is like having the city at your feet." He thinks about how much James would love this; they are both hopelessly, shamelessly in love with San Francisco.

Once, at a dinner in New York, a woman remarked that San Francisco is like a dying old dowager, rattling her jewels without realizing that it is over. Max and James didn't know quite what to say and so made themselves sound agreeable with an "I see your point," but their affection for the city went undiminished.

::

MAX TURNS BACK to see Theo sitting atop a granite kitchen counter, legs lightly swinging, flirting outrageously with a shy boy. Max smiles, asks Theo if she wants to go to Orphan Andy's, and she says, "In a minute, everything is so pleasant just now."

And it is true, the four friends are having the first genuinely good time of the evening. The party is loose, the crowd electric and amiable, the music is the right music at just the right level. People are drinking, smoking, teasing, wooing, laughing, and speaking closely with each other, or making eye contact from afar. The conversations are continuous, accommodating enough that others can join or exit, without a serious falling off. Everyone relaxes.

TENTH HOUR

GRACIE AND ROY are dancing in a parlor near a set of stained-glass pocket doors that look as if someone looted a very old Czechoslovakian cathedral; one of the doors is pushed back into the wall. Jelly is talking within the intimate circle of her beautiful girls as one or two boys inch closer.

There is a banging on the front door, which no one answers, then more banging. Very distinctly a girl's voice giggles. "I guess no one's home." More laughter.

Someone opens the door, and in fall the host from the first party and the two girls that he was hiding from with Jelly. The three of them tumble and sprawl in a tangled heap, laughing and drunk. One of the girls has lost her top and is now wearing a white-lace push-up bra with her short black skirt.

Of the girl in her underwear, Jelly says softly to Elodie, who has been talking with Jelly for the past ten minutes, "Oh, look, a classic anxiety dream."

At that moment, the host cries out, "Jelly!" with a kind of happy recognition. And before she goes to him, to offer her hand and get him to his feet, she says, "Now I think it is time to go."

Eleventh Hour

THERE WAS A WAIT to get a table at Orphan Andy's. Roy, Gracie, Jelly, Theo, and Max stood outside on the sidewalk, with Max seeming to have a speaking acquaintance with everyone. "My God," says Theo, "is there anyone you don't know?"

And when Max's face brightens with a light of sudden joy, Theo thinks it is because he is pleased with his popularity, only to discover that Max has found James.

::

EVERYONE GROWS TIRED of waiting and makes the move to the Youki Singe Tea Room. Except for Max, who has decided, at last, at last, to stay with James.

Twelfth Hour

GRACIE, THEO, AND JELLY have taken over the rustic teahouse, with its cedar and paper walls, tatami mats, low table of Honduran mahogany, and the absolute peace of the private space, separated from the larger Youki Singe Tea Room. In a tiny recess in one of the walls is a raku bowl that, miraculously, no one has tried to steal, though it has occasionally been used as an ashtray. There is a note in calligraphy attached to the shelf on which it sits that reads:

Japanese potters were known to incorporate themselves in their work, for example, leaving fingerprints in a piece. They loved the imperfect. Of a flawless bowl they might say that "it waits for no one." It is complete. You should always be incomplete.

"This place makes me feel like I am on a ship," says Jelly.

"Did you all miss me?" says Coco as she crawls into the tea-house.

They ignore her as Gracie says, "After tonight, I'm happy to be anywhere."

Theo lightly shoves her. "I was hoping you'd kick so I could raid your closet."

"What are we talking about?" asks Coco.

"Gracie's stuff," says Jelly.

"Yes," says Gracie, "I have such a fine wardrobe."

Roy is table-hopping outside the teahouse; since he is not social by nature but only social with help, this is the time when he is most friendly and accessible.

"Hey, hey," says Ginny, coming into the teahouse with her roommate Selena. "We were just at this party in Bernal Heights—"

"So were we," says Theo, "but I didn't see you."

"Funny. Anyway, we can't go home just yet," says Selena.

"The roommate?"

Ginny waves her hand. "Let's talk about something else."

"Seriously," says Gracie, sipping a glass of wine, "I wasn't feeling so hot."

"Seriously," says Coco, "can I have your bedroom furniture?"

Gracie shakes her head and asks, "Where are those nurturing girlfriends who are always There for You? Those girls who soothe you and hang on to your every confessional word with empathetic tears?"

"Oh, we're here," says Jelly.

"Yeah," says Theo, "I'll give you tears."

"If you want to cry, come home with us," says Ginny.

"Who's this new roommate?"

"We like to refer to her as the Doubtful Guest—you know, the Edward Gorey story about the peculiar thing that came to live with the normal family. Well, now it lives at our house."

"So, Jelly," says Coco, "where did you go? When we were at Ned Nickerson's?"

Jelly has been rolling a joint. She licks it, sets it on the table to dry. "Remember the girl in the hallway? I was curious about her, so before that delightful fellow at the party confessed to all and sundry his deepest feelings about me, I went out to see if she was still there."

"Was she?"

Jelly lights the joint, inhales, passes the cigarette, nods. "I asked her, 'Do you want to come inside?' and she said, 'No, thank you.' I waited, knowing of course that it was none of my business. I asked, 'Are you locked out?' No, she said, very politely, she was not locked out.

"Then she opened her hand, showing me her keys. I sort of lingered, until she said, 'She's home.' "

The girls pass the joint around the table. They are very sleepy, relaxed, crushed up against each other in the little room, and listening to Jelly, who continues, "I got to wondering, was she seeing some married man? Or was this her lover and was he living with someone? Who's 'she'?—the wife? the girlfriend? Or was the girl in the hallway the wife/girlfriend and her husband/boyfriend was with his *other* girlfriend?

" 'Have you been here long?' I asked.

" 'Awhile,' she answered.

" 'Do you love him?' I asked.

"And this time she looked straight at me. 'Who says this is about a man?' "

The girls sip the wine. They smoke.

"You know," says Coco, "when some guy neglects to call, or forgets me altogether, I consider that I might have better luck with my own sex. I leave it there, a possibility unexplored, something to fall back on. So, I must say, I don't like the sound of this story at all."

"That we are no better than they are?" Jelly says.

"Women do betray women," says Gracie.

"Listen," says Theo, a tone creeping into her voice, "why are women supposed to be better than men anyway?"

"And why do we expect it?" says Selena.

"Because we want it to be true—no, because, we *have* to be, not because we *want* to be," says Ginny.

"But we're just people," says Theo.

Coco raises her glass. "Good-bye, Angel in the House."

Ginny raises the joint. "So long, Hooker with a Heart of Gold."

Jelly says, the weariness in her voice apparent, "As the resident bitch, I say love and broken hearts all around." She stubs out the joint. "Then love again."

Roy raps on the doorframe, indicating that, if they all hurry, they can race the moon to bed.

a sundial of maidens

KITAGAWA UTAMARO
(1795–1796)

::

*An "hour" in the Japanese lunar system roughly
equaled two hours. Each day was divided into
twelve two-hour segments named for the twelve
symbols of the lunar calendar. Utamaro did two
series: "The Twelve Lunar Hours of the Pleasure
Quarters" and "A Sundial of Maidens."*

*"A Sundial of Maidens" depicts a day in the
life of the daughters of the townsmen class,
beginning with the Hour of the Dragon (8:00 A.M.),
continuing to the Hour of the Snake, Hour of the
Horse, Hour of the Ram, and finishing with the
Hour of the Monkey (4:00 P.M.).*

Primarily, it is a rotation of women.

LAKE STREET WAS WELL BEYOND THE FINANCIAL REACH OF Ginny and Selena, longtime friends and neighbors, until the day they happened upon a garage sale at a Lake Street address. Now this part of the city is not much given over to garage sales (maybe the occasional, discreet estate sale), and this one was peculiar: All the items on display were clearly worth more than the quoted prices. And the already low prices would be dropped even lower if the prospective buyer so much as inhaled before agreeing to the original price.

It was, as Selena remarked, one of those divorce revenge events masquerading as a garage sale. The woman roaming among the offered goods (the Woman Scorned, as Selena and Ginny referred to her) abruptly approached the loitering girls and demanded, "Do you see anything you like?"

Ginny, startled at being directly addressed, replied, "Your house."

The Woman Scorned turned around to study her own home, with its stairs that led up on one side to a modest recessed porch, and three stories of beautifully weathered pale moss-colored shingles, with darker trim and gunmetal gray accents. Though it was quite vertical (with barely a breath of space between it and its neighbors to either side), architecturally it seemed to suggest a bungalow. It was full of windows and backed up to the lovely greenery of the Presidio.

The Woman Scorned's expression softened and became remote as she scrutinized her house. Wistfully, not really addressing anyone, she whispered, "It has a garden that has sadly fallen into disrepair."

"I imagine it's still quite beautiful," said Ginny, embarrassed and wanting to leave.

"Yes." The Woman Scorned turned to Ginny, briskly asking her for a ridiculously low monthly rent, that is, if Ginny truly admired the place.

Selena and Ginny, caught up in the luck of this offer, chimed a single, enthusiastic yes! and were set to move within a month.

It was only after they hurried away that Ginny said to Selena, "How will we ever afford it?"

::

GINNY AND SELENA had met on the roof of their crummy apartment building on Lombard Street. Each girl was new to San Francisco, more or less without friends, employed (enough to live on, not enough to care about), and a tennis player. The party on the roof was a barbecue with two hibachis and an ironing board that held food and drinks. Neither girl knew the host very well, but they were pretty sure he dealt heroin in an empty apartment in the Castro. Actually, they were certain.

He was a nice guy as long as you didn't cross him or date him. Once or twice, Ginny heard him slap his older, married girlfriend, who would then fight back, screaming that he would never see her again. ("You'd think if she has that much wherewithal she'd hang the whole thing up," commented Ginny as she and Selena sat in Selena's apartment smoking pot and drinking wine.)

There were other things they learned about the heroin dealer: You could always count on talking to him about clothes, for example. His studio was overrun with an expensive array of cowboy, Italian, Spanish, British, and motorcycle boots. His passion for leather extended to a marvelous selection of coats and jackets.

And he had a quiet generosity; you could say something to him like, I haven't been to the new Maxwell's Plum, and he would say, Really? What time is it? and you'd say, Ten-thirty, and he would say,

I have to be somewhere at midnight but I can take you now for a quick drink because you really ought to see the place.

And off you'd go. And he would act like a friend and not like someone trying to charm you, which, at times, can carry a charm all its own.

There were other girls as well: His favorite, he said, looked just like Peter Pan. Ginny and Selena saw all his women come and go and knew that the married girlfriend was the only one he ever struck, though she wasn't his only married girlfriend. All the girls appeared to adore him. Ginny and Selena attributed it to the fact that, overall, he seemed to take a genuine pleasure in their company, the married girlfriend that he roughed up notwithstanding.

Once Ginny asked the heroin dealer about that particular girlfriend, saying, Why do you still see her? And he answered, Because she rides so nice.

In any case, the girlfriend did not appear to be a victim, so Ginny and Selena did not feel compelled toward her rescue.

THERE WERE OTHER tenants in the building more troubling than the heroin dealer. There was the insane woman upstairs who told everyone she was "targeted for murder," pointing at people ignoring her on the street and claiming that they were "assassins." She dropped cans on the ceiling above Selena's apartment and poured urine out her windows so it would splash onto Selena's windows. And that was the least of it.

There was the Russian immigrant who lay dead in her apartment for three days before anyone knew she was missing.

And a fellow they called Green Teeth.

And the lesbians who mysteriously insisted to everyone that they weren't lovers but "sisters."

And the biker couple with a toddler, who kept their 1958 Harley Panhead in the center of their minuscule studio.

And the band of gypsies, all enormously fat except for the grandmother, who drove a gutted Cadillac with a fruit crate nailed to the floor on the driver's side.

::

GINNY AND SELENA shared such an immediate and strong sensibility that people frequently mistook them for childhood friends. These same people would feel slightly excluded from the landscape of their friendship and attributed the feeling to the longevity of their time together.

When it was disclosed that the girls hadn't known each other for a lifetime, there was amazement all around; even the girls themselves were surprised at the sense of familiarity they had found in each other.

They could break it down by saying that they laughed at each other's jokes, that they liked each other's taste, that they saw the world with the same mix of sadness and humor.

That is to say, words and circumstances that had the potential to break a person's heart were reworked into a kind of laughter. Not strange, gallows laughter, more like "oh well" laughter. "What are you going to do?" laughter. "Can you believe this?" laughter.

They knew that something that didn't kill you didn't make you strong—it just nearly killed you. Then, quickly or slowly, you came back to your old self. Sometimes they couldn't laugh off disappointment or despair, making one or the other cry until there were no tears left.

Another thing they knew and shared and believed was that no one could really help anyone else, that sadness is solitude, but you could love someone, without reservation or fanfare, just love them, without expecting anything in return and, sometimes, it would be enough.

::

SELENA WAS SCRIBBLING numbers on a piece of paper as she sat at the vintage Stickley table in the kitchen of the house of the Woman Scorned. The girls had lived there two months, and though the rent was incredibly affordable, Ginny's and Selena's jobs still did not allow them to truly afford it.

"What about a raise?" asked Selena.

"A raise," said Ginny. "My boss doesn't want to pay me at all, let alone pay me more." She was smoking a cigarette while cleaning the top of their Wolf range. For all the meticulously preserved charm of the shingled house on Lake Street, the owners had poured a small fortune into modernizing the kitchen and the bathrooms. Even more surprisingly, they had proceeded with taste *and* abandon.

Ginny stepped back, admiring the convection oven, the separate sink containing a garbage disposal (as opposed to the larger, main sink), and another oven designated only to heat bread. And the gorgeous cabinetry, the wood floors, the whimsical tile work. Ginny spread her arms across the Sub-Zero refrigerator and said in a serious voice, "This kitchen has made me a better person."

"But you don't even use the kitchen," said Selena, who did most of the cooking.

"Isn't self-improvement enough for a kitchen to provide?"

Selena returned to her sheet of figures.

"I still can't believe we can afford a place with a kitchen that looks this—and a garbage disposal—and a dishwasher." Ginny sighed.

"Actually," said Selena, "we can't." She wrote on the paper before her: NO RAISE.

They were thinking.

Then Selena said to Ginny, "A roommate is the only way."

Ginny pretended to cry. Selena told her to be a man.

MILLIE

THEY SAID OKAY to Millie because she was about the same age and seemed normal. She had a job. That was all they thought about Millie.

Until she began to complain about their intermittent cigarette smoking. Their pot use drove Millie into a glaring silence. When asked if it bothered her, Millie replied that she "didn't believe in drugs" ("Is it finally a religion?" asked Selena, which drove Millie from the room in a huff of censure), even though Ginny, going through Millie's dresser drawers, found four bottles of prescription pills.

Ginny took out two capsules, gave one to Selena and kept one for herself, and the next thing they knew they woke up in Selena's car. It was parked in the garage, with the door still open, causing the girls to wonder whether they had passed out before leaving or upon their return.

Millie was also a reader of self-help books. One was called *Overcoming Rape Trauma*, and it focused on male-male assault. When Selena came out of Millie's room carrying it, she showed it to Ginny, who raised her hand and said, "I don't want to know," then added, "You need to stay out of Millie's room."

"You should talk," said Selena.

It was then they realized that neither of them, separately or together, or to each other, had ever violated anyone's privacy the way they had Millie's. And while they were careful and secretive about it, Ginny said, "No wonder she hates us."

"Do you think she hates us?" asked Selena. This surprised her; she was not accustomed to being hated—overlooked, but not hated.

"Maybe I just hate us."

So they asked Millie to go, explaining that she brought out the very worst in them, to which Millie responded, "I don't think that's possible."

JUNO

JUNO HAD A MILLION friends, and they always seemed to need a place to crash.

REBECCA

REBECCA WANTED TO escape her interfering, extended family, who lived in the avenues. " 'It's a Chinese thing,' they say, except they don't say it exactly like that," she told them.

"In my family," said Selena, "it's an Italian thing. The relatives. The guilt."

"The music. The madness," said Ginny.

Rebecca's family eventually bought her a condominium in Pacific Heights that, all three girls agreed, was pretty damned exquisite.

BETH

BLOND AND BLUE-EYED. Very cheery. It turned out she was very Christian, her room a library of Christian literature. She wanted to know if Ginny and Selena would mind if she borrowed the stereo to listen to her own records.

Ginny had bought the stereo off a Vietnam vet for practically nothing. It was loaded with knobs and lights, and was, in general, rather dated. A male friend of theirs had recently bought a CD player: new and expensive and temperamental. Most of the guys they knew were intrigued by stereo components, whereas Ginny and Selena, who still called their stereo a record player, retreated into their girl world, which, mercifully, carried no pressure to keep up in the electronics arena.

An overproduced, dramatic power ballad came on. Someone's heart was full of love. Big love. A love larger than the universe.

Ginny began tapping her foot, until she caught the lyric and understood that the object of all this affection was Jesus. And while Ginny loved Jesus, she didn't *love* Jesus, as she said, *in that way*; she loved him more like a brother. But the sensation of being lured toward the music then realizing what sort of music it is was akin to finding a particularly hairy fly in a particularly delicious soup.

Beth had a boyfriend. Also blond and blue-eyed, which made Ginny and Selena wonder if a certain genetic coloring was a require-ment of their church. Ginny referred to Beth's church as the Church of Newport Beach.

Beth and her boyfriend were engaged. He never spent the night. An enormous wedding was planned, but first they had to participate in the obligatory retreat weekend, followed by six weeks of premari-tal counseling.

It was during the six weeks of counseling that Beth began bum-ming cigarettes from Ginny or Selena. And the truth started tum-bling out, prompted, the girls guessed, by the counseling and the night they all got high.

"You see," said Beth, "this is what I want my life to be like."

"Yeah, me too," said Ginny.

"No, really, the problem is . . ." Beth hesitated. It was obvious Beth had never named the problem, "I'm bored."

Ginny and Selena did not know what to say.

"With"—a tear slid down Beth's face—"no end in sight."

Selena said, "Maybe it's just pre-wedding jitters. It will pass. I mean, you love him. Maybe you should relax and give everything a chance."

Beth shook her head. "I can't get divorced and stay in my faith."

"Why?" Ginny's tone was indignant. "I'm sorry, but isn't a little tolerance in order? Since when are Christians shunned for erring? What happened to unconditional love?"

"Oh, no," said Beth. "I wouldn't be thrown out. No. I meant *I* couldn't stay because it would mean I only believe a little. That I'm not committed."

Beth's best friend was a young woman named Georgia, who was so unlike Beth that the tie that bound them was not immediately evident. Georgia had nothing to do with Beth's faith or her church; Beth sometimes jokingly referred to her as My Secular Friend, Georgia. And yet, Ginny and Selena saw, there was some essential element within each girl that attached to the other. Georgia occasionally called very late at night, and once was so distraught over some incident in her love life that she came to stay with Beth for a week.

"Married guy," Ginny and Selena whispered to each other of Georgia's emotional catastrophe.

By the end of the week, Georgia seemed to rally, cheerfully returning to her cottage on California Street. ("He must have called," speculated Ginny and Selena.) Now it was Beth's turn to grow thoughtful and quiet. Twice she was late to her spiritual counseling sessions. She told Ginny and Selena that she was the only Protestant Christian in her family, that it was the result of falling in love with her fiancé, that her family was "rather Catholic. One of my ancestors is a saint," she said. (Ginny and Selena were unexpectedly moved by a life of purpose and devotion.) "But I'm not."

And the next day all Beth's stuff was gone.

MAVIS

MAVIS WAS GREAT.

She got all their jokes, slipped into their lazy, mildly dissipated lifestyle. Loved the house and the way they got it. Loaned them clothes and jewelry. Had a good job as a graphic designer. This was a complete novelty to Ginny and Selena.

"Let me get this straight," said Selena, "you actually—now correct me if I'm off base here—work in a profession for which you are educated?"

"That's right," said Mavis.

Ginny turned to Selena, Selena to Ginny, then both back to Mavis.

"That can't be right. No one we know—including us—does anything even remotely related to their college degree."

"We've only heard about people like you, but we have not actually met any. Not in our age-group, anyway."

Mavis made them a batch of hash brownies. After they each had one they went for a long walk in the Presidio.

"Did you know," said Mavis, "that when I lived in New York I had the phone numbers of four different people who would deliver pot right to your door?"

"Really."

"They came with what looked like a fishing tackle box, opened it while giving a rundown of the price and potency of all their merchandise. One guy even had a storefront on the Lower East Side."

"You'd think you'd get arrested for being so blatant, if nothing else."

"You'd think."

The closest thing that Ginny and Selena had come to anything like that was their friend Sal, the manager of a popular rock band that she hated. Sal told them that at the record label offices in Burbank a woman would come by, in the middle of the day, with a large basket of baked goods laced with pot and hash. "I know that's not the same thing," said Ginny. "It wouldn't do me any good anyway. I never get high when I work because it makes the day seem twice as long."

"On the other hand," said Selena, "I start in the morning and pick it up in the afternoon."

"You guys really don't like your jobs," said Mavis.

"Well, it isn't as if we are trained to do them—unless—we are—?"

"Don't ruin the afternoon," said Selena.

They came upon some bleachers in need of paint and rested, admiring the long autumn shadows as the sun gave way to an early moon.

::

LIVING IN THE interstices that existed between roommates, Selena and Ginny often fantasized that this was their house. They dreamed about the improvements and changes they would make. They wanted the carpet (expensive though it was) pulled up from the bedrooms. They wanted diaphanous cotton drapes hung from copper rods as slender as reeds, instead of the heavier "window treatments" that now hung room to room.

They both disliked wallpaper, unless it was the fabulously dear hand-painted variety that carried all the interest of a mural. The owners liked wallpaper.

It wasn't long before the frustration of rentership settled on them once more. They were used to it (having been renters all their adult lives) but thought that this wonderful house might make them immune. They were so tired of this renter's limbo where you cannot put any money into the property because it isn't yours and so all the energy you would normally spend arguing with contractors is expended trying to convince the landlord to do something he should do anyway.

Their situation did not even lend itself favorably to trying to persuade their landlord to grant their requests because of the ongoing feud between the Woman Scorned and the Man Who Ruined Her Life. They both seemed hell-bent on letting the place fall to ruin.

"I think that property should rightfully belong to whoever loves it," said Ginny.

"Is that like possession is nine-tenths of the law?" asked Selena.

"No, it is when the property possesses you."

The other thing wearing on them was not knowing if and when they'd be asked to move. Not that they could be tossed aside on a whim; city laws had seen to that. Nor could the rent be raised through the roof (that is reserved for the next tenants). But if you don't own, you will move. Maybe not today or next year, but at some point.

It makes notions of home and refuge seem useless and foolhardy.

It makes you never want to get attached.

And being unattached to one's home can exhaust a person.

A corollary to being asked to move by the landlord is the question of what happens when Ginny or Selena moves out. They know they cannot stay together forever. Even though someone once asked them if they were lovers and they said, Yes, but without the sex.

ALEXA

ALEXA SEEMED LIKE a nice girl, and all went well for three months, though she seemed to lose a bit of weight on a regular basis. She was quiet and polite and didn't care if Ginny and Selena smoked, or what they smoked, or what any of their friends did in the house, or how late they did it.

Then Alexa's habits went a little funny. Ginny found Alexa's underwear in the freezer.

"I've heard of this," said Selena when Ginny called her over and they peered in together. "I think it was Joan Crawford who used to do this on hot Los Angeles days to cool off."

After that they referred to Alexa as Alexa Joan.

They invited her to go out with them. "There is a great party in Bernal Heights and you should see the house—it's fantastic," they told her.

"I can't picture a nicer place than this one," she said. They asked her to eat dinner with them. They told her to come to the Youki Singe Tea Room. She always declined, seemingly touched by each and every invitation and gesture.

Next, Alexa Joan began playing music in the middle of the night. Not softly. Every night. Selena, cranky and bleary-eyed, sat with an equally tired Ginny at breakfast and groused, "Someone should remind her it's a school night."

Alexa had money for rent but no job, so her time was always her own.

Then, she began bringing in strangers: men and women. Not going out and getting them, no, she would stand in the front window, provocatively dressed, and beckon them inside.

"Can't we ask her to stop it?" asked Selena.

"Well, she is entitled to have friends over," reasoned Ginny.

"Don't you have to know someone's name for it to constitute a friendship?"

"Maybe we should talk to her."

::

THEY TRY TO TALK to Alexa Joan. They tell her they care. They say, We will be your friends. Alexa Joan thanks them in her sweet manner, assuring them that she is fine and happy. Truly.

Selena finds a note on her bedroom door from Alexa Joan that they are out of laundry soap and could either she or Ginny pick some up on the way home from work and she will reimburse them. The message is neatly written and affixed to the door with a steak knife.

"So," says Selena, "isn't this the part in the script where we call somebody?"

"Actually, I think this is when someone calls us hysterically, urging us to get out of the house."

They sigh. Ginny takes the knife from the door, where it has nicked the Honduran mahogany, minor damage to which they display renters' indifference.

::

FOR TWO DAYS, nothing happens. For two days, Ginny and Selena plot and call each other at work, or walk to the store together, or eat out, trying to decide what to do. Alexa remains her sweet-natured self.

The only place they can't talk is at home.

"I feel like the astronauts in *2001*," says Ginny.

::

SELENA AND GINNY are eating in the dining room with its chandelier of dark brown metal and amber glass, the light reflecting off the paned windows of the built-in cabinets. Alexa Joan walks past them, smiling her warm, polite smile. They smile in return. They watch her as she walks to one of the front windows, overlooking the sidewalk. She opens the window. Ginny and Selena catch each other's eyes, and they seem to be thinking the same thing: She wouldn't bring a stranger up from the street this early in the evening and in their presence, would she?

They wait and do nothing.

Alexa Joan leans on the window frame. The evening is crisp and fragrant with fall. Ginny and Selena resume eating and return to their conversation.

There is the squeal of brakes. The sound of people running. They look to the window, but Alexa has vanished.

::

ONE LEG IS BROKEN worse than the other, but both are fractured. The ankles are especially bad. The living room is on the first floor of the wonderful house, but, as with almost every dwelling in San Francisco, the first floor is usually above the sidewalk by about ten feet.

When Ginny and Selena rushed to the window, they saw Alexa Joan sprawled on the sidewalk, her legs at awkward angles, and someone calling up to them that an ambulance was on its way. Some other people sat with her.

Ginny and Selena were concerned and strangely removed at the same time; they thought it was because nothing Alexa Joan did could possibly shock them anymore.

::

THEY WENT TO THE hospital and brought Alexa Joan flowers and chocolate (which she did not eat). They asked if there was anything else they could do for her.

They were very well disposed toward Alexa Joan, believing she had spared them the task of forcing her from the house. They would do all they could for her in her dwindling days of roommatehood. They assumed that when she was discharged from the hospital she would want to go home immediately, for they often heard her say how much she loved and missed her family.

So it surprised them when Alexa Joan asked if they could do her a very big favor.

Of course, they said, before they knew what it was.

Well, would they mind picking her mother up at the airport? She would be coming to take care of her.

Ginny and Selena had not expected Alexa Joan to recuperate at the house but, they told each other, they could wait a little longer.

Alexa Joan's mother moved into one of the guest rooms ("I'll keep Alexa's empty for when she returns"). If you caught her mother out of the corner of your eye, you would think she was Alexa; their movements are identical and do not belie anyone's age.

Then Alexa came home.

Then Alexa's sister showed up. Ginny and Selena came home from work to find her reading a magazine on their sofa, eating the chocolates from the hospital that Alexa had not touched.

Then a friend of Alexa's sister. And no one had jobs, or anywhere to go. And they all seemed to have money for rent and food.

Ginny and Selena stayed away more and more. Eating out almost every meal. Going away on weekends. Watching their bank accounts drop dangerously low. The only people who didn't go away were Alexa and her family.

::

"I CAN'T GO on like this," says Ginny.

"I won't be able to make my rent if I don't start staying home," agrees Selena, "but I can't stand to be home."

It wasn't that Alexa and her family were unpleasant; they were easygoing and thoughtful, in their way, as Ginny observed.

Something had to give.

"Alexa," says Ginny with Selena by her side, Alexa alone in her room. "We've decided to move on."

Earlier, when Selena suggested they leave, Ginny cried, "I love this house! It's my house! How can you ask me to leave so perfect a place?" Selena also choked up; their dream departing.

But they knew they could not properly care for the still recuperating Alexa, and that as long as she remained bedridden it would be impossible to dislodge her family and friend.

Alexa does not demur or ask them to reconsider; instead she says that she will need a copy of the lease and an introduction to the landlord. And, if the girls are not mistaken, Alexa seems slightly pleased, and rather businesslike.

"Okay," Ginny says. "We'll be gone this weekend."

Selena has been watching Alexa. She says carefully, "We love this place. It is our place. I don't think you fully understand what it means to us."

And this time Alexa, the new Alexa, who seems curiously shorn of her shy neuroses, replies, "Oh, I think I do. Because it should be very clear to you, by now, that I love it more."

a collection of beauties at the

height of their popularity

KITAGAWA UTAMARO
(1789–1801)

▪▪
▪▪

Ukiyo-e *were wood-block prints, mass-produced for
the townsmen class (the lowest class) in Edo. They
often depicted the women who inhabited the Floating
World, that is, the world of pleasure. Because of the
process of production and the content, these prints
were often not taken as a very high art.*

*A young artist named Toshusai Sharaku, who
had a brief and brilliant career, made a series of
"large-head" prints of Kabuki actors in 1794.*

*It is said that Utamaro, a brilliant artist him-
self, responded (competitively) by publishing his own
large-head series—ten in all—of the most beautiful
courtesans of the most famous geisha houses in Edo.*

One of the girls holds a moon-shaped fan.

OF COURSE HER given name is not Jelly; it is Gillian, though no one ever calls her anything except Jelly, and, as a nickname particular to a particular person, it suits her absolutely.

It was a name of childhood, teen years, young adulthood (when it has turned distractingly sexual). It will not wear well past forty, but that doesn't matter now, in her twenties, when it is more of a social asset than a liability.

::

JELLY IS NOT from San Francisco proper; she grew up instead in a small town roughly an hour and a half north of the city. In terms of cultural considerations, the distance was far greater than geographical, which is why she eventually left. ("There was nothing for me there" is her standard answer.)

Some presumed it was an old boyfriend who precipitated the move, leaving her with "nothing." Or for whom she felt "nothing." Maybe it was college that pulled her away. Or kind, uninteresting parents or, conversely, disagreeable, controlling parents. Perhaps a fight with a best friend?

One or two came closer to the truth when they guessed it had something to do with her beauty, which was considerable. The honey-hued hair, side-parted and smooth; clear hazel eyes; her slim, strong stature. The unhurried directness of her voice and gaze. She was, as some would say, one of *those* girls, meaning different enough to not quite belong.

In San Francisco it is evident that she is not native. She has an aura of being a not-quite-right fit. It isn't her looks that lend that impression—it is because she is in the process of giving herself over to the city, of allowing it to come inside her being, to transform her. No native would be so open.

"Must you wear so much black?" asks her mother when her parents come to visit (her parents who are neither dull nor dominating). "And your skin, sweetie, is there no sun?"

"Not much," says Jelly. "You know what Mark Twain said about the coldest winter he ever experienced was a summer in San Francisco."

"You aren't going to start talking like a T-shirt, are you?" asks her father. "Because if you are I'm going to have to answer you by saying things like a woman needs a man like a fish needs a bicycle."

They laugh. They are a loving family. They are not the reason Jelly left.

REGARDING THE BLACK attire and pale skin, what Jelly did not explain to her parents was that daily life in the city, as opposed to a little town, is life in reverse. Meaningful relationships, conversations, exchanges, and events mostly occur at night. During the daylight hours everyone she knows is in a sort of work dormancy. Jelly herself works downtown for an accounting firm, doing the very basic bookkeeping that would be a waste of time for a CPA. When evening comes, everyone awakens.

She has a second job, sporadically waiting tables at a popular ("Yuppie by way of the Raj" is how she classifies it) restaurant bar. There she observes the mating rituals of people slightly older than she, with professions, living moneyed lives. They are attorneys and physicians and stockbrokers and advertising people and bankers. They have careers. They live in the Marina or Pacific Heights or Cow Hollow, though no one who lives there calls it Cow

Hollow. They have nice cars in garages. They have garages. They come to places like this to meet and drink and go home with each other.

Jelly never frequents places like this on her own time. No one she hangs out with does either; none of them would be able to afford it for long. More than that, the milieu is wrong. Her friends are not Union Street. Her friends are North Beach or Castro or the Mission. She knows she can always find someone to hang around with at the Youki Singe Tea Room, which is usually the first place she stops when the evening hours become her own.

::

BECAUSE OF HER face and demeanor people have a difficult time accepting the jobs she works at; they seem to expect so much more. Eventually, Jelly gets into the habit of saying that her job (bookkeeping, waitressing) isn't the only thing she does with her time. She is an aspiring illustrator.

"What do you illustrate?" they ask.

"This and that," she answers. Adding, "I'm not comfortable discussing my work."

"Oh," people say with understanding, "you're very superstitious with your ideas."

"Very," she says.

Being a beautiful girl in a city makes her feel pressured toward accomplishment. If not accomplishment, then certainly clear ambition. She wants to say that a lovely face is not something earned or worked for; that she might not want something simply given to her for what is essentially an accident of birth; and that one day she will find out who she is (maybe take a drawing class, perhaps she has stumbled upon her true calling), but, for now, that person remains hidden, even to her.

::

JELLY HAD BEEN far too beautiful for the plainness of her home-town. She did not believe that she could be a conventional model, despite the constant encouragement of the townsfolk to think otherwise. In this way ("Oh, Jelly, you should be a model!") she learned the art of politely, modestly accepting compliments. It would be rude to correct these people by pointing out all the ways in which she could *not* be a model. They had eyes, she thought crossly, they should use them to see that her height was wrong (not short but not tall either), her face lacked the proper planes, her slim figure was not slim enough. There was thin, and then there were models.

To put it another way: It was one more thing that bothered her about home, that its citizens thought she should *want* to be a model. She could imagine them rehearsing their I-knew-her-when stories.

In the little town she is extraordinary; in the larger world she is just another pretty girl. All right, maybe a beautiful girl who, under certain circumstances, could make money off her looks. She felt, however, that her most attractive quality was her mind. Her cool manner and her calm voice. Models do not speak.

It was claustrophobic, this local worship and the ease with which she could have anything. She and her pretty face.

It was exhausting.

::

ONE DAY JELLY happened into the best store in town. It was a designer store that sold clothing and shoes and jewelry and lovely objects that wouldn't have been out of place in colonial Kenya, or Hong Kong. This designer had made his career on clothes that worked a fantasy of casual wealth and privilege.

Usually, Jelly only looked and did not buy because these goods were out of her financial reach. And because she was young and really did not require that level of ornamentation.

Her parents had been talking to her about college, suggesting that she attend the school nearby, live at home for a couple of years, then transfer. What did she think? There was the money that could be saved, though what really concerned them was the emptiness of a life without her. They would get used to it, they knew, but neither thought it would be easy. What about a European vacation as an incentive? It could be the summer before school, or as a graduation present. An affordable luxury if she were to remain at home.

Jelly said she'd consider it. She was already here, surely she could manage two more years.

So, as she walked downtown she wandered into the store that was too expensive, too romantic, and too unlike anything about her life. The woman who owned the place saw her, recognized her, and talked her into trying on a few things.

"Here," said the woman, as she handed Jelly a tobacco-colored suede wrap skirt as supple as silk. "And this." A white cotton shirt, with a masculine cut and small pearl buttons. A wide leather belt that rested on her slender hips, its brass buckle rubbed to a dull gold. The leather riding boots already looked broken in, with the air of a life of adventure, the sort where you live in the wild and the men think you are not up to the challenge of the environment until you perform some brave act, which forces their respect.

The woman gave her a critical once-over. "Something," she muttered, then brightened. When she returned she strapped a vintage man's watch on Jelly's left wrist, but not before Jelly had seen the $1,950.00 price tag. The boots themselves, as worn as they appeared, were hundreds, and who knew the value of the suede skirt?

"Let's look at you," said the woman, taking Jelly's hand and leading her to a full-length mirror. "Wow," she said softly.

Jelly and the woman admired Jelly.

They were still staring at her reflection when four middle-aged women, shopping together, entered the store. The woman, without a word to Jelly, went to them. They both knew that Jelly wasn't going to buy anything, that this was just a lark, a way for the woman to see the elegant clothes on an elegant girl and to break the monotony of working in an infrequently visited, expensive store.

Jelly was lost in thought anyway, about college and Europe and her parents. It seemed a fair exchange: dressing up Jelly like a life-size doll as a distraction from the stillness and emptiness of the workday. For her part, Jelly could behold the possibility of her own loveliness.

Did she ever believe she wasn't beautiful? That wasn't the problem. The problem was believing she would never get out from under it unless she left. Soon. Right now. This minute.

This minute? Jelly walked slowly toward the dressing rooms. She felt among her heaped clothing for her wallet, then, leaving her clothes in the same disarray in which she found them, walked back to the sales floor.

The woman waved to Jelly, smiled when one of the middle-aged women said she wanted to look like that (pointing to Jelly) and the woman answered, Don't we all.

Then Jelly left.

She walked, with unhurried steps, out the door, unconcerned that she was stealing.

She thought, You all want to admire me, so admire me. She smiled and greeted people she passed, everyone commenting on how nice she looked. She said thank you. She did not subtly change the subject.

She thought, Is this really so bad? To live in a place where everyone wants to look at you? To make them feel special because they believe that you are special? To be in a place where no one else resembles you?

She walked with her head held higher.

She considered the possibility that such a life could make her punishing and cruel. It wasn't good to have such blanket permission, for anything you might do or say, conferred upon you. She wanted to cry out that she was too young to know what to do with the increasing attention and realized that she was hoping the owner would come running after her, to kindly remind her that she was wearing things that did not belong to her. Maybe threaten her with the police.

That's it, thought Jelly, I want someone to deny me, to tell me that not everything in this town is mine for the asking. Worse, for the taking.

She knew it was true where boys were concerned (she could have anyone). And she was in a not dissimilar situation with girls. At this moment she wanted nothing so much as to be caught and told no.

She waited.

She bought an ice cream and sat on a bench.

No one came for her.

She finished her ice cream and with a sigh returned to the expensive store, made eye contact through the front window with the saleswoman, who motioned for her to come inside.

"There you are," said the owner. "I was wondering if you'd come back." She went behind the counter as Jelly watched her, waiting for her to pick up the phone and call somebody. At least demand the return of the clothes and watch.

"I didn't know if you wanted these, but I wrapped them up for you," she said and handed Jelly a bag filled with her clothes from the dressing room.

"Oh," said Jelly, taking the bag, "you didn't have to—I—don't you want these clothes—the cost—"

The woman waved her away, saying, "What the hell, you know? You're young, you're perfect."

"But—"

"Tell you what, if it makes you feel better, consider yourself my walking advertisement."

All Jelly could manage was a quiet thank-you.

IT WASN'T JUST being told no; it was the invitation to the loneliness of being different. A bit of physical perfection had always held Jelly apart from everyone she knew. She knew intimately the life of an anomaly; her area of expertise was the complexity of solitude.

JELLY TOSSED THE bag of her clothes in someone's garden. And she kept walking. She threw the belt in the open window of a parked car. And she kept walking. She went on until she reached a little foot-bridge that ran over a shallow, narrow ribbon of water, located on the outskirts of town. And there she stopped.

The bridge was more like a miniature of a real bridge and the water beneath far too insubstantial to carry the symbolic weight of what she had in mind, which was to strip off her fine garments, unbuckle the handsome wristwatch (with the price tag still attached), fling it all into the water, and watch it float away.

If she had done so, the reality would have been a naked Jelly standing on a footbridge, with her clothes clogging the flow of the water and lying so close to the surface that she could have practically reached over and plucked them back out.

She could have succumbed to the admiration of others, their

eventual emulation, and her own little living-legend status, with everyone in this town knowing that if she could own this place, just imagine what she could do, away, in the world. Our Jelly. Her elbows on the fragile rail of the footbridge, knowing she had to get out before she began to believe it too.

MICHA

HE WAS A BOY so stunning that few could turn their eyes from him when he entered a room. There was the mystery of origin (country? nationality? race? No one knew for certain since he appeared to be everything and nothing) and the mystery of desire, prompting everyone to try to know him.

He, in turn, was aware that people were drawn to him as a result of a fortunate accident. His genetics had handed him the gift of uncontested beauty, and it was his job, he felt, to work the gift to the greatest good for himself. To exploit this serendipitous occurrence.

Micha laughed to see how easy, how effortless it was to get almost anything from almost anyone. It was easier than wrestling with the idea of respect for someone who would hand something over to him simply because Micha's face pleased. And he surely did not allow himself to think about what respect might mean to someone who would accept such an offering.

Yet it was to Micha's credit that early on he developed a certain charm to accompany his beauty.

::

AS A TEENAGER he had been "discovered" in Golden Gate Park. The Panhandle, to be specific. He was standing on the edge of an unkempt hippie-punk gathering on a golden afternoon in late summer, watching one man chasing another, brandishing a metal pipe.

Most disturbing was the blood that came from the pursued man's head, clearly a result of unfortunate contact with the pipe. The curious aspect of the incident was that the pursued man alternated between begging and provoking the man with the pipe, who was saying, "I told you to leave me alone!" and the unwillingness of the bleeding man to do so.

Micha was wondering if the police would arrive and if they would do anything (the SFPD were not always known for their acts of compassion as it applied to certain citizens), when a middle-aged man, and a middle-aged woman with bleached hair and black roots, approached him. Micha was so engaged in watching the bloody, darkly comic scene being played out before him that he didn't notice the couple until they were quite close and speaking in low voices to each other.

His first thought was that they might want to proposition him, that they mistook him for some angel of a street kid with everything for sale. This had happened before, ever since he turned fourteen, as if he commanded a certain strain of sexual attention, like a kind of odd fairy-tale birthday-wish gift that had finally come to fruition.

He always said no in such a charming way that whatever was being offered in exchange for his favors was immediately upped as a way of persuasion. He again said no, sweetly. A certain kind of worship from afar had begun to appeal to him.

The man asked, "Have you ever been professionally photographed?"

Micha smiled. "Not interested."

"Wait," said the man, with the woman chiming in, "You haven't heard us out."

"It's okay," said Micha politely, "I have heard it and I am very flattered, but no."

The man patted down his jacket, then pulled out a business card (not his) and said, "Give me your number. It might not be what you think," then added, "though I can see why you might be headed in that direction."

Micha sighed.

"I'd rather talk to your parents, actually."

This was new. Then the man explained that he was connected with a very well known New York clothing designer.

"So," said Micha slowly, "what are you doing here?"

"Don't all tourists come to Haight-Ashbury?"

It was true. The Haight had become a human museum of seedy proportions. It had not truly gentrified since the Summer of Love, though there had been attempts (a new shop of cool clothes, a tapas bar) here and there to fix it up a bit; it was as if it could come up only so far before it began to slide back down to what it had already been for a very long time. It was as if it was the sole district in the entire city too worn out to be spruced up.

And so the tourist trade visited (with thoughts of Jefferson Airplane, Janis Joplin, the Grateful Dead) and smiled for their cameras as they posed at the crossroads of Haight Street and Ashbury.

"Actually," said the man, "I used to live here about a century ago."

"We live in Manhattan," said his companion, raking her fingers through her bicolored hair, purposefully messing it up instead of smoothing it out. "Have you ever been to New York?"

"Not yet," said Micha. Until that moment he hadn't thought about going anywhere. He loved San Francisco.

"Would you like to?"

"Sure," said Micha with that perfectly calibrated disinterest particular to youth.

The two men who had been fighting in the Panhandle were now sitting together with a girl in a dirty madras print dress, on an equally filthy blanket. The three of them were passing around a single can of beer and two sandwiches, acting as if they had known each other so long that they were now just a bit bored with each other's company.

"Look," said the man, "I'm going to give you my number. Tell your folks to call me."

He handed Micha the business card (he had scratched over the name and information printed on the front and put his own on the back), which the boy held on to until the couple were out of sight. He walked over to the threesome on the dirty blanket and offered them the card, which they refused.

::

EVENTUALLY, MICHA'S parents allowed that Micha could participate in the designer's spring and autumn campaigns (Micha on bus stops and billboards all over Manhattan), with the stipulation that the pictures be taken in San Francisco ("He's still in school," they said).

And what began so lazily led to Micha's first fame, as he became known three thousand miles from his home.

::

MICHA GRADUATED FROM high school and enrolled in art school. This came about by process of elimination (he eliminated other ways of making a living as too difficult or too dull). He couldn't sing or dance and was smug when looking at what he said "passed for art" (without really looking, without discerning), and he thought to himself, I can do that.

Through art school, and from the magazines that carried his picture, he read about a new interest in art. Some were saying there was an approaching "art boom." This led him to believe he was on the right occupational track.

He was also learning that beautiful *and* artistic, tossed in with minor celebrity, made for a very heady mix.

Grades and prizes came his way because his work was good enough and his face, now losing some of its teenager's allure, was developing an even more exquisite aspect. And there was his charm.

But this strange life had the unforeseen consequence that when someone questioned his work too closely, or opposed him, even slightly, he became filled with a sort of angry amazement. Who was this person, after all, and why should he, Micha, be expected to listen? For he had grown so unused to being told anything contrary that his diplomatic skills were beginning to show signs of deterioration.

::

GRADUATED AND GROWN, he did go to New York. His artwork was being included in a large show that featured other "emerging young artists." His pictures were not the best of the lot; they were graffiti-inspired and so were thought to be "street." And Micha himself was trying on the persona of beautiful street kid for which he'd often been mistaken in his younger years. The fact that he came from a solidly middle-class home occurred to no one, so it ceased to occur to him. (Can anything have less sex appeal than the middle class?)

His reinvention was not strenuously achieved because those around him had started the transfiguration for him. All he had to do was show up.

The graffiti pictures were full of not very well drawn faces and bodies (some might say primitive, though it does not mean the same thing), words ran recklessly among the images, color was thrown and smudged. His work was lively. It looked like a depiction of haste and impatience; it very strongly resembled youth (some might still say primitive, though it does not mean the same thing).

It was not his strong suit to handle his materials skillfully, or to

present figure and form in any traditional or conventional manner—
he was in too much of a hurry—and this was the reason his work was
not genuinely abstract: He could not abstract what had not been
realistically rendered (or considered) to begin with. His work was
wildness.

In this way, image was everything. It might be said that he
worked on the surface.

So, he was not the strongest artist of the show but he garnered the
most attention. He came of age in a time when the people with money
were not all that interested in separating the art from the artist.

How wonderful Micha would look seated at their dinner parties!
How deliciously young and beautiful and avant-garde. Who knew
what he might say or do? My, wouldn't their friends envy them. And
if the price to have Micha as a guest was the cost of paint on canvas
(along with the occasional cigarette butt, bit of trash, or other studio
detritus), then they would gladly pay.

In this way, Micha's work was singled out from that of the other
artists at the show, Micha singled out most of all.

::

FOR A WHILE THIS LIFE suited him very well. He was making considerable sums of money, invited everywhere, asked his opinion on
all manner of culture; he was golden. He was also the perennial
houseguest, living luxuriously without spending a dime of his own
money, which he put away.

He dressed like a well-appointed pauper, arty and appealing.
Carefully, indifferently expensive. And the more thrown together
his work looked, the more it was admired.

Micha found religion—well, religious symbols, incorporating
them into his pictures. This upset Middle America, but Middle
America wasn't footing his bills, so what did it matter to him? He

liked controversy, so much so that his work got more outrageous. As usual, no one dared oppose him.

::

SOME CRITICS SAID his work was lively but ultimately shallow, that it was worth one look but not two. His defenders defended him more vigorously. If you criticized his graffiti or use of the Pietà (who someone once said was "beyond the beyond") then you just didn't "get" it. You were hopelessly out of the loop of all that is modern and postmodern and new and ironic, by failing to see what lay *underneath* (that there *was* an "underneath" seemed the true dispute). And, for some, who did profess to like it, deep inside they wondered if they weren't being taken for a ride.

Because of his social position and his beauty, it was getting difficult to talk about Micha apart from his increasingly bothersome art. Especially for those who adored the perfection of his face: Wasn't he exquisite as he sat in their living rooms? Whoever saw a boy as beautiful as he, asleep in the sun at their summer homes?

It was difficult not to think that praise (or criticism) of Micha's pictures was praise or criticism of Micha. He seemed so hard to reach behind that protected veneer of cash and coolness.

And if the scandals brought on by his pictures seemed to other artists deliberately provoked, instead of sincerely coming out of his work, what could they say without being accused of sour grapes? As if, said one artist, when I began to paint I ceased to be an audience, someone with an opinion. As if, said another artist, if I don't admire his work then I am thought to be jealous. How insulting.

::

MICHA MISSED SAN FRANCISCO. He longed for its cool loveliness. Its small, human scale, unlike New York, which dwarfed everything and everyone. New York was bigger in every way: the crowds, the money, the streets. The praise was bigger because the stage was bigger.

He was homesick and he wanted to go home.

He was tired of the privilege his face afforded him, though his sense of entitlement made him increasingly difficult to be around. If he had been intractable in art school, he was positively imperial now.

Here was the center of his irritation: He was sometimes dismissive of his art, cavalier almost, until someone else treated it as casually as he did, then he heated up. All the same, getting what he wanted was feeling less and less like what he wanted.

He fell into the life of an artist because he thought it could provide a life (and it did) he was born to live. It was a part he thought he could play.

Then a funny thing happened: He discovered he wanted to be an artist. This confusion occurred in the midst of being an artist.

And the drugs he sometimes took left him empty and bored.

So he stopped.

::

HE BEGAN TO READ about art and how artists felt about their work. This he did not discuss with anyone. On the outside, he still acted flip and clever, but there was a seriousness inside him that he showed to no one.

This is what he read:

Art could only result from love.

—JAMES BALDWIN

Mapplethorpe said that when he was working he was "holding hands with God."

I believe in God when I work.

—HENRI MATISSE

Picasso took exception to Matisse's involvement with the chapel at Vence on the ground that Matisse was not "religious."

The Nuba tribe paint their faces and hands so their bodies become works of art.

Jawlensky said, "I realize that the artist must express that in him which is divine. That is why the work of art is a visible god and art a longing for God."

In India, women paint prayers on the ground outside their homes each morning. Daily events (people walking, the weather) ensure their disappearance by evening.

In Japan, a tattoo of a cherry blossom is meant to evoke the beauty and impermanence of life.

HE BEGAN TO RELEARN how to handle oil paint and gouache and encaustic and crayon. He paid attention to the quality of his materials. He sought out artists whose work he admired and listened to them. This was one of the hardest things, since humility was a foreign idea to him.

He kept his reading, his practice of technique, and his conversations with other artists private. He did not want to have to explain to anyone that he envied the sense of rapture some people felt about their work. He thought of the writer K. C. Cole saying that stars, water droplets, and neurons viewed differently are galaxies, clouds, and minds. He wanted to make a galaxy.

It was not easy to let go of the life he had made. For years he had been admired and made wealthy. He knew what it was like to be an object of desire and discussion, and to have his work collected. But more and more it was merely out of habit that he reverted to his sophisticate's stance when talking with his money friends, who thought that being enlightened was just another way of saying you saw through everything.

ONE OF HIS NEW artist friends had asked him along to a Mark Rothko retrospective. Previously, he had not much cared for Rothko, dismissing him as nothing more than one of a handful of field painters, someone with a tragic end who made pretty pictures.

He passed through the rooms of Rothko's early, less abstract, less compelling work, looking without interest. Then, all at once, he was in the rooms where (as Micha would later describe it) Rothko became Rothko.

Micha went from painting to painting, then stood in the center of that first room, not yet ready to move on, and turned and kept turning. The colors were astonishingly beautiful, melting, blending, feathering into each other in a way that allowed him to see the change from one color to the next, yet left him unable to discern the exact location where this transformation took place. Red turned into orange, orange into rose pink, green into blue into purple into gray. The effect was of red having *always* been orange. At what point did blue cease to be purple?

Micha slowly left one room and entered another. The next room and the next left him as breathless as the first. It wasn't simply absolute color shifting into absolute color—it was light. Micha stepped back and watched the pictures around him glow. They were incandescent, illuminated with a light so convincing Micha had to remind himself it was just paint on canvas after all. How was it that this effect could be achieved with such ordinary materials?

If the colors and light transfixed him as he stood, then the spiritual element so affected him that he wanted to weep. The pictures seemed as sanctified as any Italian Madonna, or Pietà, or saint's eyes on heaven in a state of ecstasy. They had captured something without beginning or end, while at the same moment seeming so new as to have been recently hung, the paint still slightly damp.

Just color and time and light and a little divinity. Even though these paintings had an aspect of goodness, they were not about purity.

Micha, long separated from his friend, finished out the exhibit, then circled back to the middle rooms, where he had to sit down for a while.

Beautiful is a term that rarely can be applied to painting anymore . . . but in Rothko's case, "beautiful" is not inappropriate. . . . The beauty of the work has nothing to do with its bite. . . . Beauty tends to be misleading; to disguise—not express—the real content, as Mozart's tragic passion is obscured for some people by his elegance.

—ELAINE DE KOONING, 1958

ELODIE

IT WAS DURING her high school junior-year assembly, when Elodie read her English class essay about water and cities (rivers, dams, waterfalls, fountains, public swimming pools, harbors, aqueducts, reservoirs), that the least likely boy to speak to Elodie (for he was popular and she was not) whispered, as he passed by, "You have a beautiful soul."

Then walked away.

This remark caught her off guard and made her shy.

That night she replayed the encounter incessantly. She read and reread her essay, trying to understand what it was the boy saw or heard. What part of her connected so effortlessly with some part of him? The essay itself became new and unknown. Elodie became unknowable to herself. It amazed her that something so unforeseen and so insignificant could bring someone into her life who, otherwise, never would have entered it at all.

Elodie and the boy traveled in different social circles. High school life, as if in defiance of the American "classless" society, is rigid and unyielding. Once the citizens of this very undemocratic world are positioned, it is almost impossible to change the order of things. There is almost no upward mobility. It is far easier to fall down. For the high school caste system is among the strictest known to man.

It would be more likely for Elodie to marry "up" later in life than it was for her and the boy to become friends in this one.

That Elodie was aware of the boy was not her choice; he was visible and sought after, though she did not want him for herself. There was no time prior to the assembly when she had mooned over him, or stared, or contrived to be close. No fantasies of life as his beloved.

His popularity was a fact of high school; the same way that the positions of deeply fringe kids, or cruel jock girls, or equally mean socialite girls were; overlapping with the very cool girls and their counterparts, the cool guys, who did a fairly credible job of working out a genuine indifference to this stable hierarchy.

With the truly cool kids it was understood that you'd better befriend them *now* because there would be no *later*. Once they graduated, and went off to college or New York or Europe, they would not be coming back. And if they impulsively showed up at a reunion, they would be recognized as the happiest, youngest-looking guests at that strange party.

There were others, like Elodie: not popular, not shunned, not fringe, not happy, not miserable, not lost, not brilliant but sort of classroom smart. One might think of them as movie extras, providing the backdrop and the context.

So, someone like the boy did not cross Elodie's mind unless, for a split second, she wondered what it would be like to be him. To have everything given to you. But that thought would move on as quickly as it arrived. So it could be argued that he did cross her mind.

::

THE MORNING AFTER the boy had said to her, "You have a beautiful soul," Elodie could find nothing suitable to wear. All her clothes, none to her liking, seemed as if they belonged to someone else. (How had this happened?) There was nothing distinctive in her closet, just the same short skirts and 501s that all the girls wore. Her wardrobe complemented her long, straight, center-parted hair, smooth as glass. No makeup. She wondered how it was that she was so ordinary, such a follower.

How had the boy seen anything in her? How was it that her words—on civic waterways, no less—had moved him to say, *You have a beautiful soul*? His voice so natural, so conversational, as if he were simply stating facts. Yet the memory of that voice filled her with self-consciousness. Her stomach was a storm of butterflies.

She could not have predicted such a thing being said of her (to her), and in those circumstances. Maybe years from now, somewhere else, and she would be, by then, someone else. Maybe in a place like Paris. She wondered wildly if the boy loved her.

No. Boys like him did not notice girls like her; he *had* noticed her, but still. She knew she should be grateful for his attention. Clearly, she could only aspire to the position of the Chosen and not the reverse.

Wasn't being told that she had a beautiful soul being chosen? She could not say.

::

NOTHING PLEASED ELODIE. She was a new, reborn Elodie as the result of one quiet, passing remark, transformed, puzzling out who she might be.

Time had lost its meaning. An hour passed in an instant. If she watched the clock, every minute slowed to almost nothing. She could not regulate the passing of the day. Nor could she count on feeling hungry or sleepy at the appropriate times.

Elodie watched for the boy, curious about their next encounter. Wanting to see him, wanting to miss him. She lacked the sophistication to know what to say or do; she wanted to do nothing, since that was the way she had caught his eye to begin with, and having captured his attention only made her want to keep it.

::

SHE DID NOT SEE THE BOY.

::

ELODIE EMPTIED HER CLOSET. Then her dresser. The clothes she kept were dark (navy blue, black, gray) or white. She was particular about the fit, nothing that clung or hung too loosely. Nothing the hues of the violent, smog-touched Southern California sunsets. No pastels.

She wore white T-shirts or borrowed white dress shirts from her brother and cuff links from her father. Her mother allowed her to pierce her ears for her birthday, and in these she wore tiny eighteen-karat gold hoops. Her skirts were unfashionably long, either knee-length or skimming her ankles, and slim in cut. Some of them had kick pleats or vents up the back. She even dug out an old blue wool beret from her mother's bureau. Her mother was fascinated by this change in her daughter.

Her dark, sometimes tailored attire drew stares (black was unusual for sun-saturated Los Angeles), and the beret (no one wore a hat) and the matching silver cuff bracelets (lifted from her mother's jewelry box), one for each wrist, made her look like some slave of bohemia.

Regardless of the whispers, no one could take their eyes from her. These changes brought Elodie no new friendships. No dates. Just the other girls secretly, slyly watching her in much the same way that Elodie's mother watched her. Elodie's style made others see her singular beauty, even if she remained unaware of it. The girls at school, her mother—it was all a variation of wondering what someone would do next.

Elodie had lost her place in the social spectrum; she was neither high nor low; she was suddenly differentiated from it altogether. Without fanfare or warning she had moved outside the system. This took even Elodie by surprise.

::

ELODIE STILL DID NOT see the boy. Nor for the next eight weeks. Since they shared no classes, she did not realize that he was gone from school entirely. Then she heard someone say that he had come down with something.

She was relieved when she discovered that he had been ill, since she had panicked, thinking maybe he had been kidding her, or avoiding her. Now she considered the possibility that his comment was the result of a fever. Her life felt strange and foreign to her because he had made a meaningless, feverish remark.

This made her feel flu-ish too. The sheer nervousness of her system often made her feel that she would swoon. Her weight dropped, and the consequential thinness (how could she face him?) added to the new her.

::

ONE DAY, Elodie borrowed her parents' car to drive down to Laguna Beach. She was sixteen and quietly craving independence. She parked the car and strolled the main street.

She walked into a cool, shadowy, spotless place called Dilley's. It was her favorite bookstore, with its extremely high ceilings and rolling ladders used to retrieve the books. The atmosphere was more akin to that of a personal library than to that of a shop.

It was kept by an elderly woman whose face and figure bore the marks of a life well-lived. Her conversation was smart and direct, edged with amusement. In an instant, Elodie thought, *I'd like to be that sort of woman when I am her age*, though, having recently turned sixteen, she didn't give it another thought.

"You must like Robert Benchley," said the woman as Elodie handed her two hardcover books (the dust jackets soon to be tossed by Elodie, who knew nothing of dust jackets).

"I don't know," said Elodie, "I've never read him."

"Are these a gift? I can gift wrap."

"No, these are for me."

The woman's gaze rested for a moment on Elodie's face, then she went back to writing up the bill of sale in her perfect penman-ship.

"I love Dorothy Parker," confessed Elodie, though this was not the whole truth. Yes, she liked a handful of stories, but she didn't understand all the references in Parker's reviews, nor did she care for the singsong cadence of her poems (though a few made her smile). Elodie liked the *idea* of Dorothy Parker more than anything else. Much in the way she had been drawn to the woman in the bookstore. And they had the same last name, Parker. So, in her young girl way, Elodie was infatuated with the dream of Mrs. Parker. Hence Benchley.

"Why are these books so expensive?" asked Elodie.

"They're first editions," and when Elodie didn't respond, the women set down her pen, reached over to open one of the books, and pointed to a penciled "1st ed." written on one of the end pages in the same neat, schooled hand. As if that explained it.

"Oh," said Elodie, thinking, I could write that in any book.

"You know," said the woman before Elodie left, "if you're interested in Dorothy Parker, I have something else you might like. No longer in print of course." The woman handed her a novel called *The Wicked Pavilion* by Dawn Powell. "It follows a group of New Yorkers who frequent a place called the Café Julien."

"Is it a first edition? I'm only buying first editions." Elodie smiled.

The woman smiled back. "Let's call it a gift."

::

AFTER LEAVING DILLEY'S, Elodie went into a sweetshop and purchased a Moon Pie. Something she has loved since she was small and for which she has never lost her taste.

::

AS ELODIE WANDERED dreamily down the main street, she was startled by the boy brushing her shoulder in passing.

Her primary impulse was to hide, then not to hide, since she did not actually hide at school but often felt hidden. She could not be certain if the boy would notice or not notice her; she hoped not, since her mouth was full of Moon Pie.

"Hey, Elodie," said the boy, who seemed pleased to see her.

In her embarrassment (eating in front of a boy and eating such childish junk, doubly damning), she held out the pie to him. "Would you like a bite?"

He gently held her wrist in the palm of his hand and bit into the Moon Pie.

Would he now explain himself ("You have a beautiful soul"), walk with her, ask her to sit on the jetty talking, comment on her recent changes? He did none of those things; instead he said, "I forgot how good those things are," then, "I like what you're wearing."

She wore a white shirt with white enamel cuff links and two sparkling marcasite dress clips at the buttoned-up collar. Her skirt fell to her ankles. She did not feel attractive and so doubted the sincerity of his compliment (she was unused to them as well) and drew the books, tied in brown paper and string, across her upper body.

"You look like New York," he said.

"Have you been there?"

"A couple of times, yeah, with my family, but I'm going to live there. Unless I live in Buenos Aires, or Rome. Somewhere else. I don't want to stay here—that's what I meant to say, you look like somewhere else."

When Elodie had been in the midst of change brought on by the boy, she'd decided her home would be by water. And talking to him today, combined with the encounter with the woman at Dilley's, and the dream of Dorothy Parker, made Elodie understand more specifically the kind of life she wanted, and she knew, as she stood on the street with the boy, that it was not in this place. That she would go elsewhere. She would find a city that felt like home, and, of course, it would be on the water.

"Me too," she said, "I'm doing that too."

AND LONG AFTER, she went to San Francisco, living the hours of her life, writing in her pillow book (and later, those letters) in the Youki Singe Tea Room, where no one ever believed she was from Southern California.

When asked why she moved to San Francisco, she sometimes answered, "It was because I wrote an essay about cities and water, prompting a boy to tell me that I had a beautiful soul."

Everyone would sigh, *How hopelessly romantic*, but secretly believe she had made the whole thing up.

beauties along the tokaido

(OISO STATION) (FIFTY-THREE STATIONS OF THE DEMIMONDAINES)

KEISAI EISEN
(1830–1844)

::

There are a number of things happening in this picture: one, the top of the picture depicts one of fifty-three stations along the Tokaido highway; two, the girl is one of many popular beauties located at each station; three, these prints sometimes included advertising for cosmetics; four, there are haiku by various poets.

It is the beauties that stand out, and the travel on a road that brings the traveler into their sphere.

"CLOSE YOUR EYES," SAL WHISPERS.

Sal and Lucy are having an afternoon coffee at the Youki Singe Tea Room. It is Lucy's birthday (her thirtieth!), an event she cannot name without an exclamation point, so when Sal tells her to close her eyes, she does so with happy anticipation.

Something cold and slightly weighted touches her collarbone, then slides around her neck.

"There," says Sal, as she clasps the necklace, with Lucy's hand reaching up to feel what she cannot see.

It is charms strung on a chain, Lucy guesses. They are circular little wafers, possibly sterling silver (she almost always wears silver).

"Take it off, take it off," says Lucy, who loves gifts of jewelry, "I want to see it."

She can see affection and appreciation in Sal's eyes as she reaches over to remove the necklace.

Lucy spreads the necklace before her on the table. Nine miniature moons of polished and oxidized silver lie across the dark wood night sky of a Youki Singe table:

1. Young crescent
2. First quarter
3. Waxing gibbous
4. Full moon
5. Waning gibbous
6. Last quarter
7. Old crescent

8. No moon

9. New moon

The oxidation of the silver re-creates the blackness of shadows across the moon.

Lucy notices that, here and there, the sterling silver chain has been faceted so that it catches the light like minuscule stars strung across space.

"Oh"—she breathes—"it is so very perfect."

"I had it made for you." Sal wears a delicate bracelet configured into a constellation of diamonds on her upper arm.

Lucy kisses Sal for a long time. Her hand holds the necklace chronicling the phases of the moon, and though Sal has offered to clasp it again around her neck, Lucy says, "Let me admire it for now."

They push aside the coffee and order martinis with two green olives apiece ("You know what Frank Sinatra says about the olives in a martini, that you should always order two: one for you and one for your girl"). They share the olives with each other. Lucy is again wearing the necklace, her fingers intertwined with Sal's.

"I'm so happy," she says, and there is joy in the way she touches Sal. That sort of lucky-in-love kind of happiness.

And Sal responds, "Would you marry me?"

::

LUCY AND SAL have been together so long (seven years) that people often tell them they seem more married that most married couples they know. It is something about the pleasure they share in each other's company. They possess a sweet camaraderie.

They met in Los Angeles, courted in London, then settled in San Francisco. They love San Francisco; Lucy especially cannot get over how fortunate she is to live in one of the world's loveliest cities.

Though there are days when her affection wears thin, when she longs to be in Barcelona or Rome ("Someplace where staying up all night, every night, is considered a normal part of living. And not just for the young," she complains), then scolds herself for taking San Francisco for granted.

Taking for granted the graceful suspension of the Golden Gate Bridge; the steel-shade beauty of the bay on a gray day; the carnival atmosphere of a rare, hot summer night; the bohemian hangover of North Beach (and the comfort of the shabby Youki Singe Tea Room); the holiday of the Castro; the vague exotica of Chinatown.

Taking for granted the sweet, smoky smell of barbecued meat in the Mission; the wet, soft kiss of fog in Ocean Beach; the painted carousel ponies in the park; the curiosity of the Transamerica Pyramid downtown.

When Lucy dodges a cable car, she curses them. When she nearly collides with a bike messenger, she curses them. When her path is obstructed by tourists staring raptly at a sight she has seen so often she no longer sees it, she curses them. When all available parking disappears in her neighborhood, she curses all the filled spaces.

Then, in the middle of her black mood, she unexpectedly falls in love all over again. She cannot say what it is that suddenly leaves her awash in affection. It could be a young man striding purposefully down the street with a silver crown on his head, or sitting with friends in the Way of Tea teahouse in the Youki Singe, or the pages of all the daily planners, from all the offices in the Financial District, that are tossed like so much confetti from the windows on New Year's Eve day.

Sometimes it's the annual visit of the Blue Angels in the autumn, with their loud jet noise, buzzing the city in intricate patterns of daring flight.

Then she again marvels at the wonder of living someplace other people can only dream about.

::

LUCY SAYS, cupping Sal's face in the palms of her hands, "I can't marry you and you can't marry me."

"I know, but we can still have a ceremony. Invite our friends and family. It could be like a wedding."

Lucy looks in Sal's eyes, then slowly takes her hands away. "Why do you do this?"

"We've been together—" Sal breaks off. "Look, if we could get married, if it were possible, would you?"

"Let's just enjoy the day."

"I'm asking."

Lucy sighs, fingers the wonderful necklace, pressing one of the moons between her thumb and forefinger. "Do you want the truth?"

"Unless you think I'd prefer the lie."

"The truth is, I think you would prefer the lie."

And nothing more is said.

::

NEITHER LUCY NOR SAL ever pined for marriage. Even if they could have been married, it was not something they had wanted. They would have felt obligated to come home to dinner each night (which they do anyway, but they tell themselves they don't *have* to). What about kids? A pet? A mortgage? It was inconceivable that they would be married without those things; they suspected that, once they were married, all those things would simply arrive.

Certainly there was the occasional party (movie, bus ride, person at the next table in a restaurant) where one of them would meet someone and something would click, sending them home thinking,

wondering, wishing without wishing, what life would be like unattached. It seemed they did not need to act on these musings simply
because they weren't married and so were together by choice.

Marriage seemed to carry a lot of pressures: from outside (family curious if this "relationship is permanent") and inside (the
stranger at the next table).

On the other hand, it sometimes occurred to them that maybe
marriage is a closed world, but that it, paradoxically, reveals a new,
rarefied, previously hidden world. Maybe the good marriages are
always worlds within worlds.

None of their friends, gay or straight, was "married" or married.
No one was engaged, or even talked about engagements, even though
everyone was getting close to thirty.

"It's a little strange, don't you think," said Sal to Lucy, "that
there is almost no marriage in our crowd."

"Probably because no one has kids, or has a house."

"Yes, but why don't we have those things?"

"I guess they aren't things we want."

"Exactly," said Sal. "But *why* don't we want them?"

Lucy considered this question. "Maybe we do want them but
can't afford them. It isn't as if we have these big careers. Maybe it's
because we don't love our jobs, so even if we make enough money to
have something, we still don't want it because then we would be
hooked into this job we hate and can't leave, and so we're scared all
the time."

"See," said Sal, "that too. I mean, we all went to college, so why
don't we have better jobs? Feminism has been in place for what?
more than ten years—we're from nice families. We read, for chris-
sake, so what is it?"

"Well," said Lucy after thinking this through, "you know how
Gertrude Stein talked about a Lost Generation? In *Everybody's*

Autobiography, she writes that a man becomes civilized between the ages of eighteen and twenty-five and that if he is a soldier he misses the 'influence of women and parents and of preparation.'

"I guess what I am saying is that we caught the tail end of the sixties but missed the party. I mean, a social revolution took place that left nothing the same, and there we were, growing up, like the little foot soldiers who lacked the 'influence of parents.' At the same time, look when we came of age: during an economic downturn, and oil embargoes, and watching the government fail; inheriting the hedonism that came after but with none of the idealism, and so here we are—uncivilized. And lost."

"Wait," said Sal, "we're baby boomers. We're yuppies and computer nerds."

"No," said Lucy, "*we* are not. We are the second half of that generation. It's like—it's like being the younger child who gets only what the older one doesn't want. We're a lost generation within a generation. We're a new thing: We've become our own subset."

Sal took from the shelf a round metal tray with a photograph of the Magic Kingdom imprinted upon it, and a plain wooden box. Inside the box were a Baggie and rolling papers. She pulled a delicate leaf of paper from the pack, sprinkled in some pot, then rolled and licked the joint, setting it down on the tray next to a pair of hemostats.

Sal caught Lucy's eye and sang softly, "Let's get lost."

THE THING THAT neither one mentioned was the perpetual adolescence that they and many of their friends seemed loath to leave.

(There were times when Sal thought it was the result of living in weather so mild that the concept of seasons seems imposed on the calendar. Without the markers of fallen leaves, snow, the rains of spring, and the romantic, disconcerting heat of summer, who could know the passing of time?)

Sal seemed to be moving in reverse: She grew younger with each progressive year. At twenty-nine, she was far less serious than at sixteen. By twenty she had been positively disdainful (she couldn't imagine disdain today), feeling that her opinions were absolute. Now ambiguity and ambivalence ruled the day. Life had lost gravity. For a while she, along with many of her friends, had enjoyed this sensation of lightness.

Her appearance reflected her backward movement into youth. When she was younger she shunned makeup, dressed daily in blue jeans and loose T-shirts. She easily blended into all the other girls, with their equally androgynous looks.

But these days, her hair is cropped short and unkempt. It is dyed boot black, though two months ago it was streaked with red. Her boyish frame still allows her to wear men's clothes well, but now she dons beautifully tailored suits, or trousers, her T-shirts are often fitted, skinny affairs with tiny straps. A bracelet of diamonds that are set with all the randomness of stars circles her upper arm. (For her twenty-fifth birthday, her mother had given her a more conventional diamond bracelet, which Sal promptly had reset in her own design.)

Her makeup (makeup!) is smudged and dramatic, or her face is scrubbed clean. Whereas she once looked like a tomboy, she now resembles a beautiful boy model.

Lucy is a softer version of Sal, shorter and less angular. But Sal's look fits her profession, which is the road manager of an extremely successful, terribly mediocre band with a repertoire of bad party music and unbearable rock ballads. And, to top it off, they act like rock stars, which is to say they are petty and unimaginative and excessive and drink awful champagne (because they cannot tell the difference, Sal notes). They predictably consort with a not very interesting group of girls and, naturally, think highly of themselves and their music.

They get along with Sal because she is very good at her job and they like the novelty of having a female road manager. It gives them a sense of self-satisfaction when someone comments on it. They like to say it is because they are based in San Francisco and so are more liberal than most bands. But, mostly, it is because Sal does her job well.

Sal, for her part, stays as uninvolved with them as she can; she finds the lead singer particularly unpleasant and ridiculous. Once she even wrote a letter to *Rolling Stone* following a cover story they had done on the band. The letter began with a mention of their discernible lack of talent, then went on to quote their numerous unintelligent views and comments. Then she signed a fake name.

When she told Lucy, Lucy asked, "Why didn't you sign my name?" It is no secret that Lucy can't stand them.

"I was thinking we might want to eat next month. They know you know me."

"It's not like I'm your wife."

To which Sal said nothing, for if the truth were known, the idea of Lucy as her wife thrilled her. She liked the thought of belonging to Lucy always.

::

SAL'S JOB DOES PAY for their very nice place in the Marina, and they like their neighbor across the hall, Ned, who is always willing to pick up their mail or check their apartment when they are out of town.

But she doesn't love the job, even though there is something gratifying about being a woman in a traditionally male profession. Not that she is like the three-piece-suit women in the Financial District with their sneakers and those silly neck scarves that they wear ("Is it meant to be some sort of retort to the bow tie?" asked Lucy). Those women hurry around Montgomery and California and Sansome streets, acting for all the world as tough as men, at the same time beginning the rejection of feminism.

The first time Sal overheard one of these women stating to her equally businesslike friend that she emphatically *was not a feminist*, Sal had to stop herself from staring. She didn't understand; did the woman think her job was manna dropped from heaven just for her?

More curious was the fact that Sal (or Lucy or a number of their friends) never went around announcing that she was or was not a feminist. Why would you? What would it mean? They didn't run around waving a banner because feminism was just who they were, a part of them. Though none of them had ever been a radical feminist, and they had been uncomfortable with some of the more extreme stances, it had not occurred to them to distance themselves from something from which they had benefited.

And it got Sal to thinking, What was the point of the three-piece-suit woman talking to her friend (an attorney, as it turned out) making such a statement? Was it to please men? ("I like men," she had heard more than once lately. Many people thought feminists were gay anyway.) And humor, when did humor disappear?

Sal began to laugh. The women had changed the subject and now were on to Jazzercise. Sal thought what a strange time this was shaping up to be for girls: when being feminist means you hate men, but making out on the dance floor with your straight girlfriends is every man's dream.

::

NOW SAL HAS FINALLY, finally brought up marriage (impossible legally, of course, but still), to hear Lucy say, "I don't see myself as a wife. I'd only disappoint you."

"How do you know?" asks Sal, curious.

"You'll have expectations."

"Luce, did we just meet?" Sal asks. "Listen, I don't even know what our marriage would look like, so how can I have expectations?"

"Maybe I'll have expectations." Lucy bites her lip. "I don't think I'm noble enough for marriage."

"I have no idea what you mean, but keep talking and I'll catch up in a minute."

Lucy takes a deep breath. "I don't know how else to say it."

"Are you ignoble?"

"Yes. That is what I am. In some way, I'm not sure I can be trusted. Something is wrong with my fiber, or I lack fiber, or my stuff needs to be sterner."

"I see."

Lucy punches Sal on the arm. "You do see. You know me. Oh, you play dumb but you know me."

Sal does know Lucy. She gets her. And in *getting* her she understands the difficulty of actually *having* her. The complexity of the thing is that Lucy is a faithful girl. But she lives with her head in the clouds. She is hard to reach.

::

SOME PEOPLE SET OUT to find other lovers; some do not. Some simply wait. And even those who do not pursue, do not wait, do not actually want someone new, still somehow end up finding them anyway.

Here is how it began:

In Los Angeles, with her awful, mediocre band. They were all at the record label's office when Sal excused herself to have a smoke out in the interior courtyard of the offices. On the far side of the courtyard sat a girl with copper-colored hair and a pencil in her mouth. Sal noticed that her clothes were wrinkled, not very fashionable, and, if she was not mistaken, her shirt was inside out. The girl was somewhat small, with a slightly square build, making it difficult to determine her age, though Sal guessed mid-twenties. Her feet, shod in those British cop shoes that were becoming popular here among the L.A. set, were demurely crossed at the ankles.

The girl, so engrossed in her book, wasn't even remotely aware that she was being observed. Sal watched her and realized how long it had been since she'd looked, really looked, at someone else. There was an echo of Lucy about the girl (though Lucy would not be quite as thrown together as this girl), which set her to thinking about Lucy.

Sal's love for Lucy scared her. She thought, as she continued to watch the copper-haired girl chewing the pencil, that she could not live through the loss of Lucy. Could not fathom Lucy as a "friend" in the aftermath of all their years together, because their friendship would kill her. Of course, to not be friends and never see her again would do her in too. Sal adored Lucy, who was as lovely and elusive as the moon.

She had spent almost their entire love affair letting Lucy go her own way because she knew Lucy would not allow any sort of restriction. In letting her be, Sal bound Lucy to her. It was Lucy's paradox: The open hand was the one she would grasp.

But something was changing for Sal; she was starting to understand how hard she worked giving Lucy the rhythm of life she required. How sad it was not to marry her. She wanted to marry her. To stand by her side and make the world see them. But Lucy would not say yes, so Sal could not ask again.

The copper-haired girl looked up.

She would not say yes.

The copper-haired girl was startled by Sal's attention; it was evident in the way she had lifted her eyes from her book, to gaze off into the middle distance, when she caught sight of Sal.

She could not ask again.

When Sal met Lucy in Los Angeles, she told her, *It is as if you radiate. As if light gathers upon you.* Then laughed, embarrassed by the clumsy, unpoetic statements. But Lucy seemed taken with them.

"I radiate?" she said.

But Sal was thoroughly humiliated by now and muttered, *Forget I said anything.* Lucy came with her and stayed.

⠶

"OH," SAID THE copper-haired girl, "I didn't realize anyone else was here."

"I was wondering"—indicating the bitten pencil that the girl had held between her lips like a cigarette but now had in her hand—"if you needed a light."

Sal still dreamed about Lucy. In her dreams, Sal was always in love.

The copper-haired girl laughed, waved the pencil in the air. "Sometimes I underline."

Sal wondered which was stronger: love or the fear of losing love.

"Are you in school?" she asked.

"Not anymore. No, this is how I read."

"I didn't think anyone in this business read," said Sal. "Unless they are 'artists' being interviewed."

"Yes," said the copper-haired girl. "It is lonely at the bottom."

Talk turned to books. Books turned to dinner. Dinner led to Sal's hotel. And no one asked if anyone was seeing anyone else.

⠶

SO LOVE WAS NOT part of it.

The band went on tour again, and since Sal didn't participate in the party life, she was up and around during the day. She was resourceful, finding entertainment at every stop (except Milwaukee, which she found uninviting). There were libraries and museums full of art and artifacts, and landmarks and historical sites. Monuments. House and garden tours. There was always some eccentric side attraction; some Enchanted Forest that would promise a defiance of gravity (!!!), or a Haunted Shack, or a wax museum, or an extravaganza concocted by an imaginative individual, as with Scotty's Castle or (her favorite) the Winchester Mystery House.

And places like the Edgar Allan Poe Museum, or something like a room in the Philadelphia library where a very wealthy man had donated his country estate library: books, furniture, wall paneling, windows, and all.

Or someone who'd amassed a weird collection of famous murder weapons or portraits made from hair, or acres of sculptures where the collector had removed the names of all the artists so they wouldn't "overwhelm the work" as he drove you around in his golf cart.

Foreign films and documentaries. Lectures and readings. And, in all these places, there were girls.

Girls who provided conversation and companionship without any complications. They were smart and lovely, and they became, for Sal, like charms or talismans that offered protection from the uncommitted Lucy.

The trick was that Sal had to believe in their powers of protection for them to work. She was prone to disbelief. Sal was confused about her parallel life.

At one museum she saw a traveling show of Japanese prints covering the eighteenth and nineteenth centuries. One series was called "Beauties Along the Tokaido." Fifty-three pictures depicting fifty-three beauties.

This all started when Lucy said she did not want to marry. And the fear of losing her was beginning to take on elements all its own.

Lucy, who had given no indication of leaving, would surely leave if she knew of Sal's double life.

It is as if Sal thinks she can split her single life into two lives, hoping for one to provide an alternative to the other. Thinking maybe this will save her from heartache. But she knows the reality: There is no such thing as two complete lives, only half-lived lives. The same way that all fifty-three beauties along the Tokaido cannot add up to one Lucy.

::

SAL DOES NOT tell Lucy the exact time of her return. Lucy says, excitedly, "Call me as soon as you know. I've missed you more than I can say."

Fortunately, when Sal gets to the apartment her neighbor, Ned, is having another party, with muffled sounds of guests within, followed by the sharper sounds of Ned's door opening and closing as guests come and go, masking Sal's own arrival.

She slumps against the wall opposite her front door. Her bags have been misplaced by the airline, so she is empty-handed. Her black makeup looks tired, and she wears a pair of gorgeous men's trousers, and a tank top with her diamond bracelet visible as it caresses her upper arm.

More guests for Ned.

Sal waits and waits before entering her apartment. She can hear music from within, the volume increasing or decreasing as Lucy answers the ringing telephone. She hears Lucy walking from room to room, singing.

Sal thinks of an expression she read in a book in one of the museums she visited, regarding paintings. *Inherent vice.* It means that the destruction of the painting will come from within. That the flaw lies in the materials of the painting.

A very pretty girl comes out of Ned's apartment and asks if Sal wants to come inside. Sal shakes her head. Then this girl (who reminds Sal of Lee Miller) asks if Sal is locked out. Sal shows her her keys. She wants to tell this pretty girl all that Lucy means to her and that she thinks, in safeguarding her heart from Lucy's improbable defection, she has begun to endanger something that was safe all along.

What she says to Jelly instead is "She's home." But she can see that this pretty girl misses her meaning entirely.

love deeply concealed

KITAGAWA UTAMARO
(1792–1793)

::

This print is part of a series that Utamaro made based on some themes from classical Japanese love poetry. It is said that he is "capturing fleeting emotional states" with his close-up depiction of women.

In this picture, a woman can no longer hide her deeply concealed love, and sighs.

SUZANNE LIKES BEING AROUND OTHER PEOPLE; SHE JUST ISN'T particularly comfortable talking to them. She supposes that she is some variety of voyeur, enjoying the spectacle, breathing in the atmosphere, while experiencing uneasiness when asked to become part of it. None of this makes her unhappy. The life of a wallflower, she often thinks, is not such a terrible life.

Even her job as a bookkeeper for a downtown accounting firm agrees with her. Working with numbers (though they represent money) causes her little stress and is devoid of spontaneity. Things like excitement and unpredictability, highs and lows, are not desirable in her field. She likes the boundaries, so well-defined, that numbers provide, impulse and surprise forced from the picture.

There seemed a rhythm to the figures that she moved about each day. Sometimes she dreamed of numbers, and they were always soothing dreams. Maybe, she reasoned, because it was not her money. Suzanne makes enough to live on, and her needs are few.

::

HER SISTER COCO called and demanded that Suzanne go with her to a friend's annual Last Days of Autumn party.

"Can't you go with Jelly?" asked Suzanne. Suzanne and Jelly work for the same firm, but Coco is the one who mostly goes around with her.

"No," said Coco. "I want to go with you."

"I'm busy."

"I haven't told you when it is," Coco said. "Suzanne, you have to go out once in a while. Really. Just to keep your hand in with the human race. Otherwise, they might ostracize you from the tribe."

"But that doesn't sound that unpleasant to me," said Suzanne.

"Oh, yes, you can be with your cats. Too bad you have such mismatched life spans."

"Don't," begged Suzanne, who cannot entertain thoughts of losing her two middle-aged cats.

"I'll pick you up Friday. Ten o'clock."

One of Suzanne's cats slid its body across her calf. "All right, all right," she said, absentmindedly petting the cat, then worrying about what to wear.

::

SUZANNE'S FLAT in the avenues is a sweetheart of a place; its living room has two giant picture windows that tilt on their respective axes. There's a fireplace, a dining room with archways leading in and out of it, into the hallway. The kitchen has a black-and-white linoleum-tiled floor that picks up every foot and paw print no matter how hard she tries to keep it clean, and a service porch in the back with a washer and dryer. The washer and dryer rescued Suzanne from any more years of laundromats, where she routinely forgot loads of linens (resulting in endless mismatched sets of sheets and towels), well-loved pairs of jeans, and underwear. And, once, an irreplaceable quilt that she later learned shouldn't have been washed in a machine in the first place.

It also meant an end to one of her favorite pastimes, people watching, though she still sometimes accompanied friends, which sort of negated the need to people-watch since it is an activity of the alone and bored.

The flat had two bedrooms, one with a picture window allowing her to gaze outside, and two bathrooms (almost unheard of). There was a glassed sunporch from which she could step out into her small, square garden of Japanese ornamental grasses, carpets of baby's tears, impatiens, dusty miller, fuchsia along the fence, crisscrossing with violently hued bougainvillea and myriad wild roses that scattered and climbed and insinuated themselves all over. There were purple iris, daffodils, and ranunculus, dahlias, daisies, peonies, and, her favorite, a blossoming cherry tree.

The flowers had brief, beautiful lives, falling around her like so much gorgeous snow when they dropped; when anyone asked her the best feature of her flat, she always answered, "The cherry tree."

That, however, would not be the answer given by many of her friends, who would say that the most marked feature of Suzanne's nearly perfect home is that the generous space is practically empty.

A love seat in the living room faced the fireplace. A cardboard box sat, in place of a table, on the black-and-white modernist kitchen floor. Suzanne covered it with a sheet because she got tired of the comments. It could seat four people comfortably, for it was a rather large box, though Suzanne had only a pair of folding chairs.

A stereo that was once kept in her bedroom was stacked on the floor of the dining room, with the music echoing in the empty room with hardwood floors, underscoring the absence of furnishings.

Suzanne and her cats slept together on her futon on the floor, flanked by a fruit crate; her clothing was neatly folded into a second-hand dresser of indistinct design that someone had given her. A drafting table stood alone in the second bedroom, unaccompanied by so much as a stool.

WHEN COCO PICKED her up that evening, Suzanne met her at the curb. As soon as Suzanne got into the car, she noticed Coco giving her the once-over. Coco then said, "I hope we can find parking."

"You want to say something about what I'm wearing," said Suzanne, "so just speak and be done with it."

"Now that you bring it up," said Coco, as she merged with traffic, "what have you got on? It looks like some sort of, like a . . . is that a men's bathrobe?"

"It is." Indeed, Suzanne had on a very elegant, expensive silk men's robe, indigo with a pattern of saffron butterflies so small and finely drawn that it was hard to tell what they were from a distance.

"Did you buy it new or is it a vintage item?"

"New."

Coco sighed.

Suzanne had discarded the sash, replacing it with a wide scarf of clouds in an evening sky (the crescent moon, hazy, hanging on the edge of the scarf), wrapping it around herself so the effect was almost, though not quite, as formal as an obi. Everything was held together with a tarnished silver brooch of an open fan, more than one hundred years old.

Around her throat were imitation pearls and, below them, the white silk of an undershirt. She wore dark red stockings and penny loafers.

Her hair, thin and uninteresting, was pinned up but already coming down, as if it were the end, not the start, of a festive evening.

"Suzanne," Coco began, then, "Suzanne." She started searching for a place to park. "Well, at least you are going out. Little steps and all that."

::

AS SOON AS THEY ARRIVE, Coco sees some people she knows, and though she drags Suzanne over with her, she is soon gathered into a conversation that doesn't include Suzanne. The conversation expands slightly to allow Jelly (she greets Suzanne) to join the group, then someone else, until Suzanne is forgotten entirely. This works out well for her, since it allows her to enjoy the magnificent wall of music, and the dancers, and the milling crowd dressed in their finery, and the thousands of tiny, white lights strung to and fro and giving the illusion of the roof having been lifted off the place.

The party is being held in a converted church on Potrero Hill, and Suzanne is lost in the bliss of the place, for she has always longed to live in a church. She thinks of a converted church as some kind of spiritual loft.

In imitation of an Italian cathedral, someone had painted a starry sky on the vaulted ceiling, and when combined with the bright, white lights, it gives Suzanne a feeling similar to the one the cherry tree gave her when it snowed its delicate petals: like a fairy-tale tree, this fairy-tale sky.

::

AS SHE SAT in the balcony that had held a choir—the pews had been removed and a variety of worn, once-elegant sofas, love seats, and fainting couches were strewn about—a young man said to her, "That's a great outfit."

Suzanne turned to find herself face-to-face with one of the most beautiful men she had ever seen. He was so breathtaking she immediately wondered why he was talking to her.

"Your bathrobe," he said, "I have one exactly like it at home."

Suzanne blushed. "It's not really a bathrobe," she said, but she knew her voice lacked conviction.

"Oh, I don't mean anything by it. I love mine. Though I have to say, yours looks better on you than mine does on me. Perhaps it's the jewelry." His fingers brush the one-hundred-year-old brooch so quickly and lightly she thinks she might have imagined it.

"Maybe you should accessorize."

"I understand that it is an important thing to know," he says, then gestures with his hand as if to ask if he might join her. She makes room for him on the chaise longue.

"Are you an artist?"

"Oh, no," said Suzanne. "I'm a bookkeeper."

"Now this is awkward. No one I meet is ever anything like a bookkeeper—everyone is usually Something Else. A writer or an artist. . . . Look, are you sure you don't want to be an artist?"

"I could be like that artist who hammered himself to a Volkswagen. Or maybe someone who sits in a gallery reading *Moby-Dick* while people look on."

"No, I see you more as the slather-yourself-in-chocolate type."

"That's a type?"

"Actually, it is. In my experience."

"I never ask anyone what they do for a living. I like it better when they tell me who or what they *think* they are."

"Who do you think I am?"

She took in his genuinely distressed leather coat, which fell nearly to his knees (and clearly cost a mint originally); his boots, his Levi's, his pristine white T-shirt. No jewelry, no tattoos, yet neither would look out of place on him. Though there was little that was obviously hip in his attire, you knew he knew what it meant to be cool and creative and apart, and that was why he didn't need the tattoos or the jewelry.

Before she could answer, he said, "I've got to ask you—what is happening with your hair?"

Suzanne's hand went to her head in time to catch the complete collapse of her clipped-up hair. Bobby pins clung to various fallen strands, which hung about her shoulders. "Oh dear," she said, wanting to get away, though the young man seemed in no hurry to see her go.

Instead, he set his drink on the floor, then reached over, taking out each bobby pin and holding them in his palm until he had collected them all, while Suzanne sat without moving. Then he smoothed her hair and handed her the pins, saying, "You look good this way too."

"Do you read?" she blurted out.

"All the time." He picked up his drink and watched the dancers below, while Suzanne marveled at the ease of this meeting. It was as if their parents had known one another when Suzanne and the young man were children and now, having had no interest in each other before, they are now meeting as adults, with all awkwardness erased.

Did he remind her of someone she already knows (the only other person she has ever known that was as beautiful was Jelly). Is it a pheromone thing? Is that how we recognize each other, is that the thing that makes us feel—nothing to do with intellect, emotion, or what the eye appreciates—we have known someone forever?

For Suzanne, who seldom feels at ease with anyone, the effect of this young man was quite unusual indeed.

::

THEY EXCHANGED NAMES AND NUMBERS.
Suzanne. Micha.

::

MICHA TOLUCA began seeing Suzanne. The first time he came to pick her up at her flat, he walked around, then asked, "Moving in or moving out?"

"Neither," she said.

"Oh, in that case, I love what you've done with the place."

"Which is nothing."

"Well," he said, "just making sure you know."

::

SUZANNE FELL FOR MICHA so effortlessly that it shocked her. Since she had spent so much of her life apart and alone (without loneliness), this sense of connection was for her as full of wonderment as a Gershwin song.

After their first date, she bought a Christmas tree, something she had never done. When it was delivered, she stood back, examined its shape. It resembled the grown-up version of a pathetic Charlie Brown tree, too full at the top, nipping into the center like a lady in a corset, then splaying out again, but not evenly. And the branches were sparse. She turned it to get a better angle and discovered a large hole of missing branches.

At the tree lot she had purchased boxes of bright, white lights (reminding her of the Last Days of Autumn party) that flashed on and off with an almost undetectable tinkling sound that one could only really hear if one was very quiet and very near.

Since she had not had a tree before, she was without ornaments. She opened her jewelry box and took out all her earrings and hung them on the irregular branches. But unless the lights were near enough to reflect on them, they ended up lost among the deep green needles.

When Micha saw the tree he said, "Putting it up or taking it down?"

"Neither."

"Well, in that case, I love what you've done with it!"

She laughed.

The next day he brought her a box from the Guggenheim Museum that held a large ornament, cut from a sheet of silvery gray metal, that depicted Santa and his reindeer flying over the Guggenheim, his impression on the enormous moon that dominated the scene. She had not ever seen an ornament like it.

"It's wonderful," she said as she put it on the tree.

::

THE FIRST TIME MICHA spent the night at Suzanne's he came out in the morning wearing his blue silk bathrobe, the one identical to Suzanne's from the party. She walked out to find him drinking coffee and reading the paper at her cardboard kitchen table, his robe held together by a brooch of a Japanese woman holding a fan.

"I feel more 'finished' this way," he said.

When he told her that the pin was from the 1930s and a gift for her, she unpinned it from his robe, which fell open, and that took care of the morning.

::

AFTER THAT, they wore their matching robes around the house together. He told her he liked dressing like her.

::

THEY WALKED AROUND the Presidio (once having a run-in with some military retirees on the golf course who got rather ugly with them) and the ruins of the Sutro Baths, and went to the movies in the Castro. They had dim sum at Yank Sing and listened to the pianist in the Redwood Room, which, they agreed, was the most beautiful room in the entire city. They spent weekends in Sonoma and Carmel.

They often stopped by the Youki Singe Tea Room, where they ran into Sal and Lucy and Jelly and Ginny and Max and James and Coco.

::

HER FAVORITE PLACE to be is Micha's studio because it is like being enveloped by Micha. Inside Micha.

::

THERE ARE DAYS when Suzanne tries to watch Micha without him realizing what she is doing, and her heart fills and falls and seems to dematerialize, only to reassemble in such a quick progression that it renders her breathless.

She thought she was in love twice before, but those times were nothing like this. I'm a cliché, she thinks to herself, believing that her heart sings! That she flies on gossamer wings! I am so ordinary. And this fascinates her: the idea that something as spectacular as falling in love could render her so commonplace. For this alone, she could thank him.

::

MICHA WAS COOKING in Suzanne's kitchen when she casually said that she thought it would be great to live in a hotel. She said this without weight, just in passing.

"And what is it that appeals? The transient quality of the people or the anonymity of the decor?" He wasn't looking at her, he was wrestling with the single, bent serving spoon she possessed. It went with the two very dull knives and crumbling rubber scraper. And the crummy pots that didn't come all the way clean. And the four mis-matched plates. His voice was tight.

"Actually," she said quietly, hearing the tension in his voice, "both."

Micha threw the spoon into the stir-fry he was making. "How can you live like this? Not changing, not caring. You live as if there is no tomorrow, giving nothing to today."

She said nothing as he left the room, grabbed his coat, and slammed out the front door.

Then he came back.

::

IN THE MIDDLE of the night, Micha rose and dressed. Suzanne awakened, asked where he was going. She wanted to know if he was coming back but couldn't bring herself to ask the question.

He sat on the edge of her bed and tried to explain that he couldn't undo the love he felt for her but he couldn't continue. Her empty flat frightened him.

He went on to say that she did not know the man he used to be, when he lived in New York and didn't need a home or money because everyone took care of him. And how he gave himself over to nothing, not even the pictures he painted, and how he lived a life in which he felt his actions were without consequence. It was a life of pleasure and drifting, and how one day it came to him that he was lost.

And that when he saw her at the converted church, under the artificial stars and looking perfectly happy by herself, he was drawn to her. She seemed to be enjoying the moment. And that he had read somewhere that enlightenment is a result of no longer having desire, of being happy with the way things are.

Then he saw her flat, and knew that its emptiness wasn't the result of being without desire. The same way that his New York life wasn't without desire. And then he fell in love with her, but he recognized emptiness when he saw it. Because they were so very much alike, he knew that this nothingness in her life didn't have to do with material things—that wasn't the point—but that people with nothing have nothing to lose. He *knew* her, he said again. And that is why I have to go.

SUZANNE CRIED INTO the palms of her hands as she sat at the cardboard box in the kitchen. She took the sheet off, no longer willing to pretend the box was something it was not. Why her place was so bare, she could not say.

She only knew that when she tried to buy things she panicked, her breath caught up short—the dizziness, the light nausea, the airlessness of it all. That is not to say that she liked the way her flat looked.

She loved her friends' houses, admiring their things, the touch and feel of their possessions. The smell of fresh-cut flowers in a Chinese vase. The intricate patterns on a dish, the pleasing luster and weight of a silver spoon. Even her friends who had little money still made homes out of nothing.

COCO SAID, "Let's spend the day together."

"I miss him," Suzanne said, but she agreed to go to the Museum of Modern Art ("Won't it make you cry?" asked Coco. "Everything makes me cry," replied Suzanne).

They wandered, together and apart, and Suzanne did not feel like crying. They wandered silently, happily from room to room, largely uninspired by what they saw; still there was a soothing joy to being surrounded by these pieces of art. Then Suzanne happened upon a work by Marcel Duchamp called *Box-in-a-Suitcase*.

She stopped.

She stared and stared at it, under its protective Plexiglas, as she turned insensible to her surroundings. Her mind went lively with a sense of discovery: If she had to sum up the way she lived, it would be *Box-in-a-Suitcase*.

Calvin Tomkins wrote of Marcel Duchamp: "The Anschluss in 1937, the Munich Conference and Hitler's annexation of the Sudetenland, the Nazi-Soviet Nonaggression Pact, and the menacing build-up of Germany's armed forces all pointed to the inevitability of conflict, which Europeans awaited with fatalistic resignation. Duchamp, like many others, was packing his bags."

BOX-IN-A-SUITCASE (*BOÎTE-EN-VALISE,* 1941)

Duchamp was packing his bags.

Duchamp's response, in 1938, was to begin to reproduce his own well-known work—*The Large Glass, The Bride, Tu m', Glider*—and the ready-mades—*Fountain, Paris Air, Traveler's Folding Item.* He included *Why Not Sneeze Rrose Sélavy?* His "box" within a box eventually held sixty-nine items.

It took six years to finish the first box, which involved a suitcase and pictures that pop up and slide out. A little portable Duchamp museum. The one that has Suzanne so transfixed.

SUZANNE THINKS, So it is the war that creates *Box-in-a-Suitcase* and the truth that an artist's work cannot easily be transported. It does not lend itself to flight. And if a work of art is the heart of an artist (Duchamp cannot bear to leave his work behind), then how can one be asked to abandoned one's own heart to the fates?

R. B. Kitaj, an American expatriate living in England, said that "painting is a great idea I carry place to place. It is an idea full of ideas like a refugee's suitcase."

Suzanne reads that Joseph Cornell, himself someone who made boxes and could not bear to sell them, helped with the *Box-in-a-Suitcase* series.

The idea that a heart can be packed up and carried off, that you can keep pieces of yourself, contained and portable, that you can leave nothing behind. No trace.

::

AS SHE LOOKED at the Duchamp piece she thought, *This is me, I am like a refugee.* This chilled her—a refugee from what? No war threatened her; yet she could not understand her constant need to be ready to flee.

::

SHE FINALLY MOVED away from *Box-in-a-Suitcase* and on to another room, when a young man with wire-rimmed glasses and some kind of heavy, engraved silver bracelet (it looked Japanese; the drawing, not the bracelet) came over, seeming as caught by the work as she.

::

THERE WAS A TIME when Suzanne thought her lack of belongings (and the lack of desire to have anything) was generational. Her generation seemed attached to nothing. Content to float along, not caring, not owning, to remain in the moment. And, of course, they were all young.

Now they were all getting older, and she began to see that she didn't know anyone like her, that is to say, as detached as she.

It made sense that her monastic-seeming life scared Micha, but then she got angry and resolved not to call him, or speak to him unless he spoke first. But then, the emptiness of life without him was upon her; she felt his absence most keenly and could not stand it.

Whereas once the silence of her flat calmed her, now it made her restless. She paced and cursed. She broke down and called him.

She remembers saying, *Please*, though she was not begging, and remembers him answering with a surprising kindness, *I can't live with my suitcase by the door.*

She remembers him saying her name, because his remark about the suitcase forced her into silence. How could he know? And then remembers that he is the one person who does know her. Suzanne desperately wanted to persuade him to come back but did not know how, so the conversation ran out.

And, afterward, she no longer has to ask what she had been running from: it was the impending cataclysmic event, not of a war but of her own loneliness.

::

SHE TRIED TO TAKE her Christmas tree down many times and finally got around to it in February, when the needles dropped with the provocation of the smallest breeze. She liked the way it filled up a part of the living room. But it had to go.

She collected all the earrings and carefully took off the white lights. When she went to put the Guggenheim ornament in its box, she hesitated. She held it aloft by its string, contemplating hanging it somewhere in the flat. Thinking she could glance at it for a few more days, or weeks, or however long it takes (to get past this sensation of love).

There was nothing to hang it on. Of course.

Spring pressed on. Suzanne thought she could lose herself in the splendor of the days. Spending time in her garden, lying on her back beneath her beloved cherry tree, reaching an arm over her head to touch the trunk.

Going to the Youki Singe, seeking out the people she knows more avidly than she ever had before, and pleased at the reception she received.

Pulling the silk indigo robe with the saffron butterflies from her closet and smoothing it out on the bed beside her. Holding one of the sleeves in her hand and falling into fitful slumber.

::

ONE MORNING SUZANNE unlocked her nearly empty storage room and located the moon ornament. Took it back upstairs. She called Coco and asked her to drive her to Union Square, where she had seen in a window a metalwork floor lamp that had a stained-glass scene of a caravan crossing the desert at sunset. She purchased the lamp, loaded it into Coco's car, and went home.

When she set it in her living room, she took the moon ornament and hung it from the switch.

::

THE LOVE SEAT NEEDED a mate. A sofa stuffed with down and upholstered in pale moss velvet took its place across from the love seat. Another floor lamp, of Italian silk, arrived. Behind the lamp and sofa is a standing floor screen of oxidized silver engraved with lilies. There is a second floor screen, of gold paper illustrated with snow monkeys and clouds, in Suzanne's bedroom.

Plants nestle in terra-cotta pots of cracked white and blue. Strings of lights hang in the bathroom, Japanese paper lanterns in the sunporch and, eventually, out into the garden.

Drapes of amber velvet, and red, and silvery green silk. A print by Utamaro called *Love Deeply Concealed*; a blue painting by Bob Tavetian, and one by Vilallonga of a naked woman happily plucking flowers from the cushions of the blue sofa upon which she reclines.

A coffee table made of a sheet of glass that rested on the rusted metal backs of two crocodiles walking in opposite directions.

She clears a large portion of her savings on a used Stickley dining room set of table and chairs, and a vintage kitchen table with two chrome-and-Naugahyde chairs from a garage sale. In the dining room is a framed square of black wool on which someone stitched century-old silver *milagros* (miracles).

Stars are painted in one bathroom; grass wallpaper is hung in Suzanne's bedroom, which also has a vanity with an enormous, moon-shaped mirror.

Suzanne walked room to room, touching, straightening, mostly thinking, So this is what I like, not having had any way of knowing. Her things were old and new, some cost quite a lot and others, not much. Everything was all mixed up and punctuated by something she considers a luxury: books. Not her usual library books (though she still goes) but her own, making this house *her* home.

::

AND MICHA? Micha happens by around Thanksgiving, almost a year to the day of the Last Days of Autumn party where they met. When she opens the door, they kiss and kiss and kiss.

moon of the pleasure quarters

YOSHITOSHI
(1885–1892)

::

Moon of the Pleasure Quarters *is a picture that
can be read like an essay on cherry blossoms.
Cherry blossoms refer to courtesans;* Night cherry
blossom *is eighteenth-century slang for a prostitute. A cherry tree was situated at the entrance to
Shin Yoshiwara and was called the "cherry tree of
first meeting."*

*John Stevenson writes, "Cherry blossoms were
noted not only for their fragile beauty but for the
transitory nature of that beauty," their petals
falling prior to full bloom. "To compare a girl's
beauty with cherry blossoms is to imply her beauty
will soon fade."*

*This picture is an illustration inspired by a
chapter of Lady Murasaki's eleventh-century
novel,* The Tale of Genji, *which is possibly the
world's first novel, and certainly Japan's. In it a*

ghostly girl, who lives alone in a run-down house surrounded by yugao (moonflowers), is discovered by Genji during his travels. Since she will reveal nothing about herself, not even her name, he calls her Yugao, after the flowers in her garden.

He falls deeply in love with her and asks her to come home with him. They have a brief love affair, which ends with her death, though she is so insubstantial during her life one can see the moonflowers through her figure as she floats in her garden.

Moonflowers and cherry blossoms, pleasure quarters and gardens in gorgeous disrepair, all serve to remind that beauty cannot be possessed because by the time you fall in love with it, it has vanished.

A Museum Meeting

ON FIRST GLANCE, the young man gazing at *Box-in-a-Suitcase*, with his wire-rimmed glasses and longish hair held back in a short ponytail, appears to be a young graduate student, Coco guesses the sciences. He caught Coco's eye in one of the rooms of the San Francisco Museum of Modern Art as she was looking for her sister Suzanne. But now he has sidetracked her completely because, upon closer inspection, Coco notes that the matter of his attire spoils the notion of a life in academia, for everything about his appearance indicates money.

His shirt she recognizes as the work of a Japanese designer who uses fine materials and favors asymmetrical designs, with small, industrial fastenings made from used copper or steel. She would say it cost him about five hundred dollars, give or take a hundred. His glasses are from a very hip Los Angeles company and run about as much as the shirt.

Coco moves a little toward him, nearer; he takes no notice, still studying some kind of sculpture, she thinks it is, under the Plexiglas. She can make out the details of his wide, silver bracelet, with its intricate design of Utamaro's *Two Lovers*. It is a detail and not the entire picture.

The bracelet is inlaid with traces of coral, onyx, and pearl. The figure of the woman is mostly clothed, with one leg raised and her robe falling back to expose her nude hips. Her hands hold the man's face as she kisses him on the mouth; his face is obscured by her kiss. An open fan is held between them; there is a rail behind them, a flowering plant beside them.

Money, thinks Coco.

It is then that Coco, without plan or thought and fueled by unexpected desire (desire lain dormant, actually), abandons her search for Suzanne, moves quickly to his side. She doesn't know what she thinks she is doing but cannot stop herself.

Money

COCO FINDS HERSELF thinking endlessly about money. It so often crosses her mind that it crowds and colors all other thoughts. For example, if she sees a play, she wonders how much of her ticket goes to the actors' salaries, the producers, or other elements of the show. If she admires someone's hair, clothes, home, car, jewelry, or skin— it doesn't matter—her brain begins an involuntary analysis of monetary value.

She thinks this preoccupation is brought on by the times in which she lives, that is to say, a flaunting of wealth. (A wealth not shared by everyone, and set against a background of increasing poverty for many others.) There is no shame in openly wanting what you want, and thinking those who do not want anything are foolish, or worse, jealous. As if it were not enough for them to have German-made cars and Marina flats and a wine country retreat—no, they want you to *envy* them as well.

Other times she wonders if it is because she lives in San Francisco and cannot really afford any of the luxury of the city. The building that houses her studio apartment is shabby, despite the proximity of not one but two rather exclusive neighborhoods. Her car is old and unreliable, the furnishings of her home unremarkable, and most restaurants are out of her reach. No nights at the opera, a play if someone takes her or gives her tickets, and all the clothes she cannot have. Her lack of funds for travel wouldn't bother

her half as much except that San Francisco is such a well-visited tourist destination that there are seasons when she is surrounded by the accents and languages of the world. A world that comes to her and that she cannot visit in return.

Maybe it's because San Francisco, small and graceful, makes explicit its social stratifications. Coco does not live in the street, nor does she dine in a Pacific Heights mansion, and, because the city is so compact, she is constantly reminded of where she is and where she is not.

Being among the working poor in San Francisco has the insidi-ous quality of making you think that you are richer than you are because it is an intimate city lacking the bombed-out viciousness of poverty so common in other American cities. This lures you into thinking that the income discrepancies are slight, that you *choose* not to have the German-made car, the expensive night out, the wine country weekend, the opera tickets. And you go about your day thinking that because you don't live in the street (and rightly think yourself blessed), and you have a San Francisco address (in an awful building with storefronts, with increasingly crazy, sometimes dan-gerous neighbors), everything is the same for everyone. We are all San Franciscans. Even when you find yourself at the Museum of Modern Art, on a free admission day, shadowing a young man who looks like money.

What you mostly think is, Well, I just live in a different city. Same geographic location, different details of daily life.

Coco was once inexplicably invited to a formal dinner-dance by one of the clients of her firm, and all the other secretaries wondered why Coco was asked and not them. (The whimsical prerogatives of the haves, is what Coco guesses, then explains that twice she was mistaken for one of the caterers and handed dirty plates to bus by some of the guests.) As she made conversation with four couples near the buffet—her MUNI anecdotes, her crazy, dangerous neighbors, her street stories and Youki Singe tales—actually, you could pick any random day of the week and something had occurred, some moment—

"So many things happen to you! And to your friends!" a woman in pale blue sparkles remarked.

Coco started to say, but stopped herself, It has to do with income: high income, no stories. Low income, many stories. Whether you want them or not.

She wanted to say, High income and you can regale people with the description of that fabulous hotel in Venice. Or that fabulous hotel in Bangkok. Or in Morocco. And the guides you hire so you are never lost. And the food that is seldom a risk, and menus that translate into English in more ways than one.

It just seemed to Coco that, while she increasingly craved comfort, a five-star hotel anywhere in the world is really all the same place, all the same experience. Everyone speaks English, nothing is left to chance, the world conforms to you, so why leave home, really?

But lately she found herself less entertained by the vagaries of her life and more impatient and dissatisfied; tired, really, of all these daily adventures for which she does not volunteer and from which she cannot extricate herself without a significant change in her financial life. The kick she felt a few years ago has grown old.

And maybe the most enviable aspect of having money was being able to say those little words, "It's only money," and mean them.

Lenny's Suitcase

LENNY, THE YOUNG MAN who has so captivated Coco, is in the middle of an involvement with a very famous woman painter, forty years his senior. He had arrived, penniless, at the door of the painter's beautifully old, slightly fatigued house in the desert. The place was surrounded by a strong stucco wall, adorned with brilliant bougain-villea and some kind of wild vine, giving it the look of a closed com-pound as it sat high above a slender river, with trees and painted hills all around. The sky was the color of blue one dreams about in the midst of winter.

That was two years ago.

Prior to his coming to the woman's house, he had been knocking around the country in the years following college (no degree), end-ing up in one or two foreign locations, living on the cheap, unable to make any sort of meaningful decision in his life because he was infected by the belief that whatever he attached himself to would prevent his pursuit of the better thing that, he was sure, would come along.

And so he lived without any true love of person, place, or profes-sion.

Then he moved to Washington, D.C., spending the cold days of winter in the warm museums with free admission. He went to gal-leries and libraries. Anyplace where he could find shelter, since he was always trying to make his barely adequate trust fund last (his trust fund, he used to say, was primarily symbolic, in case anyone mistook him for wealthy). He read some, but mostly he looked. And the more he looked, the more he wanted to look. Until the time when the air was filled with spring and blossoming cherry and dogwood trees, and still he went to the museums and galleries.

His life had been itinerate, so he really didn't have any friends, and the art he visited became, for him, his connection to other peo-ple. Through art he saw who and what the artists loved, and what made them angry, what they believed in and what they rejected. Their entire lives (religion, philosophy, love) existed on canvas, Masonite, paper, cloth, in stone and marble and metal.

Lenny developed opinions regarding what he liked (or didn't like) and, for the first time, felt affection for something. It meant something that art was made by human hands. He started sketching the things that caught his attention in a notebook, so he could recall them later in his room. It was cheaper than buying postcards, and his copies were not half bad. He had a proficiency in imitation.

There was a traveling show at the National Gallery of a group of "emerging young artists" out of New York. It was when Lenny stood before three pictures by Micha Toluca and thought to himself, as a statement of fact, untouched by arrogance, I think I could do that, that he decided to see what his future held.

::

HE PACKED HIS SUITCASE and had left Washington, D.C., traveling to a village in the Southwest, when he heard of the famous woman artist, who lived like a nun on the outskirts. He was caught by surprise when he realized how the mention of her name and the proximity of her home excited him. For the first time he understood the effect of celebrity.

Since his sensibilities involved art, as opposed to sports or television or movies, it was natural that the prospect of actually meeting an artist would carry a certain thrill. This woman painter also had a persona that enhanced, and sometimes transcended, her art. (Gertrude Stein had said, as her own charisma threatened to, and eventually did, overcome her work, that people seemed more interested in her than in her work, though it was her work that brought her to their attention, so shouldn't they be interested in her work? "This is one of the things one has to worry about in America, and later I learned alot more about that.") The woman painter was old and handsome and had been married to a famous photographer who, in turn, made her famous, along with her work. For him, she had been wife and muse and lover and client.

These days women admired her independence, underscored by her choice of the desert as her home. Her image was of someone willingly, absolutely, magnificently alone. The truth is there was a seriousness to her marriage that went unnoticed and unremarked, until she was asked why she continued to return to New York every year instead of remaining in her beloved desert. She replied, mystified at the question, "My husband was there."

LENNY FIRST KNEW her art, then he wanted to know the artist.

He contrived to meet her through some casual acquaintances, arrived penniless at her door, offered to help around her house, and soon entered the world of this rather reclusive woman.

TO BEGIN WITH, she was surprisingly unpleasant. Demanding. Impatient. Lenny thought that artists, making sense of the life around them, would be wiser, more forgiving, well past the pointlessness of cruelty and forgetfulness.

Then again, he could say something that delighted her and she would laugh a full, truly wonderful laugh and he would, briefly, see the shining girl in her.

Her home and clothes were spare, monotone, monastic; her pictures extravagant with azure, rose madder, alabaster, cadmium yellow, and manganese violet. Mint and smoke.

He loved her work from the start, with its smooth, unbroken surfaces of color. She told him that when she was an art student she had fallen for the flatness of Japanese wood-block prints. He liked her flowers, abstractions, and skulls, but what he deeply adored were her city scenes of buildings and streetlights and shadows and moons. In one city picture, she had painted the name of her husband on a neon sign, lost among the other signs on the street.

What he learned, primarily from the woman painter, was contradiction. Night and light; wonder and callousness.

WHEN HE FINALLY confessed that he, too, had artistic ambitions, she demanded to see his work, for he had been working on some very small paintings in his free time.

He brought them to her. She said, "Why don't you work larger?"

"I can't," he said, not wanting to say that he would work only on pieces as large as a suitcase. Some part of him was still homeless and moving restlessly about the country.

Then she said, "Why don't you move in with me? You can work here." She gazed at his pictures, and he thought he heard her say softly, "You remind me of someone I used to know."

HE DROVE HER to the market and took care of the details of her life. Helped with her correspondence, travel arrangements, and requests for shows or appearances. He was her buffer from a larger world. They took trips together, some business, usually leisure. They actually got along quite well. It turned out that they liked each other, laughed together. Their conversations wound in and out of time spent waiting in airports, or, more often, on long driving trips, or making a variety of decisions regarding her life and work.

Though he could not get accustomed to her difficult side, he began to understand it by knowing her well. It was ironic that once he made this leap, he seldom saw this part of her anymore.

::

SHE ASKED HIM for a great favor. "I was married once," she said, "as you know." Then she said, "I want to make a substantial donation of photographs to a museum in New York, and I'd like you to help me." For all the times he'd acted as her secretary in dealing with museums, she had not involved him beyond letter writing. That is, she did not consult him.

So while it was flattering to be asked to work with her, he was also irritated; she was aware that he had just started a series of pictures and was anxious to work them through. He was preoccupied these days, mentally already having begun the project, considering form and shape and color, pictures existing in the abstract, if not yet in fact. He wanted to get to work.

By now she worded her demands as requests, behaving in a more "feminine" way toward him. But they were demands, nonetheless. He tried to explain, politely, that he was actually needing a little more time to himself these days, not less, saying, I know you understand.

Her response was to say that whatever he was doing could wait, with the implication that her work should take precedence over his. Whatever pleasure he had experienced when he was asked to help with her bequest was lost to him in his anger at her. It also reminded him of the traces of inequality left in their friendship. When he began to argue this point with her, she said, "Just like my husband," and left the room.

::

THE PHOTOGRAPHS, fanned out and grouped loosely on the floor around them, took his breath away. There were hundreds of pictures of the woman artist, a biography comprised of photographs saying as much about the subject as they did about the photographer.

It was kaleidoscopic—her youth, her middle age, her moods refracted and repeated in each pose and expression. Now she is young (twenty-nine: a year younger than he is now) and nude, or in partial states of undress, clearly someone's mistress. Now she is married. Now she is middle-aged, no longer someone's mistress, but more like someone's companion. Her emotional life an open secret.

It is a marvelous, almost unmanageable valentine. It is as epic as the Taj Mahal, another husband's adoration of his wife. It is a time line, a thousand-year-old Japanese novel that unscrolls and unscrolls.

::

IN THE COURSE of organizing, cataloging, sorting, the woman painter tells Lenny stories about the pictures (that is, stories about herself). When she was young, she spent her late teens and the entirety of her twenties in and out of school, living here and there. Restless for something. And how much she loved her time in the West with all that unused space.

She was twenty-nine when she met the man who was to become her husband. And how she loved him, and how they had trouble with devotion (of all kinds), and how so many arguments turned on the difficulty of conforming her workday to his; eventually, her entire work life to his.

In this way Lenny came to understand that the remark about being *just like my husband* was not directed at him; it was leveled at herself.

::

DAY AFTER DAY, sorting through the images of her: sexual, barely dressed or unclad, the haiku of her hands, her still beautiful middle age; her unknown years, her famous years. The dark hair, the white skin. The intelligent eyes, the infrequent, charming girlishness of her smile and laugh, rare and elusive. She mentioned that she had "broken down" twice in her life, when she was well past forty and suffering from a kind of distress of the heart. Her recoveries were long and tough, and Lenny knew it to be true because he could identify a sort of surrender or sadness in a handful of shots.

All of this brought him closer and closer to her, even as it took him farther from his own work, which he did not seem to miss much.

Lenny changed toward the older woman; he searched her face and hands (my God, her hands) for the young woman in the pictures. He got to thinking about youth and age and wondering, Where do people go? Babies are nothing like children, who are nothing like teenagers, who are nothing like middle-aged adults, who are nothing like the elderly. How is it possible to be the same and not the same? Here he sits, with a woman close to seventy, and he can barely discern the young girl in her.

::

SHE IS BREAKING his heart and doesn't even know it; Lenny has fallen in love with her. It is all confusion because he doesn't know what to do with these unfortunate emotions. He feels he loves the essential her, which must be timeless, he believes; then again he is attracted only to the young woman in the photographs. He subtly withdraws from their friendship, because his every impulse is to pull nearer, to take refuge. The impossibility of age stops him.

::

HE FINDS A PICTURE among the photographs of a young man who is not her husband. The date on the reverse is too early for the man she eventually married. The young man is handsome and happy.

"Oh," says the woman as Lenny holds the picture, "that's not part of this. It's a little more personal."

She says, "It didn't work out. Maybe I should say, it didn't work out for me. He thought we were great friends."

She gently takes the picture from Lenny, places it to one side, but not before Lenny notes the resemblance between himself and the man in the picture; they could be brothers.

It occurs to him that he and the woman artist are both melancholy with love for what they cannot have. Perhaps he should say for *whom* they cannot have. Lenny learned from her, early on, the effect of time and money on an artist's life; what he is now learning is that time touches love as well.

He tells her that he needs to go away for a couple of weeks but he will be back, leaving her no choice but to let him go.

Box-in-a-Suitcase

WHICH BRINGS LENNY to the San Francisco Museum of Modern Art, where he is so fixated on the work before him that he never notices Suzanne (who has left the room), or senses the proximity of her sister, Coco. He continues to look at *Box-in-a-Suitcase, 1941* by Marcel Duchamp because it reminds him of his previous life. The life in which he loved no person, place, or profession.

Now his life is tangled with various attachments: He loves museums, loves the work of other artists, he loves working on his own pictures, but, most of all, he loves the woman painter. He loves her and cannot have her.

Now he is thinking specifically of the young woman in the pictures. He loves her straight, dark hair, almost black, and her wide smile. Her loves her slender frame, and her hands, and her white skin. He loves her dark eyes. And he loves the artist she becomes.

He gazes again at *Box-in-a-Suitcase* and knows that his previous, uncaring life is over.

He loves her and he cannot have her.

Coco

COCO HAS QUIETLY MOVED around Lenny, with his Japanese designer shirt and his Utamaro bracelet of two lovers. She should not be here, she should find Suzanne, but Coco is so weary of a life in which she barely gets by that she feels she could be capable of almost anything—pursuing a stranger, for example, who looks like money—just to see what it would feel like to indulge her smallest whim. To not have to hold back and think about what you are about to do. She often imagines rich people simply acting on harmless impulse, and now she is behaving impulsively.

This is not who she is, she reminds herself, as she stands across from the young man. She almost blurts this out to him, as if he has been listening to her inner thoughts the entire time; she wants to defend herself, saying, I don't really think this much about money. Then she is lost again, just wondering what it would all be like.

Lenny

WITHOUT HOPE.

He lifts his gaze from *Box-in-a-Suitcase*, and it falls on a young woman, maybe in her late twenties, situated across from him and looking at the Duchamp. She is delicately built and has straight, dark hair, dark eyes, and very pale skin.

She doesn't look exactly like the girl in the photographs, but they are the same type. The girl in the photographs is more arresting, a little more unusual, while this girl is commonly pretty.

The young woman continues to study *Box-in-a-Suitcase*, but something in the way she holds herself seems to him as if she is not only very aware of his interest in her but subtly inviting his attention.

The Question

CAN THE PURITY of love be muddied by the way of love?

The Recklessness of
What He Wishes For

LENNY WATCHES COCO while turning something over in his mind. The longer he stares at her, the more familiar she becomes. She is beginning to feel so known to him that he wonders if she *would* be shocked by what he has in mind. Somehow, he doesn't think so.

The Recklessness of
What She Wishes For

COCO WAITS. Dreams of rescue are clouding all thoughts of caution. He seems to want to speak to her; she doesn't want to question why. She tells herself, This is exactly the way lovers meet, by chance. Then has to remind herself that she is long past notions of chance and is already onto methods of design. All this could be seen as a bit unsavory, but she is far past caring.

The Kiss

COCO LOOKS UP and into Lenny's eyes without coyness, without reserve. He does not hide the fact that he has been observing her.

This is how they stand, separated by the Duchamp with its box and suitcase and miniature works of art.

Their desires are so different and yet so fatally matched, it is as if the gods conspired to allow this moment.

Lenny's fingertips rest on his lips (something he often does when thinking something through), then he surprises himself by placing a kiss upon them. He reaches across to Coco, lightly brushing her mouth with his fingers, leaving the kiss, like a covenant, behind.

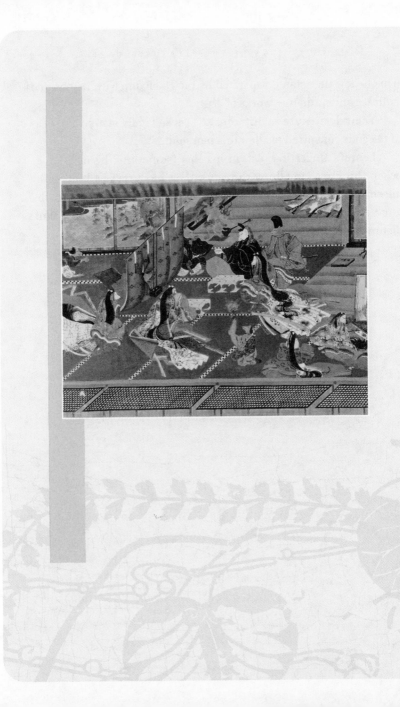

tale of a strange marriage

UKITA IKKEI
(1850)

::

This narrative scroll was done during the last twenty-five years of the Tokugawa rule, which began in the first years of the seventeenth century and ended, along with Japan's isolation, in the mid—nineteenth century. It depicts the courtship and betrothal of a fox and a vixen.

It was not uncommon in the nineteenth century for insects, animals, birds, and imaginary creatures to represent the intrigues of humans. Often, the intrigues were political.

This particular scroll was once thought to have political marriage overtones. On the other hand, since Ikkei did not leave a written explanation, this picture could be satirical or whimsical.

One could think of it this way: It is impossible to choose who we love.

The book is a love story, the New York love story of a triangle marking time. The love story is serious and important and tragic to the people in it, but a matter of comic burlesque to all casual outsiders.

—DAWN POWELL, *The Diaries of Dawn Powell*

PIROUZ

HOW DOES LOVE BEGIN?
For Pirouz, it started with a photograph.

::

HIS FAMILY, originally from Tehran, lived in the tiny French Alps town of St.-Cloud. Pirouz, who was fluent in English, thought it was called St.-Cloud because it was up among the clouds, then learned that the French word for *cloud* (obvious since he was in France) was *nuage*, as in *nuage entre mal vu*, meaning to be under a cloud.

Pirouz missed the heat of Iran, the exquisite, lush garden of his family home, and their villa by the sea. St.-Cloud was often beset by dampness and gloom. Not a deep grayness but enough to cause Pirouz to experience a kind of lethargy and general disinterest.

Tourists seldom stopped because St.-Cloud was a place almost without charm. There was a main road that traveled the short length of the place, and a dirt yard where the old men played bocci. The only true point of interest was a deep, rocky gorge halfheartedly protected by a low rail meant to discourage the curious. It seemed to perform its function, since there were no gorge-related deaths, which may

have been because the drama of the rocky drop that terminated
St.-Cloud quickly grew commonplace until no one noticed it at all.

::

THE HOUSE THAT PIROUZ'S father bought was magnificently
unusual in that it was built against a cliff of irregularly formed
smooth stone the stormy color of slate. It served as a wall for all four
stories of the house; it was as if a giant had heaved an enormous rock,
breaking through one side of the house, causing itself to lodge in its
place. It was startling and impressive and poetic all at once.

There was an elevator that ran four floors up, and down to the
basement. Moroccan arches and twisted columns connected the
rooms, while gorgeous tile work of ocher, sky blue, coral, and pale
olive green adorned them. There were spacious public rooms and
smaller, intimate rooms. The plate-glass windows were cut in solid
sheets to fit the Arabic windows, which actually did not look authen-
tically Arabic. They allowed the inhabitants of the house to view the
main street and the almost forgotten gorge.

Pirouz's father adored the place.

The family also owned a very nice apartment in Geneva, where
Pirouz's father spent most of his weekdays, looking after his financial interests. The family took trips to Geneva for fondue and chocolate and concerts. Living between two residences felt normal, like a
continuation of their previous Iranian life. Not that they spoke of
Iran; not that they spoke of why they did not speak of Iran. Whatever
longing, or regret, each member felt was kept to him- or herself.

Pirouz was twenty.

::

THEN IT HAPPENED THAT, all at once, a homesickness settled on
the house built against the smooth cliff the color of storms. The

mountains made them homesick; the spring made them homesick; they talked among themselves exclusively in Farsi. Pirouz's teenage disdain for Iran (since he assumed he would always be able to live in Iran, he had indulged in the luxury of mock dislike for his parents' home) gave way to a nostalgia for a life he would never have.

Some of their friends in Geneva, refugees like themselves, said that it was only a matter of time before they could all go back, but they said it without conviction, while increasing their efforts to make Switzerland home.

Pirouz didn't believe it because he saw that his father didn't believe it, as he too tried to warm to these new countries.

THE SUMMER THAT Pirouz graduated from the university had him doing absolutely nothing, day after day. His parents allowed it because he had done very well in school and they trusted him not to turn to dissipation.

On this particular day he was sitting on a bench, smoking a cigarette near the bocci players with an open, upturned book (an English translation of *The Immoralist*) next to him. He was watching a small group of girls, American tourists, he thought, judging from the sneakers and blue jeans and general well-fed appearance. They looked like college students, except they had a rental car, no backpacks, and were poring over a gold-covered guidebook.

The five of them seemed to be lost. One girl was shaking out a map while the others concentrated on the guidebook. Why no one else cared about the map, he could not say, but the girl who held it (uncommonly pretty she was) caught him looking at her.

In an instant, he saw how essentially apart from her friends the pretty girl was.

Pirouz's first impulse was to avert his gaze, out of politeness, though for some reason he ignored it. The girl with the map smiled at him. Pirouz smiled back. She left her friends and languidly walked toward him, bold and confident. As she approached, it came to him that she knew she was pretty, and that she and her friends were older than he'd originally taken them to be.

"May I have a smoke?" she asked.

Pirouz picked up the pack, shook out a cigarette.

She stood in front of him, still holding the open map in one hand and an unlit cigarette in the other.

"How did you know I spoke English?" he asked.

"The Immoralist."

"Are you lost?" he asked.

She laughed, said, "Sometimes. Of course, I can't speak for the others."

"Hey," he said, "I think your friends want you."

The girl glanced over at the other girls, one of whom shook her hand in a cartoonish gesture of physical appreciation of Pirouz. The pretty girl turned back to Pirouz, who gave her a puzzled look, and she said, "That is the international hand signal that you are quite something."

"How can she tell?"

"Well, from a distance then, you are quite something."

"Oh."

"I'm Jelly," said the pretty girl.

"Pirouz." To which Jelly said, "Pruz?" He corrected her, but it still came out "Pruz" when she repeated it. He let it go. He liked how she said it.

"Are you in town long?" asked Jelly.

"God, I hope not."

"Where do you live?"

"Here. In St.-Cloud."

"Oh," said Jelly, who, having left a small town herself, understood the shorthand of dissatisfaction.

Her friends started toward them. Jelly, still holding the unlit cigarette, said quickly, "Maybe I'll see you tomorrow."

"This place is quite small, so if you are still here, I'd count on it."

"Then I'll count on it."

Pirouz watched her walk back to her friends with the same unhurried stride with which she had approached him. Her friends gathered around her, touching, talking, behaving playfully. He could hear their accents and note the unguarded warmth that seemed, to him, so superficial with Americans (who knew what their easy openness masked?). That incessant smiling. He wondered if they ever guessed how they appeared to others, how strangely unfriendly and insincere. This national characteristic seems to inspire trust and suspicion at once.

They were so different from the girls in Paris, miserly in their expressions of warmth, and their cold distance. Of course, those girls were wonderful to look at.

He wouldn't mind seeing Jelly again.

Perhaps it was the slowness, the laziness of her smile that made Jelly seem a little more mysterious than her friends.

::

THE FOLLOWING DAY, Jelly was strolling down the street when she looked up to see him, unexpectedly, lounging in one of the huge, arched windows of the remarkable house. She waved with delight as she stood below, unable to capture his attention; he was gazing at some point well above her head while at the same time seeming to focus inward, preoccupied.

Jelly knocked on the front door. The housekeeper answered and called for Pirouz, who reluctantly set his book down. It was written by Paul Bowles, lost in his dream of North Africa, spinning Pirouz into his own dream of sun and Tangier boys.

Pirouz appeared pleased but not particularly surprised to see Jelly standing in the front room of his house. He did not ask how she came to be there; it was as if he expected her.

"You have a housekeeper," Jelly said.

"Of course. Why not?"

"Merely commenting."

Then her eye caught the gorgeous gleam of the jagged, polished surface of the enormous rock face, with the sun upon it. She walked past Pirouz, her hand outstretched, and ran her palm over the beautiful facade.

"This is extraordinary." She glanced up.

"Four stories, and beyond."

"You know, I was so certain that you were a tourist like me."

He laughed. "Oh, but I am. Tell me, what gave it away?"

"You don't seem native."

And, recalling Jelly with her girlfriends, he wanted to reply, I could say the same of you.

::

PIROUZ THINKS, Our lives are made up of such small occurrences: the chance encounter, the correct observation. We connect over things as insubstantial and as necessary as air. He thinks, Love is in the details. The minutiae of love; that is all there is. Nothing big. Or maybe it would be more accurate to say that the enormity of love springs from the littlest of things.

::

THE DAY THE TWO SPENT together is a moment, something without beginning or end. At least that is what Jelly and Pirouz would have said if asked. A beautiful accident; a small incident. So perfectly contained.

When Pirouz thought back on that day he recalled only scattered impressions: a bicycle race that suddenly surrounded their car on the road between St.-Cloud and Geneva. The riders descended like a flock of birds (A herd! A pride! A gambol! A chorus! A cluster! An exultation!—

"How many of those expressions do you know?" asked Pirouz in the middle of Jelly's litany.

"One year's worth," said Jelly. "Someone gave me a book of days full of them. My favorite is a murder of crows."

"Yes, that is lovely," said Pirouz).

They ventured into a dozen chocolate shops, passed a dozen banks, and ate lunch at a place that served a dozen different kinds of fondue.

She explained that this trip was a gift from her parents, who'd offered it to her if she would stay at home and go to college; then she told him why she had declined and left. And how they gave her the trip anyway.

The rain came down in a soft drizzle. They visited an excavation beneath a cathedral. The maze of catwalks allowed them to walk above the dig, the length and width of the cathedral, the floor of the church serving as the roof above their heads. It was in the depths of the excavation site that Pirouz saw Jelly privately lose her confidence and turn quietly nervous. She kept wiping her palms on her jeans, subtly, trying not to call attention to herself, and taking deep, audible breaths. He thought he heard her talking to herself in whispers.

"What do you think?" he asked.

"It's great," she said with false cheer. "Fantastic that all this should lie below—" Her voice began to deflate, her color to fade, so he said quickly, "You know what? I think we should get more choco-late." Then she slipped her hand wordlessly into his as he gently led her out to the street.

::

THEY WENT TO a park ("This is truly the tidiest city I have ever vis-ited," said Jelly) with a life-size chessboard painted onto the con-crete. Jelly pushed the enormous plastic pieces to and fro, from square to square, with Pirouz standing nearby, watching.

"I'm not playing," she said, "I'm arranging. Not being a good strategist."

"What about with words? Word games? Crossword puzzles? Scrabble?"

"I do love a good crossword puzzle," she said without looking up. "I happen to do them in ink, you know."

"I'm impressed."

"Well, it is very impressive. I ink in the word that fits without regard to the words it intersects. And when I get to those words, I do the same thing. Sometimes the words cross correctly, and other times I just write over them."

"My God, what does that look like when you are finished?"

"You can imagine."

"But, then, what is the point? If it is illegible?"

"I find it relaxing. And I like the idea of doing a crossword puz-zle in ink. The confidence of it"—she looks over at him—"like intro-ducing myself to unknown men in foreign parks. I like surprising myself."

Pirouz came closer, examining her handiwork, caught her gaze. He held her face in his hands as she said quietly, "Ah no, you're not going mushy on me are you?" Kissed her anyway.

::

THE FIRST LETTER he received from Jelly arrived so quickly he wasn't sure she sent it from home. But after he spilled the contents of the envelope, he knew that he was wrong.

A photograph fell out. It turned out to be the first in a series of what she called *A Personal Jelly Map: A Guide to Home.* Someone (he fleetingly wondered who and if there was more than one photographer) had taken pictures of Jelly against an ever-changing backdrop of San Francisco.

Jelly on the Golden Gate Bridge with the skyline behind her.

Jelly in Chinatown, holding a Peking duck in front of a window strung with Peking ducks, all colored that strange, sweet reddish hue. A circle of polished sea green jade on one wrist.

Jelly in the doorway of a place in North Beach called the Youki Singe Tea Room, holding a glass with a bit of lemon rind floating in it and a notation on the reverse saying, *I'm not drinking tea.*

Jelly smoking a joint in the Haight at the Jimi Hendrix Electric Church, her eyes averted from the lens, watching some punk kids nearby; ditto at the Palace of the Legion of Honor (without the punk kids); sitting in the band shell in the Music Concourse.

Jelly eating lunch at Leon's Barbecue and, later, Jelly at the zoo, next to the capybara cage, another note on the reverse, *I adopted this animal.*

Jelly at Kezar Stadium; in front of a mural in the Mission; pointing out a WPA mural in a Financial District building; the view from the thirtieth floor of the Transamerica Pyramid; at the Ferry Building.

Jelly at the Haas-Lilienthal House, the Octagon House, Fort Mason, Fort Point, the Japanese Garden, the Mission Dolores, Washington Square, Grace Cathedral, in front of the Castro Theatre.

A hot dog being eaten outside Macy's; the ruins of the Sutro Baths; and Jelly's beautiful face in the lower corner of a shot of the women weeping on the columns at the Palace of Fine Arts. Jelly wrote on the back, *They are crying over a life without Art. Foolish girls.*

This final photograph contains a note with the words "This is my offering. Love, Jelly."

::

PIROUZ SAT IN HIS ROOM in the wonderful house at St.-Cloud. The San Francisco pictures had skies of blue blown with white clouds; some had fog, but when the sun was present the city glittered.

He added each successive picture to the previous one and thought about Jelly, with her cool, assured walk and her restrained fear beneath the cathedral. The way she moved toward him in the park, and the moment he held her beautiful face in the palms of his hands in the other park, the one in Geneva.

They slept together because the day provided such a profound sense of connection. They felt they might not ever meet again.

Then the pictures began to arrive, and he was reminded of how much he liked her. They had gone to an uncrowded, rather second-rate Asian museum in Geneva that was featuring a wide and mostly uneven range of Asian art and artifacts from the eleventh century to the nineteenth, with great gaps of logic and continuity along the way.

One thing the exhibition emphasized was the role of poetry, in the form of letters, commemorating events, and as communication between lovers. It was customary for lovers to send each other a morning-after poem following a night spent together. That is what came to mind for Pirouz when he put all of Jelly's pictures together: that she was sending him an epic poem of love and location.

Without meaning to, Pirouz fell in love. And the experience had all the attendant emotions of recognition, discovery, wonder, and a sense that there is home in the world. This realization came by way of beautiful, cool Jelly, though it was not Jelly that he fell for: It was San Francisco.

DEFINITIONS

Kara-e:	Chinese theme painting.	Public, formal.
Yamato-e:	Japanese theme painting.	Private.
Onna-e:	"Feminine" painting.	Introverted, emotional.
Otoko-e:	"Masculine" painting.	Extroverted, physical.

JELLY

JELLY SITS IN THE GROWING darkness of the winter afternoon. Her elbows rest on the tabletop, her fingers holding a cigarette she is not smoking. As her mind wanders she censors none of the random thoughts that blend, melt, give way, and transform into other random thoughts. This inconsequential circling around a central, pressing thought. It is pleasant to sit this way, allowing her mind to clip along, relaxed, feeling its muscle as it sorts through the ridiculous and the profound.

She is reading a book about *ukiyo-e*: the art of the floating world (a time and place of careless pleasure). Ever since that day in Geneva with Pirouz, when they discovered the out-of-the-way exhibit of Asian art and artifacts, Jelly has been learning about it. The funny thing about art for Jelly is that she can seldom tell if she loves it for itself or because it becomes, in one way or another, intertwined with certain events or memories or emotions particular to her life.

That day in Geneva with the oversize chessboard and pieces, and all the chocolate and the chocolate hangover the next day. Her friends had sometimes complained of the effects of chocolate: the flush of the cheeks, the used-up physical sensation, while she dismissed their complaints as fantasy. Until Geneva.

And the sweetness of Pirouz at the cathedral excavation site. He didn't mention her fear, or act angry, or mocking, or tell her how silly it was to feel that way. Instead, he gently guided her out of the artificial, underground light as if it were something he had done countless times before.

When they spoke of home, she knew that he understood her sense of dislocation, and that she could have a good life full of friends and live in a comely city and still miss the experience of belonging. And when they slept together, there was no awkwardness, and though he wasn't the first, or only, boy she slept with on that trip, he was the one she remembered.

So, when Jelly was in a bookstore at Heathrow Airport on her way back to San Francisco and she saw two books relating to Japan—one on *ukiyo-e* and the other on Edo and its art—she instinctively picked them up. They were reminders of her time with Pirouz; it was impossible to separate the Asian exhibit in Geneva from that day, and now these books from that show. It had all become a single thing.

When they were at the Asian museum, she had read a seventeenth-century poem by the poet Basho:

> *Even in Kyoto—*
> *hearing the cuckoo's cry—*
> *I long for Kyoto.*

It was about wanting something that you have idealized to the point that, when you have it, you are still longing for it. Something can be yours and not yours in the same breath.

This was close to how Jelly felt when she was pressed against

Pirouz, after night fell on that pristine Swiss park, with its chessboard and carved wooden animals, and they were alone except for a sliver of moon—she felt lost and found and lost.

When she got back to the United States, Jelly began a letter to him, telling him of her travels after their time together (he had promised to write once he heard from her). Words failed. And so she sent a picture. Then another, and another, very sure that he would recognize a nextday poem, from one lover to another, when he saw one.

JELLY WAS NOT given over to closeness with others. Most men she treated casually and missed briefly when it ended. Her girlfriends were chosen for their independence and bright minds and humor. There was a lack of need among them and easy laughter. And because Jelly was uncomfortable with being needed she had trained herself not to need in return. When she went through her difficult moments, she did so in solitude. Sometimes cursing herself for her lack of deeper connection.

Even when she was social, she was alone, not unhappily (or so she thought), and was seldom depressed. It was as if neither happiness nor sadness went deep enough.

Her beauty inspired a constant parade of admirers, male and female, though her tendency was to stay closer to her friends like Coco and Gracie and Theo and Kit. Men she meets at parties call. She hears from her friend James. Makes her appearances at the Youki Singe Tea Room, smokes pot in the teahouse, wanders the night with a variety of friends that she meets there. Her jobs mean nothing though she is not ready to pursue a job that would mean more.

And still sometimes she wants to meet someone who will affect her so absolutely that he can break her heart to pieces. Then she reminds herself to be careful what she wishes for.

::

SHE TOLD HER FRIEND Kit that she saw marriage as an either-or proposition and that it seemed to her a cancellation of another life (what other life, she did not know), while not being enough of a life in itself. She also mentioned that she might be in love with being in love.

"You are so seldom in love," said Kit.

"Then maybe I am taken with romance," for she looked forward to the breathlessness, weightlessness, sleeplessness of it all; the way in which her life converted to the pure energy of sensation (often thinking this was the main attraction, since an overabundance of energy was a reversal of her usual pattern of lethargy. In love, she could get things done). She liked what she termed the "strange stability of a love affair."

The inevitable breaking point was when the man wanted marriage or a more permanent arrangement while she didn't want to live with anyone. She wasn't interested in children because she lacked the imagination to live for tomorrow, even though she would not say of herself, "I live in the moment."

And while she liked the effect of dancing with her beautiful girl-friends in public places, girls didn't interest her either. The one or two she went out with, once or twice, bored her as much as men did with their talk of "relationships."

Before she left on her trip to Europe, she had begun to feel a new sort of fitfulness, and all her love affairs began to seem like one rock after another that she endlessly rolled up a hill, only to watch it roll back down before it reached the summit. At the bottom she finds all these loves that are not all that deep, yet pile up so effortlessly.

She believes she cannot change.

"One day I shall be alone," she tells Kit with the sly affectation of a nineteenth-century coquette, "and old, and I will be sorry. I will be older, my looks faded, and willing to say yes to anyone who asks."

"You think too much," Kit says.

But the truth was she really didn't like looking at her life too closely, preferring to live what one old boyfriend called Your Unexamined Life.

That is why she would not have predicted Pirouz. Homeless, restless Pirouz, for whom she felt an affinity, each of them a variety of tourist who travels and travels but never arrives. His company made her see the possibilities of belonging to someone and having them belong to you.

::

AFTER THE RUSH of photographs, he wrote to her, and she wrote to him, Come stay with me. No strings. No obligations. (She was a master at evading obligation and knew that sometimes even vague responsibilities would prevent people from doing something small—say, visiting—at the risk they would be asked for something big—say, staying.)

When Pirouz arrived, it was unmistakable that she affected him, though not romantically. When this fact came to light, Jelly laughed while Pirouz looked confused, and Jelly was unable to explain how she had spent so much of her young life (she of the honey-colored hair and slender hips) being the object of desire, of having what she wanted, in many ways, on her own terms, and when she finally found someone she wanted back, she could not have him. She ruefully, sadly whispered to herself:

> *Even in Kyoto—*
> *hearing the cuckoo's cry—*
> *I long for Kyoto.*

"What?" said Pirouz. "What did you say?"

"Nothing," she said and reached out to reassure him. "It's better to have a good friend, anyway." She knows he will be a very good friend. They will hang out and gossip about the people they know (she will introduce him to all her friends and they will warm to him because it is so easy to like Pirouz). He will live with her though they won't share a room or a bed, and he will come to know her very well (and still like her, she believes). She cannot put into words why he won't be her lover, but she knows it, instinctively, to be true. Yet the intimacy of their friendship will be something, she thinks, but not everything. It is the way of her life, perhaps her fate. When intellect fails, Jelly falls back on fate.

::

THAT WAS FIVE months ago. Jelly stubs out her cigarette, rises from the kitchen table. She and Pirouz are meeting Kit and Raphaella at City Hall because they are to be married. Pirouz and Jelly.

Afterward, Max and James (if he is feeling up to it) and Gracie and Roy and Coco, Suzanne and Micha (she thinks Elodie is coming, but Elodie has been so elusive these days it's hard to know) are going to dinner at the Tonga Room at the Fairmont.

The Tonga Room has an imitation lagoon in the center of the restaurant, and a fake rainstorm pours down three times an hour. There is a band that sometimes plays on a barge floating in the lagoon, and a girl who wanders, table to table, with a camera, offering to take black-and-white glossies that can be placed in a paper frame or made into matchbook covers.

In all likelihood, that girl will take Jelly and Pirouz's only wedding photograph. She imagines the girl stopping by the table and the laughing encouragement of their friends as Jelly and Pirouz pose.

Her wedding dress is not a wedding dress but a vintage ivory beaded cardigan that she already owned, paired with a pale pink (almost white) rustling shantung silk skirt, full and sweeping, that moves in whispers. The skirt is left over from a black-tie soiree that Jelly went to last year.

She adorns her smooth, side-parted hair with a pair of ruby-and-pearl clip earrings. Applies her minimal makeup. Then examines her face in the mirror.

Does she appear bridal and radiant? Happy? About to embark on her new life with her new husband? No, she does not. She looks like she is in unrequited love (a little hungry, a bit forlorn).

They are marrying so Pirouz can stay in San Francisco. Because he is in love. But not with her.

::

ONE NIGHT, when Pirouz had been living with Jelly for two months, Kit invited them to go and hear a friend sing.

They met up at a place in the Theater District called Onnagata. Kit was standing near the entrance as she finished smoking a joint.

Inside, it was crowded and dark and scented with pot and cigarette smoke. Kit led them to a dime-size table, next to the stage, that had been reserved. When Jelly's eyes adjusted she noticed the number of very fine-boned, sometimes exotic, arresting women.

Raphaella stepped into the spotlight. She began to sing a song she wrote; it was operatic in form and content, like an aria, and sung in a mezzo-soprano of such purity that Jelly's first thought was, What is she doing in this place?

All her songs were affecting and inexplicably heartbreaking. The words were English but carried the romance of Italian or Spanish, something less Germanic. The songs were not opera, they just seemed related to opera in the way they roamed and came back, having a looser structure than a torch or pop song.

During intermission, Kit turned excitedly to Jelly and Pirouz, saying, Isn't she something? then went on to explain they had met fairly recently; that she is Filipino and Italian and Japanese. "And she's not from here. I think she lived in France." Kit said, "You lived in France, didn't you, Pirouz?"

The clothes she wore added to her aura of the unfamiliar: layers of luscious silk in shades of very light yellow, apple green, plum, scarlet, indigo, and pearl gray. Her kimono was cut short, exposing worn jeans beneath and platform sandals that seemed almost Latin, increasing her height by many inches.

Not surprising, for Raphaella is small and fragile and could be described as exquisite herself. Jelly, accustomed to being the beautiful girl in the room, felt thrown off being in such close proximity (physically and in friendship) with Raphaella. Then she dismissed her mood as a waste of time and unworthy.

When Raphaella's show ended, she joined them at their table. Jelly suggested they go to the Youki Singe because she could no longer stand to be in this place with other patrons looking longingly over at their table, wanting to talk with Raphaella themselves.

This newfound jealousy deeply disturbed Jelly; she was not given over to envy. She felt it diminished her and insulted everyone involved. She would never allow herself to indulge in it, not once thinking it might be not an indulgence at all but a response that could not be controlled.

For Jelly, who had recently discovered love (and the possibility of losing love), was now learning the unhappy truth of unrequited love and gaining this wisdom through jealousy. This awful spiraling down of experiences she does not want.

She thought if they went to the Youki Singe, her haunt, she would be able to pull everything into control. She hoped she could, because what was truly fueling her outlook of hopelessness was

Pirouz. As he smiled and chatted with Raphaella, she was reminded not only of the love she did not inspire in him but of the effect that Raphaella was having on him: It was written all over his shy, shining face.

⠿

GROW UP, Jelly tells herself as she puts the final touches on her wedding outfit. Grow up, as she brushes on more mascara. You are a sophisticated girl. You have had a couple of experiences all your own. You know the score; you've seen the movie; you've *starred* in the movie, once or twice. This is nothing new: Everyone always seems to love someone else. No, that's not true. The truth is, requited love is rare and unanswered love is so very ordinary.

As much as she wants to be modern about it, Jelly finds it hard. As she told Kit yesterday, "I act cool and hip and ironic until my emotions run wild and then I revert to all that is primitive. I look to harm; I only care about saving myself. At anyone's expense. Of course, this is under a veneer of understanding."

"So, what are you going to do?" Kit asks.

"I'm going to marry Pirouz."

"Really."

"He is in love. I love Pirouz and I cannot lose him. If I have to marry him to keep him here, then I will."

Kit smiles. "You've just got to love our generation. I can't imagine my mother or my father marrying someone to secure a green card so he can stay with his American lover."

⠿

JELLY HAS TO WRESTLE her unkind thoughts, the ones provoked by jealousy. She tells herself there are many people Pirouz cannot love the way she wants him to love her—a senseless notion because she truly feels that everyone is capable of winning Pirouz's love *but* her.

Why is it that love and jealousy push us to such extremes of logic, leading us so far afield that logic is no longer logic? So extreme that all thoughts defy what is known of human behavior.

Jelly drags a chair from her bedroom, places it in the center of the bathroom, climbs up to see as much of herself as she can in the medicine cabinet mirror.

She is ready. She loves him. And she actually looks rather beautiful.

In front of the lens, I am at the same time: the one I think I am, the one I want others to think I am, the one the photographer thinks I am, and the one he makes use of to exhibit his art. In other words, a strange action: I do not stop imitating myself.

—ROLAND BARTHES, *Camera Lucida*

RAPHAELLA

THEY ALL—Pirouz, Jelly, Kit, and Raphaella—left Onnagata and walked to the Youki Singe, which took close to half an hour, but the early spring evening was mild, though damp with fog, and the lights shown in the night as if they were on the other side of opaque glass. No stars visible. No moon.

Raphaella was answering Pirouz's questions as he walked beside her, reflexively taking her elbow when they reached a deep curb with a wide, muck-filled gutter below. She was saying, "It's true. I might make more money in a larger room—and I have been asked—but I like Onnagata." Raphaella smiled shyly. "I don't mean to sound immodest, but my songs play better in a small room, and I need that a lot more than I need a large audience. For now, anyway."

"I think you're wonderful," said Pirouz.

Raphaella is not insensitive to her influence on men; she can see it clearly in Pirouz, for example. It is one of her greatest achievements; that, and her voice. With its true and crystalline sound, it transports. People want to be in motion, they want to go, to be elsewhere, they want to be lifted from one place and taken to another; Raphaella's voice and unusual operatic songs provide such a journey.

Along the way, people often become besotted with her, though she wants to say, It is not me that you love, it is my voice. It is the places it takes you. You are just confused. You are mistaking this feeling of soaring for a sensation of love.

If someone loves your voice, it doesn't necessarily follow that they love *you.*

And, for all they think you possess some sort of insight into them because they connect with your art, it doesn't mean you know them either. Not that they will readily believe it, or how would it be possible that you could depict them so faithfully, getting it all *just so right*?

Out of all this proffered friendship from strangers, Raphaella had learned the art of appearing accessible while remaining remote. Her elaborate clothing was a part of being visible and hidden simultaneously, leaving her to wonder sometimes where the outside her left off and the inside her began.

::

THEY WERE AT THE Youki Singe Tea Room: Pirouz, Raphaella, Jelly, and Kit. Ginny was there with Coco and Selena as they all crawled into the rustic teahouse for a smoke. They discussed their days, San Francisco stories of street-corner dramas and comedies, snatches of strange conversations and comments, other people's clothing, the way people act (as if they are alone and unobserved), travels on MUNI (travels on BART did not elicit as many anecdotes, unless you counted delays and being stopped beneath the bay).

"I was on MUNI," said Coco, "heading up California, and the bus was so packed it was frightening. I wanted to get off but I was trapped. We're halfway up the hill when the bus slows, slows, slows. Stops."

Kit visibly pulled into herself. "It didn't . . ."

"Roll back down? No, thank God, but I was sure that was next."

"I know someone who was on a bus that rolled backward. She cracked three teeth in the accident and was hysterical for days afterward," said Pirouz.

"Does anyone remember the woman," said Jelly, "who got in the cable car accident and claimed it turned her into a nymphomaniac?"

"Right! And she sued and won."

"You know, I was downtown one time when one of those highrise windows blew out," said Kit.

"What did you do?"

"I heard this explosion and I jumped under one of those recessed doors, you know, that some of the newer buildings have? and, within seconds, these glass shards rained down. It was almost biblical."

"What happened on the bus?"

"The driver told everyone they'd have to get off and walk to the top, where he would meet us and let us back on."

"I've done that more than once," said Ginny.

"Yeah, but this lady refused to budge unless the driver guaranteed her the exact same seat when she reboarded. The driver, of course, acted like she wasn't talking to him, except that he wouldn't move the bus until she got off. The rest of us are out on the sidewalk, standing in the rain."

"I love a good MUNI stalemate," said Selena. "You know, someone doesn't pay and the bus doesn't move. Someone is disruptive, and the bus doesn't move—"

"Once, I was on the bus and this guy wouldn't pay so the driver got off and had lunch at Zim's, while we all waited on the untended bus," said Raphaella.

Coco said, "That's why I walk everywhere. Really. I just couldn't stand it anymore. If I was rich I'd get my own driver, I swear. You know, I even got caught in a MUNI door once, with one foot on the pavement, and the bus started to take off. I yelled, 'Wait! Wait!' until the driver stopped and opened the door, acting like I was *bothering* him." Coco shook her head. "I mean, I *am* human life, aren't I?"

"There's human life all over this city that no one seems to care about," said Pirouz.

"Amen to that," someone else said, then it was forgotten.

AFTER THE POT came the martinis.

Someone mentioned the Café du Nord and how it used to be an old speakeasy, and mentioned the martinis there.

"The best are still at the Persian Aub Zam Zam Room," someone else said, to which they all agreed. The Persian Aub Zam Zam Room was a room and an alcove, with a large circular bar, a few tables, and a juke box with music that had not been changed since 1940. The problem with the Persian Aub Zam Zam Room, besides its being in the Haight, was the unpredictable behavior of Roscoe, the elderly man who had inherited the lounge from his father.

Roscoe's hours were subject to constant change (he might actually close at eight on a Saturday night, or he might *lie* and say he was closed to anyone new entering). You could get kicked out with the words "There's a place down the street for the likes of you" for walking in the bar, for ordering the wrong drink, for laughing, for talking. If you were ensconced at the bar (he almost always tossed people who sat at the tables—"I don't know why anyone would come to a bar and sit at a *table*," he would announce sarcastically, then throw you out), it could be quite entertaining to watch the baffled expressions of patrons who did not know if Roscoe was kidding or serious. The tentative way they tried to stay, and tried to go.

On the other hand, if you weren't in the mood it was far too much trouble.

Kit said to Raphaella, "Have you decided if you are going to New York?"

"I've only been there as a child," said Pirouz.

"Maybe you should see it as an adult," said Raphaella.

"Maybe." Pirouz was smiling in a way that left Jelly feeling bereft.

::

"I'M ACTUALLY VERY happy at Onnagata," said Raphaella.

She and Pirouz spoke closely and intimately.

"What's *onnagata*?" he asked.

"It's a Japanese word—"

"Do you speak Japanese?" Pirouz's body subtly leaned toward Raphaella, and since she was not moving away he took this as encouragement.

He whispered, "Do you want to do something, sometime? Maybe go for a walk? To a museum? Sit by the water somewhere. We could go for a drive—I have a car—the Marin headlands, perhaps. Wherever you want to go, I can take you there."

"You don't even know me," Raphaella was saying.

"My point exactly."

::

JELLY HAD LEFT to use the bathroom, and when she returned Lucy had joined the party in the rustic teahouse. Pirouz sat to the left of Raphaella, as she talked with someone on her right. Though Pirouz laughed, nodded, and was involved with the conversations around him, Jelly could see he was keeping himself available for Raphaella, to engage her when she stopped speaking with the person next to her. It came to Jelly that this is how she looks in Pirouz's company. He is so happy to be near the object of his affection that he is not bothered by the casual attention she gives everyone else. The happiness of being in a loved one's circle, which, like most happiness, is bound to be short-lived.

::

"I INVITED RAPHAELLA to dinner tonight," Pirouz told Jelly.

"Should I leave?"

"No, no. I'd like you to stay."

"You aren't cooking, are you?" Jelly knew that Pirouz's repertoire of dishes was limited and not altogether successful.

He held up a Thai menu. "I might want to see her again."

Jelly was quiet, then left the room. Pirouz followed to find her perched on the edge of the sofa, her elbows on her knees, her face in her hands. He had never seen Jelly cry or, for that matter, seen any sort of chink in her cool, beautiful armor.

He crossed the room to sit beside her; at his very touch, with her hands still covering her face, she turned and leaned into his chest.

"Jelly," he said, gently winding his finger in her hair, "I love you in my own way. This you know."

"This I know." Her voice was muffled and flat.

They said nothing more: Pirouz holding Jelly and Jelly allowing herself to be held. When she pulled away, he traced his thumbs down her cheeks, as if they too were tears falling.

RAPHAELLA RANG THE BELL, with Pirouz upstairs cranking the handle that opens the front door of their flat. It is the single interesting antiquated feature of the place. It is like having a ghost in the house, a year-round Halloween trick, because the door unlatches itself, then, without a sound, slowly swings open.

"Hey," called Raphaella, as she gingerly climbed the stairs. "Hello?"

Pirouz was waiting for her at the top.

WHILE THEY WAITED for the food to be delivered, Jelly fixed her face, collected herself in the privacy of her room, and Raphaella toured the living room. Pirouz poured wine in the kitchen.

Raphaella reached for a large book, opened it as she sat on the sofa.

"What've you got there?" asked Pirouz, handing her a glass.

Her finger marked her place as she closed the book to sip the wine, then set the glass on the floor. "Man Ray."

Pirouz sat down next to her, and they scanned the pages together. Until they came to this picture:

RROSE SÉLAVY

Raphaella lingered.

"Do you know the story of Rrose Sélavy?" she asked.

"No."

She said: "Marcel Duchamp invented Rrose Sélavy—pronounced *c'est la vie*—in 1920. He said it was not to change his identity but to have two identities. He kept her around, making art and puns and bon mots in her name; posing for Man Ray"—Raphaella indicated the picture in the book—"until 1941, when she left as quietly as she had arrived."

Pirouz studied Rrose.

"Wait," said Pirouz. He walked over to the bookcase and came back with a book of photographic images of gender crossing. "I never paid attention to this picture before, but seeing Rrose Sélavy reminded me." It is by Yasumasa Morimura. They looked at it together:

"A woman's hands and a man's hands," said Pirouz. "I like that."

Then Jelly interrupted them, the food came, and the three companionably sat down to dinner.

::

WHEN RAPHAELLA DECLINED Pirouz's offer to take her home, he wasn't sure what to say. He didn't know if she was letting him know that she wasn't interested or if she had her own way home and didn't need him. Or maybe she was afraid Pirouz would expect to stay.

Pirouz and Jelly were up late, smoking, talking, long after Raphaella had gone, with Pirouz coming to the conclusion that perhaps he should back away for a bit.

::

THIS WAS PIROUZ's first spring in San Francisco. He and Jelly were living in a flat in the inner Richmond, one block from the park, inherited from Gracie Maruyama and Theo Adagio when they decided to go their separate ways: Theo to live alone and Gracie to move in with her boyfriend, Roy, the man to call for whatever your heart desires, as long as it is drugs.

It is so unexpectedly suburban out here, so at odds with the more citylike sections of San Francisco. Given the compact size of the city, these distinctive neighborhoods are actually kind of a miracle.

The inner Richmond streets are wider and quieter, parking is challenging without being impossible, and the neighborhood is full of families. (Except for the yuppie couples who cannot spare the time to have children, let alone love them.) Love demands time and attention, and they can bestow such riches only on their jobs and, years from now, when it is almost too late and children are hard to come by, they won't even remember why this was so.

As Pirouz walks along Geary he notices a slight, graceful figure some distance away. His breath catches—he believes it to be Raphaella—and his heart goes into a kind of unexpected rapture.

Then he thinks, No, it is only someone who resembles her. He squints at the slim, supple build, the long, shimmering black hair, the tilt of the head, and realizes that he has begun to pick up his pace in a kind of pursuit.

Pirouz sees the girl climb onto a bus heading downtown. The doors snap shut and the bus lumbers off before he can reach it. He hails a cab that swerves so dangerously to the side of the street to pick him up that Pirouz hesitates for a second, thinking he would never get into the car of a friend who maneuvered so recklessly, with such disregard for other cars. Then he jumps in.

Pirouz tells the driver, "Downtown," and as the cab goes to pass the Geary bus Pirouz cries out, "*No no no no,*" startling the driver, who almost clips the lurching, sluggish bus.

"I want you to follow that bus."

"Really."

But Pirouz isn't listening; he's watching for the figure he wants to be Raphaella's.

::

"HERE," SAYS PIROUZ, overpaying the driver in his haste to catch up to the girl, who has now left the bus. They are on Market Street, the girl walking up Montgomery. He and she are separated by a red light. Pirouz suppresses the urge to dodge traffic, never taking his eyes from the girl, who actually moves with a looser, more boyish motion. She wears jeans and black motorcycle boots, very beat-up and down-at-the-heels. A thin tweed overcoat falls to her knees, making her thin frame look thinner. Her hair falls just past her shoulders. Pirouz recalls Raphaella's exotic costumes as a contrast to this girl's very ordinary clothing.

They are on Montgomery, Pirouz crisscrossing California on the diagonal, the girl with her wide strides. Still she is graceful and, at times, almost sexually indistinct. It makes him hurry faster.

He hesitates, allows the girl to gain a little distance, because he is bewildered by his own actions. Am I so overwhelmed by love that I would shadow a stranger across an entire city? Still he moves in her direction.

The Financial District is crowded in the middle of the day, in the middle of the week. Pirouz, with his trust fund, had almost forgotten that everyone else works during the day.

The girl pushes the heavy glass doors of a tall building with a carved facade and dull brass detailing inside the lobby, and goes inside. Pirouz follows. There is a slick marble floor and a newly built reception desk, where a man in a suit and a uniformed security guard sit, side by side, not talking. No acknowledgment of each other.

When Pirouz rushes in the man in the suit asks if he would like some help, and Pirouz answers, No, he is meeting a friend.

The man openly stares at Pirouz, as if sizing him up, while Pirouz glances distractedly at the entrance to the alcove, with a bank of elevators, where he has seen the girl disappear.

"Well," says the man, "why don't I call up for you?"

"She doesn't work here."

"Does she have an appointment?"

"Yes, no, I'm sorry." He reaches the elevators as the doors start to close, allowing Pirouz to briefly glimpse the girl in the tweed overcoat. He lunges forward, placing his arm in the way of the doors, causing them to spring back.

Pirouz finds himself face-to-face with a small, delicate boy with shimmering black hair, in motorcycle boots and a tweed overcoat.

Shocked and embarrassed, Pirouz looks away quickly, mumbles an apology, steps back from the elevator without looking at the boy, then hears, "Pirouz?"

At the sound of his name, Pirouz turns again toward the elevator doors (toward the sound of the voice), which again close, obscuring the boy from view.

"I WASN'T SURE if you knew. I thought you knew. I thought it was evident." Raphael is talking to Pirouz in the afternoon, on the first day of spring, in the nearly empty Youki Singe. They sit at a table near the window, not drinking, not smoking, just facing each other. Pirouz leans on his elbows.

Raphael goes on to explain how early in his life he knew that being Raphael was not going to be enough, that there was a sort of greed at work inside him. He believed he was an artist and not beholden to any sorts of rules, a singer with a gorgeous honeyed voice that sounded male and female. The music he wrote and sang was in a style (his operatic style) particular to his voice.

What he says is that he wanted to be doubled. Twinned. He wanted more than a single life; his compulsions of identity ran male to female, though he often wished it were not so because it sometimes made him tired.

"But it was harder to choose, to settle for one thing. I don't know—look at me. I'm not even a single race, why should I have to be a single anything? It isn't my nature. Still, I thought you knew. Didn't you notice the women in Onnagata?"

Pirouz too shy to say, All I noticed was you.

"You know what an *onnagata* is? Where I sing? Onnagata? It's a male actor who specializes in female roles. And I'm talking about offstage and on. Sometimes more real than real women—"

Pirouz cuts in. "Listen, I'm an exile with little hope of ever returning home, so I can never blend in, as they say. People in this country would sooner take me for a terrorist than a fellow citizen." Raphael laughs at the idea of sweet, generous Pirouz as a heated fanatic. "My family name is recognizable in Persian circles, but here, it is meaningless." Pirouz smiles. "And," he says, "my attractions to others have seldom been predictable."

"Foreign you and foreign me," says Raphael.

"But the thing is," says Pirouz, "when you called my name I was not the least bit surprised. It was, really, a kind of relief, even though I didn't *know*. I mean, you might not be what I expected, but you are exactly what I want."

Drinks are served.

And in the following months, though it is clear to Raphael that Pirouz has found sanctuary in him, and that he had proposed to Jelly as a way of staying with him, he, unfortunately, cannot share the range of his affection.

"I'm getting sick of crowds," Bill said one night at a particularly noisy gathering. "Let's take a walk." After ten minutes on the moonlit road, none of the lights from the school were visible to interfere with the vast, heavy, velvety blackness of the sky, nor did the sounds of laughter and music penetrate the almost terrifying hush. We stood still, enveloped by the awesome multiplicity of stars. "Let's get back to the party," said Bill, "the universe gives me the creeps."

—ELAINE DE KOONING,
Selected Writings
(1948 Black Mountain College)

KIT

Kit is getting sick of crowds (Pirouz, Raphaella, Jelly, and her). Kit loves Jelly.

They were friends, close and fast, who had spent much of their free time together. Their lives quickly overlapped; Jelly's friends became Kit's friends, Kit's friends became Jelly's friends. It reached a point where one was seldom invited anywhere without the other. It wasn't that they didn't date, they did, but none of the men lasted, and so the constant for each girl became the other. Even when it was understood that either girl could bring a date (to a wedding, a party, a dinner), they often chose to bring each other.

They began to kid about their "marriage." They'd say, "My lovely wife, Jelly," or "This is my better half, Kit," until everyone played the joke.

The girls were so good together that they were in demand for dinner parties, since there was no chance that they would argue or snipe or bring any sort of discord.

Flirting was not going to be a bone of contention (they were skilled flirts with different styles: Kit sunny, Jelly sultry). And they in no way threatened a couples world, since neither actively strived to be part of a couple. It was as if each enjoyed their odd-wheel status.

And so it went for a while.

Then Jelly returned from Europe. Then Pirouz arrived to stay with Jelly. Then Kit saw her life for what it was: a life attached completely and willingly to Jelly's.

On Saturday night, as she cleaned her apartment, purged her closet of a few things, stirred a pot of tomato sauce, she thought of how much she missed Jelly's company. They were still close friends (although, in truth, how close can anyone really get to remote, mysterious Jelly?), but Jelly was so taken with Pirouz these days, leaving Kit to question where her other life, her life without Jelly, had gone.

She used to see Gracie Maruyama, but she rarely sees her now, between Roy and her job. Her phone used to ring steadily with boys asking her out, and old boyfriends wondering what she was up to, had they mentioned they missed her? Now it was silent.

How had she let it all slip away?

It was her marriage to Jelly. It was all the times she said she had plans with Jelly, waited for Jelly. It was the way Jelly made their shared activities a source of amusement: the dull dinners with mutual friends, a drink at the Youki Singe, walking through the park, getting a haircut, sitting in North Beach, smoking a joint and running into the people they knew casually. The migration from parties to bars to someone's home. It was doing the laundry, going to the corner store, eating at Mai's Restaurant on Clement, dreaming at Satin Moon Fabrics about the clothes they wanted to make (and never did), or sitting on the cliffs above the beach, watching the ocean tide. It was the seemingly continuous conversation that ran a range of topics, and emotions, but was always, always founded upon a kind of lightness.

::

THEY BEGAN TO CARRY each other's history. Three years passed in a moment, with Kit believing that, without Jelly to refer to, great chunks of that past would vanish. All those late-night discussions, confessions, and recent memories made the thought of life without Jelly frightening. Why, thought Kit, it would be as though I had not existed.

::

EVEN THOUGH KIT KNEW that this best-friends-at-camp life could not continue indefinitely (someone would have to grow up and away eventually), she still could not believe it when it changed.

When Kit was a child she had the usual fantasies about doing whatever she wanted when she was grown. Her parents naturally tried to explain that such a life was illusive and unreal, and that we all have to do things we'd rather not do. And that it was possible to hate all your choices, and waste the wealth of your own life. Kit listened to her parents, looked at them, and knew what they said was true. Still, she held to her dream of a life of all desires met.

Despite her roommateless apartment on Clay Street, working at a job she did not hate (but did not like, either), having casual affairs, enough money to eat cheap Chinese food and Mission District burritos and pay the rent, and Jelly as her friend, Kit thought she had defied her parents at last by proving them completely wrong.

::

JELLY ACCEPTED KIT with her faults and flaws (to be fair, that was Jelly's usual approach to everyone), celebrated her little successes until Kit realized that what she got from Jelly—acceptance, humor, a kind of undemanding intimacy—were the things she had previously looked for, and, often, could not get, in the boys she dated. This made it harder for her to meet boys who *could* offer what Jelly did, until Kit could no longer see what these boys were offering at all, so caught up was she in Jelly.

Now, there is Pirouz, commanding Jelly's attention.

::

AT A SMALL, SLIGHTLY DERELICT dinner party, Kit ran into her friend Raphael. Since Kit was the only person Raphael knew, he hung around her for the evening. Kit and Raphael always had a nice rapport, always liked each other.

They embraced. He offered Kit a sip off his drink, which she accepted.

"Where's your friend?" Raphael knows Jelly by name and reputation but has not yet met her, since he came into Kit's life around the time Jelly returned from Europe and began lavishing her free time on Pirouz.

"With her new friend."

"You don't like this new friend?"

"No. I mean, yes, I do like him. He's very kind, and smart. He's rich and generous, but not in an icky way, and he's an easy laugh."

"Can I have him?" asked Raphael.

"Oh, I wish you would," muttered Kit. Then louder, "They aren't exactly a couple."

"Why is that?"

Kit took another swallow of Raphael's drink, then shook her head. She didn't know the answer because she had been too close to her own feelings toward Jelly to see that someone might not feel as Kit does.

And now, talking to Raphael, Kit sees what she could not see before: that Pirouz cannot be entirely won by Jelly. That he carries an affection for her that is not a passion; that he is like someone waiting, and that Kit has no idea who it is he waits for but, now that she thinks about it, it may not be a girl at all.

Raphael said to Kit, "Listen, unless you are having the time of your life, would you like to drop by the Youki Singe for a drink?" While Kit thought, *Raphael*.

::

THE RESULT OF PIROUZ falling for Raphaella was not Kit spending more time with Jelly (who was a little withdrawn and heartsick); instead, her days and evenings and conversations were taken up with Raphael.

He would talk about Pirouz ("Pirouz is nice, don't you think?"), with Kit wondering why someone was always talking to her about someone else. Still, Kit accepted this consequence of her romantic machinations, sometimes laughing about the way in which the gods really do grant every wish.

::

RAPHAEL AND KIT are at the Youki Singe Tea Room, upstairs at the sex show on the other side of the heavy velvet curtains. They sit side by side in the nearly empty theater, observing a girl in a dog collar, a G-string, and truly impressive cellulite thighs do some sort of gymnastics across the little stage. Periodically, a man in a suit with suspenders stands on the side of the stage and watches. Then disappears.

"Do you think he's part of the show?" whispers Kit.

"I can't tell," Raphael says. "He seems like a patron."

"An audience participation thing?"

"Yes. Like when you see a musical and they come out into the audience to involve you."

"I hate that," says Kit. "One time I was watching some musical production when I had to go to the bathroom. So I very quietly got out of my seat, but the minute I was in the aisle, I suddenly was hit with lights. Not only am I completely startled by the lights, but now the cast have leapt off the stage and are coming right up the aisle. Well, I began to hurry, then I started to run, and the whole time they're singing." She pretends to shudder. "It is very unnerving being chased by a band of very exuberant, very insistent show folk."

"Everyone probably thought it was part of the show." Raphael laughs.

"Oh, God. Probably," says Kit, laughing.

They are quiet again, sipping the drinks that the bouncer had allowed them to bring in, though it was probably against the rules.

Now the dog-collar girl is standing before a full-length mirror that the man in the suit and suspenders had dragged out onto the stage. She seems to be admiring her beauty.

Low, bass-heavy music is playing on a bad sound system, further muffled by the speakers being situated behind the curtain behind the girl.

"Who do you think this appeals to?" asks Kit.

There is one other man, besides the bouncer, in the theater.

"From the look of it, I'd say no one."

"But do you think this is meant to draw someone in?"

"Well," says Raphael, "we're here."

"That's different."

"Maybe, but the girl on the stage doesn't know that. For all she knows we could be in love with her."

"Maybe," says Kit distractedly. "Maybe you're right. I could be in love with her."

::

RAPHAEL CALLED KIT the next day, asking her to the park.

"I have errands."

"I could have errands too." So she invited him along.

They began to develop a pattern of everyday, uneventful time together. Marketing, dry cleaning pickup, laundry, haircuts, movies, and shopping. Watching TV late into the night when Raphael wasn't working (or seeing Pirouz). Kit still missing Jelly.

One day the telephone installer had to be let into Kit's apartment and Raphael offered to wait around while Kit was at work. Another time Raphael needed a late bill paid downtown, and Kit said, "Give it to me. I'll take care of it."

They made dinner for each other, not always inviting Pirouz and Jelly.

And so it continued, the endless series of domestic chores they now shared.

::

"DO YOU EVER THINK about getting a roommate?" asked Raphael.

"In my studio?"

"No, in my place." Raphael was pretending to search in his satchel as he made this suggestion.

"Speaking of moving," said Kit brightly, "don't you sometimes think that you and me and Pirouz and Jelly ought to just be done with all this and get a house together?"

"You know, Pirouz wants to marry me—"

"—so he's marrying Jelly. I heard. I understand that afterward we are going to the Tonga Room and meeting Gracie and Roy and Theo and Sal and Lucy, some other people, oh, and Max and James."

"How is James these days?"

"Not too good."

CITY HALL IS PACKED with people.

"I thought marriage was out," complains Raphaella.

"Yeah," says Kit, "but look at them."

Pirouz and Jelly are the only couple there even remotely resembling anyone of their social circle, meaning young (well, not as young as some of the prospective marrieds here), confused, much attention paid to their appearance, living hand-to-mouth with a kind of threadbare style. As Raphaella says of the other prospective brides and grooms, "These couples look like Real People. Like they work for a living—" And this remark sparks a round of conversation among the four of them:

"Hey, we work for a living—"

"Not the same thing at all. These people look as though they are exhausted each night. Like they have responsibilities and are trying to get somewhere—"

"We're trying to get somewhere—"

"Really. And where would that be?"

The foursome falls quiet, then begins again.

"In any case, that couple over there looks like they are still in high school—"

"Maybe this is the best they can hope for—"

"What is it about certain people or situations that brings out the elitist in one? Can you hate yourself for an attitude you don't even try to change?"

"The poor working class—"

"You know, with the exception of Pirouz, we're a kind of poor working class ourselves—"

"It's true. Someone once told me when he saw me washing dishes at a catered party where I was a guest that I didn't know how to handle 'help,' and I said, That's because I usually *am* help. And still I felt divided from the woman hired to do the cleanup, even though I stood by her side, performing the exact same function—"

"And isn't it a particularly bad feeling when you do something nice for someone completely disadvantaged and they show no gratitude and you feel yourself growing indignant?"

"Making you question altruism and what's in it for you—"

(Jelly laughs.)

"As if you cannot do a single, unselfish thing—"

"Well, what sort of person are you? And you truly disdain all those yuppies—"

"And would like to kick them for their ambition-at-all-costs. For their undisguised selfishness, and their greed and their material goods—"

"That we covet—"

"But I'm not like that—"

"Oh no, sweetheart, and neither am I, but when it comes to having a little extra disposable income, what do you think of first? Wardrobe or soup kitchen?"

"I want nice things. Is that so wrong?"

"Not wrong. I'm just saying it's the infection of the times, hard to keep out of your system, and maybe the only difference between us and yuppies is the size of our savings—"

Then someone, maybe it's the bride, suggests that perhaps the main difference between the four of them and the other people here is that they are marrying for love. "Our love," Jelly says, "is so mismatched as to be almost useless."

::

IT IS DONE.

They leave City Hall, four across, to hail a cab for the Tonga Room. With Jelly's arm through Pirouz's, as Pirouz gazes with love at Raphaella, who in the past weeks has been falling for Kit, while Kit still misses Jelly.

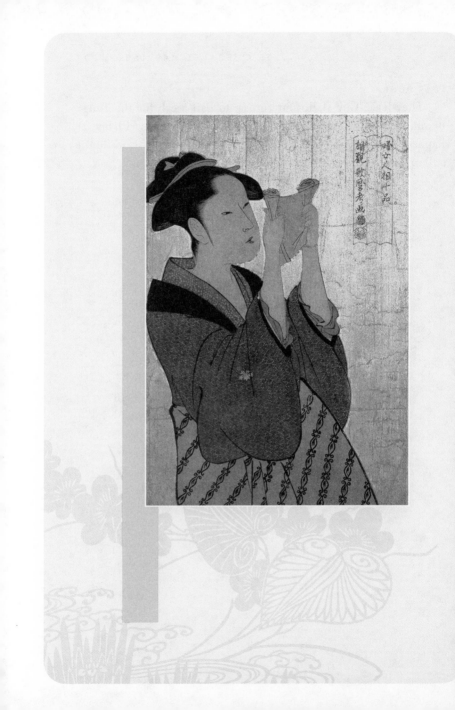

woman reading a letter

KITAGAWA UTAMARO
(1792–1793)

Judging from the woman's total absorption in the letter, and from the fact that she is exposing as little of it as possible, this letter is one of a romantic nature, received from an illicit lover. At this time, an adulterous relationship . . . could have fatal consequences for the wife. The feelings of the woman in this print, hopelessly caught between desire and despair, are suggested in her slightly open mouth, her narrowed eyes and rapt expression, and her tight grip on the letter.

—TADASHI KOBAYASHI

ELODIE, THE GIRL WITH THE TEMPORARY *INOCHI* TATTOO, with its eyelash-thin tail that trails down her inner thigh, arrives with two suitcases, having just splurged on a cab to get her up to the beautiful house, situated among other beautiful houses, on Buena Vista Avenue, above the less appealing Haight.

The Haight displeases almost everyone: the punks, the old hippies, the street folk, the tourists (who come looking for—what?), the renters, the landlords. It is as if it cannot quite come to terms with itself and, in attempting to be all things to all people, somehow finds itself without grace.

Buena Vista Park, held in the embrace of Buena Vista Avenue, is a sort of shy cousin of nearby Golden Gate Park. These days it functions mostly as a trysting place, romantic and otherwise, which provokes neighborhood disagreements.

The Panhandle is part of the park, yet not part of the park. It's a freestanding strip of green that is different in atmosphere from the larger park.

Golden Gate Park is without parallel in the city as it runs from Stanyan to the sea and, in many ways, is like a place from a nineteenth-century children's book of stories, with its merry-go-round and the De Young Museum and the Conservatory of Flowers, patterned after the conservatory in Kew Gardens. There is Kezar Stadium and the arboretum, and the aquarium with the marvelous fish roundabout. There are horse-drawn carriages and pedal boats on Stow Lake and buffalo in a paddock and a band shell and a place called the Garden of Fragrances designed for the blind, with its perfumed air.

A wall of limestone blocks from a twelfth-century monastery backs up to the Japanese Tea Garden, which a man named Makoto Hagiwara tended and refined. Until he and his family were sent off to a camp during the war and he was not permitted back afterward.

The story Elodie likes about Makoto Hagiwara is the one that has him inventing the fortune cookie for the 1909 Midwinter Fair. Stuffing cryptic notes into crescent-shaped cookies. Words and the moon, thinks Elodie.

::

THE BUENA VISTA HOUSE, with all its full-blown loveliness, is just another job for Elodie. She came to house-sitting with the same shrugging accident of fate that she brought to her various temp jobs. She often thought, as she sat in another vacated home that she was tending, or at her desk (where she didn't need to bother to learn the names of the other employees since, again, she was only taking care of the job for a real employee), that this is how you end up if you do not see to your own life. With minimal self-guidance, this is who you become.

She began house-sitting straight out of college, when her degree and intellect meant nothing to the world, and her roommate family (toward whom she did not feel familial, really) disbanded. All five of them had shared a generously proportioned, semi-sunny, once pretty bungalow, now used and tired from its many thoughtless tenants. This left Elodie open to suggestions. Her boyfriend-at-the-time's parents were traveling to Asia for eight weeks and wanted someone to look after the plants and the cat, turn the car engine a few times, but mostly just to collect the mail and newspapers and give the general impression of a house being lived in. Elodie told people that she was basically a decoy set against misfortune, that she wasn't a genuine inhabitant but provided the affectation of one.

It was similar to her temp jobs, where she was hired to work then treated like someone on an inverse office vacation, just lazing about. (When there was nothing to do she read—she had developed the habit of carrying a book when she was quite young—people seldom realized how much downtime there is in life, existing in the interstices of daily activity.) It was as if Elodie, who did the work of the absent employee, was looked upon as a cardboard cutout of an employee, with a brain to match.

It was so easy to live up—or down—to the expectations of those around her. Every time she walked through the door of a new company, she was identified as a loser. Someone not very bright (after all, why didn't she have a Real Job?). She knew people saw her as some sort of office machine. A rental of a different variety.

Much of the time she didn't care what they thought of her since it released her from the treacherous and shifting loyalties of office friendships. She was not expected to be true or to deceive; she lacked the substance for any sort of action. Layoffs did not affect her, or firings, or changes of location, transfers, shake-ups at the top, buyouts, mergers, or anyone's ambitions.

They occasionally offered her a permanent position, which she politely declined because she rather liked temping. She told herself she liked the freedom, then had to remind herself that temp work was so low-paying she couldn't turn down too many jobs, so what was the point of that freedom? She couldn't be fired, but she couldn't get ahead either. The companies and faces changed, but the tasks remained the same; her work life had achieved stasis.

She thought about what it actually means to live in the moment, behave as if tomorrow will not come. If there is no tomorrow, then one could act without regard to consequences, but since there is a tomorrow, how can one live in the moment? Who wants to live with the consequences of poor judgment?

::

HER LOVE LIFE seemed to follow the same pattern of temporary attachment. One boy she loved lived in a large, drafty flat on Telegraph Hill, overlooking the bay. He slept in a glassed-in sunroom (his room-mates having claimed the bedrooms), which was unheated. He would turn on his electric blanket and they would lay on his futon on the floor, peering up at the stars on cold, crystalline nights, and she would think, How happy I am! Life can be so perfect if you just let it. Now he is gone and what she most vividly recalls is the chill, and their frosted breath.

Another boy was more typical of her paramours. They had met at the Bohemian Cigar Store, where she was having a sandwich, and they got to talking. They went out once or twice, and she had two days between house-sitting jobs and asked if she could stay with him (he had stayed with her already).

"What's wrong with your house?" he asked.

"It's not my house," she said. "I house-sit."

And he began to laugh. Then explained that he was without a home as well, that he mostly lived in his car.

She laughed too, said, "You are so ideal for me you make me want to cry."

::

BOOKS AND WORDS were the saving grace in her life.

With books, she had entire worlds in her hands.

With books, she had a refuge and structure to her life. She lived inside stories.

Even the house-sitting jobs and the myriad offices contained elements of, if not full stories, a collection of anecdotes. And because her life was so ill-defined, she could try on different lives through books.

It seemed safe to love something so abstract because her life did not seem to offer her a way to have anything, and so she spent her time not learning to let go but training herself not to want.

::

ONE THING IN ELODIE'S PAST that she seldom thinks or talks about is that when she was a young child she had been chosen for a smart kid television show called *Another Wise Child*. Since she did not feel "wiser" than her peers, she always assumed her inclusion on the program was some kind of happy mistake that would be corrected once the producers discovered how unremarkable she was.

Later on, after the show had long finished (and really having nothing to do with it anyway), Elodie moved away from being that wise kid. Had grown quieter, asking for nothing and, as is so often the case, getting exactly what she asked for.

::

THE HOUSE-SITTING OPPORTUNITIES are many. Certain San Franciscans of a certain class like to travel. And they have nice houses and nice things and they like Elodie because she is trustworthy, admiring but not craving what they have. She would not think to take anything; with the way she lives, anything more than necessary would weigh her down, or ruin her with worry over loss or breakage, or theft. House-sitting gives her a life of luxury that is someone else's responsibility.

Her life looks like this: No car. No insurance. No furniture. No credit cards. No debt.

::

SO ELODIE SPENDS her evenings (and some afternoons) at the Youki Singe Tea Room, with her pilfered stationery, her pillow book, her outsider's eye, her love of words.

::

THOUGH SHE SELDOM admitted it, Elodie went through the belongings of some of the people in the houses she watched. It began with medicine cabinets, moved to closets: broom closet, hall closet, bedroom closet. She tried a few things on. She would adorn herself with jewelry if the jewelry box was left out. (The pirate's treasure aspect appealing to her.)

This house on Buena Vista Avenue received more of a once-over than any other place she had stayed, because it looked like, well, like Elodie. That is to say, its furnishings were things she would choose to fill her own house. And that surface familiarity provoked a certain level of investigation; she wanted to know *why* the house felt like hers.

There had been times in the past when Elodie was living with roommates or house-sitting, studying the taste exhibited in each place, and wondered what *her* taste would be. What would she buy? What colors and textures would draw her? And now she was in this house, taking care of its shy little tailless cat, picking up mail and catalogs, and she instantly felt that this was where she belonged. Since belonging is such a rare experience for Elodie, she sat up and took notice.

Normally, she did not read letters or papers or diaries of others. As much as her curiosity might prod her, she refrained. It was too much, really, to have that insight into the people whose lives she briefly borrowed.

In short, she didn't want to know what she wanted to know.

But this place was different. She had never met the family who lived here, and their departure was so hurried that they asked her on faith and the recommendation of friends twice removed. Still, she had the feeling that if it occurred to them that Elodie might invite a tribe of friends who would stay, or lift the silver when she left, this family would not have cared. Their absence seemed less like a vacation and more like a hegira. It was as if they were narrowly escaping something that threatened to crush them.

She was aware they had barely planned this trip, calling her three days before they left and indefinite about their return, though they guessed "six months, maybe more" and was that suitable for her?

::

A MONTH WENT BY. The little tailless cat always happily came when Elodie called. The housekeeper cleaned the house and told Elodie that she made her life easy because she was so very tidy in her habits. And Elodie loved the lightness of the place: the spare, expensive furnishings, the palest hues on the painted walls. The many windows inviting the light all day long. She felt she was living in clouds. The city was well into spring, and it was uncharacteristically gorgeous.

::

SHE HAD TAKEN to borrowing the man's overcoat, made of cashmere and lined in silk, a blue so deep and dark at first she thought it was black. It was knee-length, so it hung longer on Elodie. The first time she wore it she had grabbed it out of the hall closet when she was running out to get the paper and, after that, it became a kind of bathrobe for her in the mornings. She continued to retrieve the paper, and answer the door, while wearing it. Soon she was feeding the cat and eating breakfast in it. Once the morning had passed, however, she hung it back up and forgot all about it.

Until one day she was hurrying out of the house to see a movie. She raced to the closet, pulling out what she thought was her coat, only to realize it was the blue cashmere. She went to hang it up then, and for no good reason she threw it on and went out the door.

The entire time on MUNI she panicked, worried that she had sat on the wrong seat, one that carried remnants from Ocean Beach, like sand or, worse, gum or food, or other things she could not think about. Then she calmed herself and settled into the luxury of the garment and let the worry wash over and away from her.

::

SHE REACHED THE MOVIE with fifteen minutes to spare. She ate the chocolate Flicks she had bought at the concession stand until she emptied the tube. A *San Francisco Chronicle* lay spread across a nearby seat, but, on closer inspection, she saw that it was the car ads and the classifieds. She slumped in her seat (cursing herself for not carrying a book) and dug her hands into her pockets.

Her fingers found an envelope and, without thinking, took it from the pocket. She debated whether to read it; the ownership of the overcoat was becoming blurred to her. It actually did not feel as if she were prying since she felt close to the owner of the coat, with only his best interests at heart. And it wasn't as if she knew him or any of his friends.

It was boredom that finally got ahold of Elodie.

She tried to make out the cancellation stamp in the dim light: *San Francisco*. She recognized the name as that of the owner of the overcoat (she had picked up enough mail in the past weeks), but it was not the address of the house in which she was staying. She was too intrigued to leave it alone.

"Dear Nash," the letter began. She stopped. Nash was the name of the man of the house. Her eyes ran quickly to the end of the letter without reading the body. It was signed Georgia. Georgia, Elodie knew from weeks of mail, was *not* the name of the woman of the house. Nor was it the name of their young daughter.

::

THE LETTER WAS NOT a letter: It was a poem. And the poem whispered everything about Georgia and Nash, without Georgia having written an original word, save her own name and Nash's. And just when Elodie finished reading the poem, the theater went dark and she began to cry.

::

AFTERWARD, ELODIE DECIDED to walk back to the beautiful house on Buena Vista Avenue. It was a distance, but she needed time to unwind her emotions. The movie, which was inconsequential at best, was made forgettable with the distraction of the letter.

She tightened the blue cashmere coat around her, for the spring day had turned to dusk and was cooling down considerably. Elodie stopped in the Hunger Moon Café and Restaurant to have some coffee. She preferred the Youki Singe across town with its crazy decor, her customary table near the door, by the front window, her stationery and pillow book spread before her as she greeted friends, recording what she saw and heard and felt. The way she could recite their stories: Max, James, Sal, Lucy, Ginny, Selena, and the rest.

This letter made her feel cut adrift; no, that was not accurate, it reminded her that she is unmoored, with nothing to keep her tethered.

There is the matter of her friends, whom she knows far better than they know her; she often tells herself this is because her interest in their stories is stronger than theirs in hers, but that is inaccurate. Elodie has not let herself be easily known. If she can be closer to them than they are to her, she believes herself a little less fettered, since it is nearly impossible to give up the people who know us well. It may be the bond that occasionally chafes, but it is undeniably a bond.

There is the airy house of Buena Vista Park, which Elodie fundamentally recognizes as her own, that is, she can imagine living in it indefinitely. And the way in which the letter in the pocket of the blue cashmere coat indicates the unraveling of the lives that truly reside there.

What is laying Elodie so low, as she sits in the Hunger Moon Café, is that the people who live in the house have lives to unravel. They have somehow thrown in their lot with one another; they move in areas of hope. A belief in all the things that love can provide. They seem, to Elodie, to possess faith and its contradiction, knowledge that there is the equal probability of loss (*the art of losing isn't hard to master*).

The house is not really hers.

She had come to San Francisco on the strength of a romantic remark by a boy she hardly knew in high school.

And those letters she writes, in the dim light of the Youki Singe Tea Room, alongside her pillow book of observations, are part of a curious love affair in which she is involved.

edo castle and the nightless castle

::

Edo Castle was the home of the shogun, and "Nightless Castle" was a slang term for Yoshiwara, the first government-sanctioned pleasure quarters, home to courtesans. Both were located in Edo, the ancient name for Tokyo.

Kitao Shigemasa, in the eighteenth century, made prints of all four pleasure quarters, including the "snobbish" Yoshiwara, and called his series "Beauties of the Four Directions." They were often referred to by direction (east, west, north, south). There were male prostitutes in the western quarter and "unpretentious" courtesans to the east and south; Yoshiwara was in the north. Though Yoshiwara's pleasure quarters was the most elite because it was frequented by the elite, Edo offered something for everyone's taste.

*Ukiyo-e are the wood-block prints of this "floating world."
They became popular for a number of reasons, but one was
that they were relatively inexpensive to produce and so
brought art to the common man. The beginning of* ukiyo-e
was influenced by two types of published books: e-iribon
*(books with inserted pictures, that is, text with illustrations)
and* ehon *(illustrations with little text).*

*It was in 1657, the year of the great fire that destroyed
most of Edo, including Yoshiwara, that the first mass-
produced illustrated book,* A Tale of Manly Love, *was
published.*

NASH HAS A RECURRING DREAM, A MORE OR LESS RECURRING
dream in that the circumstances (the props that dress the dream)
might change a bit but the core of the dream is untouched.

In the dream there is a statue, about the size of a teenage girl.
Most of the time the statue is Kannon, a Buddhist goddess (sometimes called the Goddess of Mercy). Nash stands in a public place (a
street, a park, a railway station) with his back to the statue.

Each time, the statue reaches an arm around Nash's neck from
behind, which so startles him that he causes the statue to lose her
balance and fall.

A young girl appears to gather up the pieces.

::

BETH ANSWERS THE PHONE.

"Beth, it's Nash. Are you busy?"

"No, I'm not doing much of anything." It is ten-thirty at night.

"Listen," says Nash, "I'm leaving Georgia."

::

NASH HAS BEEN seeing Beth's best friend, Georgia, for a little over
three years, and Beth knows Georgia is very much in love with Nash.
Georgia has been Nash's secret for a long time.

Beth remembers Georgia telling her how it began; how she met
Nash and liked him instantly, for he was generous and sweet-
natured in all the right ways. She liked the way he dressed: thin silver bracelets that slid up and down his left arm, a vintage watch on
the right (how she coveted that watch); the way he hung his reading

glasses around his neck on a piece of leather so he wouldn't misplace them, which gave him a kind of hip librarian, slightly fussy air.

She described his clothes: wonderfully made, wonderfully worn, timeless tweeds and cottons and gabardines. He had the sort of good taste that wasn't really translatable to others, because the primary element that made Nash's clothes was Nash.

He did not look bohemian, the silver bracelets notwithstanding. He came from old money, then designed a little chip, which he sold, enabling him to buy the large, graceful house on Buena Vista Avenue.

When Georgia asked him if he was married he said no, not exactly, then went on to explain that he had lived with his "would-be wife," Catalina, for the last ten years, and that they had a daughter, but, technically, no, he was not married.

Georgia listened patiently, then replied, "Does your girlfriend, Catalina?"—trying on her name for the first time—"view you as attached or unattached? Are you free to roam?"

"God, no, no, I don't think that she would warm to that idea at any time."

"Then you are as good as married, which makes you pretty much not my type."

::

"I'M SORRY FOR CALLING," says Nash, "but you are my last resort."

"How flattering," says Beth.

"You know what I mean. About Georgia."

"What about her?" And Beth can feel her heart begin to toughen, almost imperceptively, in a loyalty reflex.

Nash sighs. "I just need to talk to someone about her."

"I may not be that person," says Beth slowly.

"You know," says Nash, "I love her too."

"Well, we might not be talking about the same thing here. Maybe we should define love before this conversation goes much further."

"I think about her constantly. Whenever I see that ad that says 'Come Visit the State of Georgia,' I am so overwhelmed by the desire to run and find her, and to do mundane things together and listen to her talk. I want to see her across a crowded room. And I find myself repeating, 'The state of Georgia, the state of Georgia.' "

"Why tell me all this?" Beth asks, even though she can guess why he is telling her. It is because she is Georgia's best friend, and she knows how Georgia will take this news. It will break Georgia's heart, and she has such a good heart.

"Because it is over and she won't let it be over."

"I thought you loved her."

"I do—but—I have another life. As you well know."

::

BETH DOES KNOW. She knows that Catalina is the name of the woman with whom he shares his home, and has shared it for something like thirteen years. And that they have a little girl. She's heard from Georgia about all Nash's friends and family and all the obligations (some pleasant, some not) of his life. Beth even knows something herself about living one life while being tempted by another.

She was a Catholic girl who had loved a Protestant boy, attracted, she realized, by the happiness he had found in his beliefs. They became engaged, and it was during this time that she came to live in the most wonderful house with two other girls, Ginny and Selena, who she secretly thought had not much of a life at all.

Sometimes she felt sorry for them, then castigated herself for her pride. One evening, after she had said good night to her fiancé at the door, she heard them laughing. She waited in the foyer and heard them opening wine, smoking cigarettes. She listened quietly to the duet of their conversation—which was light and aimless and not profound—and she envied them. Their easy intimacy made her long for her friend Georgia.

But it was more than that; she understood, with heartbreaking clarity, that she was not suited for the life her fiancé offered. Her belief was shallow, her conversion never really took, and she wanted to be no one's wife.

To his credit, Nash never made any promises to Georgia (as Georgia would be the first to admit), and to her credit, she never asked for any. Once, they tried to end it, and it was so hellish that the breakup lasted little more than a week, with Georgia temporarily moving into the house that Beth shared with Ginny and Selena. She slept in Beth's room; Beth often awakened in the night to hear her sobbing in the library. She found letters—written and destroyed—in the trash each morning. It was a preview of the inevitable (which was not lost on Georgia, Nash, or Beth).

Beth is suddenly irritated at her friend and at Nash. She knows what this call is about, Nash is trying to enlist her help in soothing Georgia. As a matter of fact, it is possible that, at the close of this call, Beth might call Georgia and relate this entire conversation.

Then, in a difficult and discomfiting moment, Beth wonders if that is Nash's intention.

::

"LISTEN," SHE SAYS, "you should be careful what you say. I might talk to Georgia," explaining, without stating, whose side she's on even before it is clear there will be sides.

"I don't want to put you in the middle. I don't have anyone else to talk to."

Beth snorts through a drag of the cigarette she has just lit, sending the smoke out her nose. "Oh, really, Nash. You are the only man I know who has a plethora of friends."

He is quiet. "No one knows about her. Except one—we've sometimes sent letters through him—but I've never talked about her to him, so who knows what he thinks."

"Oh." Beth marvels at the difference between Nash and his friends and her and her friends. She is amazed by and genuinely curious about this limitation of friendship and how attractive it sounds. In theory.

"I worry she might do something a little crazy," he says.

"To you?"

"Oh no. To herself." He sighs. "Which is exactly like her, don't you think?"

He does know her, thinks Beth. Nash understands that she would harm herself before going after anyone else. It is part of her goodness and part of her narcissism.

"Tell me what I should do." His voice breaks slightly.

::

NASH REMEMBERS WHEN he first met Catalina. They purchased the house on Buena Vista Avenue and made it look exactly the way they liked it. They took expensive, adventurous vacations, often to out-of-the-way places. It was exciting. They had a life. And they did not bother to marry because they already saw themselves as belonging to each other and had no need to formalize what was an obvious fact. Their families finally stopped asking about marriage and accepted them as mated.

Then they had their daughter, and they traded the adventurous vacations for doing things around the house, or involving themselves in their daughter's school (whose schedule cut into their old, impromptu trips), or seeing friends. The funny thing was this domestic life seemed to intrigue Nash.

He liked saying, "Gee, I'd love to but I have to clean out the garage." He talked about mowing the lawn and trips to the nursery and hardware store. The minutiae of ordinary life (dinner at seven-thirty, pruning the roses, waxing the car, kissing his little girl good night after telling her in his Stern Dad Voice, which she did not take seriously, to go to bed right now) seemed to him remarkable.

And he especially liked that the last thing he did each night was to go, with Catalina, into their daughter's room to check on her. They busied themselves retucking her slender arms and legs, which fought free of the covers regardless of room temperature. They kissed her good night again.

Was the window open enough? Was the night-light too bright? Should it be extinguished, with only the hall light left burning? Perhaps they should have admitted that none of these things—the lights, the window, the covers—was the real reason they came into her room; the real reason was they simply wanted to look.

Before Nash had a child he would've interpreted this need to gaze upon his girl as an aspect of self-love (See what I have made!); then he became a father and knew this was not true: that the wonder of his daughter was that she seemed so complete and apart from him, as if he had almost nothing to do with her being here at all.

Then there were the times with Catalina. Ever since he had sold his business and "retired" to marketing and cooking and picking their daughter up from school and all the rest that went with such a life, Catalina had been making jewelry. The slender silver bracelets he wore on his left arm had as much meaning for him as a wedding ring, for she had made them.

"Sweetie," Catalina would say, "let's see how this looks on." And she would affix brooches, or necklaces, or golden cuff bracelets to his body, neck, and wrists. "Ah," she would remark, "it is a shame you don't have pierced ears."

"I would look marvelous in a nice pair of drop earrings."

Catalina would laugh. "You would. Someday I'll do a men's line, just for marvelous you."

"Actually, I think I can pull off this girl stuff. I mean, I have the right mix of yin and yang, you know. But you tell me." And he would catwalk across their bedroom in all his glittering adornments. When he arrived at one end, he would spin around, one hand pinning back his bathrobe to expose his underwear, the other raised as if to hail a cab.

"Yes," Catalina would say, "you're so very in touch with your girlish self."

::

"WHAT DID YOU THINK would happen when you took up with Georgia?" asks Beth. No answer. "Nash?"

"I remember waking up one morning, restless, longing for something. I was thinking about summer—" He broke off. "You're from up here, aren't you?"

"Yes."

"In Southern California everything smells like jasmine and eucalyptus and suntan lotion.

"And there are those really hot, shirtsleeve nights when you can't sleep, and just turning over is way too much effort. That kind of night is so rare here that when it does come along I'm—I am *weary* with nostalgia. And so that morning, I was thinking of all that, almost able to feel the heat on my skin, and that was the day I met Georgia.

"The joke is I often think I'm having some kind of pre-midlife thing, except she and Catalina are almost the same age. It makes me wonder what I'm looking for—"

"Isn't that an ordinary story?"

"—in Georgia."

"So, you are breaking my friend's heart, and asking me to be a little disloyal, over a midlife crisis that arrived early?"

"You don't know how many times, since I met Georgia, when I've made Catalina laugh, made her purr [he laughs shyly], or have been lying down next to my daughter until she fell asleep, when I have thought, Why can't I be a better person? Why did anyone fall in love with me? And, of course, I can't ask for comfort from the woman I am wronging because it is so selfish, and then I think, I already miss her."

"Miss whom?"

NASH DOESN'T ANSWER. He is thinking about Georgia. They used to meet in the Japanese Tea Garden.

"I like that I rendezvous with you," said Georgia. "It makes me feel as if I live an exciting, international life."

They would wander through the park, particularly loving the Victorian Conservatory of Flowers, with its humid atmosphere, so thick with heat and moisture that every breath feels weighted. It is a risk going to the park because of its proximity to the Buena Vista house, and who knows what Catalina does with her days. Where she goes.

San Francisco is an almost perfect miniature city. This is one of the aspects that makes it so livable. But it also makes it difficult to lose yourself, impossible to hide. When Nash first moved there from Los Angeles (which is less like a city and more like a series of villages), he was surprised at the rate at which he ran into people he knew.

And yet, the possibility of colliding with Catalina doesn't bother him as much as one would think it would.

They would end up at Georgia's place, a funny little cottage on California Street, set back from the street and incongruously located next to a hospital. The very English architecture was enhanced by the wildly untended garden miraculously full of thriving climbing roses, and palm trees, and some other parasitic vines.

There is a photograph by Ruth Orkin of the view outside her window on Central Park West (one of the hundreds she had taken) that Georgia had hung next to one of her windows. It sits over a chair that Nash and Georgia bought together. A Victorian hat tree that is actually a tall, silvery metal tree with hooks extending from its branches sits by the front door.

When they saw it at the estate shop, Nash said, "Look, a coat tree that is a coat tree."

"I must have it," said Georgia, to which Nash agreed, "You must have it. I shall get it for you."

Now it is strung with butterfly lights, necklaces, and an old stretched-out sweater that Georgia wears to garden (and sometimes falls asleep in). When Nash first saw her in it he said, "I see you dressed up for me." But he was secretly pleased to see her clothed as if she were alone. It was as good as if she had said I love you.

::

EVENTUALLY, GEORGIA BEGAN to request articles of his clothing (a jacket, a shirt, the cashmere blue overcoat, even trousers rolled at the cuff, the sweaters that held his scent) to be left with her. She would tell him, prior to their assignations, what she wanted to borrow, and keep it until the next time they met.

While this increased the possibility of being caught (her in his distinctive clothing), Nash liked the idea of Georgia walking around in something of his.

⁑

BETH SAYS, "This will wreck her when you say it's over."

"I know."

"You'll be calling me again, won't you?"

"Probably. Most likely."

"If I continue to talk to you when this is over, I won't be able to tell her."

"I understand."

"Once behind her back is forgivable. More than once and I risk my friendship with her. Over a friendship with you."

"If it is any consolation, my departure may not come as a complete shock."

⁑

EVER SINCE THE DAY at Enrico's, something has changed.

The April day was luscious and warm, the sort of day that slows you down with a kind of perfect happiness. As they walked along Broadway, Nash spied Georgia sitting on the terrace of Enrico's. His impulse was to rush to her, embrace and kiss her; in an instant, forgetting—then remembering—that he was with Catalina. And the thrill of running into Georgia seemed so tangible, he was certain he had inadvertently made their relationship obvious. He thought, This is it. I have been found out and this is what it feels like. The rush of adrenaline.

Except.

Except, Catalina had no idea who Georgia was; for her she was just another stranger and nothing more.

Nash noticed that Georgia wore one of his shirts, unusual in that it resembled the top of a boy's pajamas, pale yellow with cowboys and broncos and lariats.

"Nash! Hey, Catalina!" Their friends Max and James, whom they had not seen since their housewarming party (they had moved in together) a few months ago, were sitting outside, drinking coffee. James looked a little thinner. Max was still a knockout.

"Hey, Max. James." Nash went to take Catalina's arm, out of habit and affection, but the proximity of Georgia prevented him from doing so. Catalina did not seem to notice and was immediately taken up in conversation with Max and James.

Georgia, Nash could tell, was sizing up Catalina. Then Catalina said something that made James laugh, then knocked playfully into Nash. He could've sworn he saw Georgia tense. He couldn't be positive about any of Georgia's reactions, though, as he was sneaking side glances at her.

"An Ansel Adams show," James was saying. "It's not what you think."

"I'm not really a fan of Ansel Adams, though I do like that New Mexico picture that everyone likes," said Catalina.

"You should go," chimed in Max. "It is a replication of his first show, and there is none of the grand nature stuff—more like leaves in gutters and corrugated metal."

Nash was unable to say that he had already gone to that show with the woman sitting not more than eight feet from them.

"We need to get together," said Catalina.

"It has been a while," said Max.

"Nash—" said Catalina.

He was distracted. He felt their eyes upon him and was aware that Catalina, especially, was looking in the same direction he was, to see what had captured his attention. She was looking in the direction of Georgia.

A funny expression crossed Catalina's face, then vanished.

"I've heard good things about that show," said Nash, to which Catalina replied, "Nash, we've moved on." Her tone was soft but firm, and Nash, caught in his own inner drama of the moment, could not read her. In the same vein, he could not truly tell if Georgia was amused or disturbed by this chance encounter, seeing Nash so casually happy with Catalina, and talking about social engagements with old friends, making plans that she would never, ever be a part of.

His adrenaline surged again. He could feel his heart pumping; his mind moved in various directions. But he wasn't afraid—he was thrilled.

She had seen him staring at Georgia.

Then Catalina said, "Hey, don't you have a shirt like that?" and gestured toward Georgia.

She had misinterpreted his interest.

Georgia, in the meantime, returned to her book and the thin milk shake before her. He thought he might have seen her hands tremble slightly; he couldn't be certain, since she did nothing to give herself away.

::

"LISTEN, NASH," says Beth, when he asks what he should do. "Don't tell her again that you love her. Even if it is the truth."

::

THEY HANG UP, with the agreement they will speak again. Nash suggests coffee, and Beth says we'll see, but he knows he will see her. He has no romantic interest in Beth, nor does she in him, but this isn't about them.

He knows that Georgia will also be calling Beth, in the middle of the night, crying tears that threaten never to end. He can imagine the anger and the moment of blessed relief when she has worn herself so thin she has no choice but to let go a little, to give her heart a rest.

Then it will all gear up again: the rehashing of the past three years, what she could've done differently, and the continued contact with Nash, who in his heart is a decent, albeit flawed, man. There will be letters passed through his friend. Until the breakup seems less like a separation and more like an extremely altered version of their affair; that is to say, contact will remain by phone and letters, the emotional level of the contact as profound as ever. They will be bound at the heart without being physically in touch.

::

NASH LOOKS AT the clock. It is now very late, and his house on Buena Vista Avenue quiet. He is thinking about Beth and how something has begun for them, even if she doesn't know its exact nature.

It will start with the occasional phone call, talking about Georgia, then other topics will begin to thread in and out. Current events. Daily anecdotes. A bit of personal history. Books. Casual talk will give way to coffee, which will become movie matinees, or a museum trip, an evening out.

It could go like this: What are you doing tonight? Nothing. You? Catalina is spending the night in Sonoma, and I have some tickets to ———. Or they could just as easily meet at Green Apple Bookstore to browse. An outing so casual and ordinary, no one even notices.

Being secretive comes so naturally to him; the same could be said for loving Georgia and wanting to be with someone who loves her too.

::

HE KNOWS HOW EASY it is not to be found out (altogether different from hiding). He explains this by saying that, most of the time, people don't want to know. The truth, the secret, the life that someone is leading on the quiet. Ignorance *is* bliss; truth is trouble.

And, curiously, out of the duplicity of his life, the falsehoods that blur fact and fiction, comes an existence full of trust.

Catalina does not examine his life too closely, she does not monitor his friends and activities. He trusts Georgia not to go to Catalina. He knows Beth will not speak of their friendship to Georgia. It is not that he demands this trust; it is all implicit. It is all such a fragile structure.

::

NASH HAS A RECURRING dream of a statue of a young girl breaking from her own fall. Gathering up the shards.

::

HE IS A MAN in love with disaster.

One night, in the midst of his love affair with Georgia, he went to a large dinner party with Catalina. Despite the numerous guests, he felt himself alone, though not unpleasantly so. He half-listened to the conversations that drifted and settled around him, commenting occasionally, but not very involved.

He let his eyes wander about the quiet money evident in the rooms of his hosts, all their Beautiful Things, musing on the connection between comfort and beauty, until his gaze fell on Catalina.

He observed her speaking to two women seated near her, Catalina laughing, listening, expressing her opinions with her usual high spirits, and he thought to himself, Catalina is the most beautiful, absolutely the loveliest thing in the room.

One of the silver bracelets he wears has minuscule words stamped on the outer surface. It says, "Without you, I'm nothing." In

French, because that was part of Catalina's joke. Another bracelet says, in deliberately uneven print, "Heaven." In English.

He loves her. Without her, he is nothing. In English. No laughter. He loves Georgia as well. And, after Georgia, it is fair to believe that he might love someone else. That someone else might be a neighbor, a stranger, someone's wife, an old friend. Someone not yet discovered by him.

He suppresses a chill when he thinks that this might eventually lead to the loss of Catalina (cannot even consider the absence of his daughter), yet he persists in this clandestine life.

That is when he realizes that he is a man in love with disaster.

It is the disappointment and relief of returning from a country newly collapsed in revolution. It is missing the earthquake violent enough to break a suspension bridge in half. It is the canceled ticket on a plane lost in a hurricane. It is selling his home a week before the brushfire that reduces his neighborhood to blackened rubble.

Catalina is gorgeous and remote. She is an embodiment of her name: named for a small island off the California coast, named for a saint. Both, in their way, shining and inaccessible. Remote. He has never understood why Catalina does not press him for marriage, and maybe that is why he cannot leave her—knowing she might leave him at any moment.

He thinks: It is the car accident I walk away from; it's the bombing of the building where I rescheduled an appointment; it is the flood, the blizzard, the catastrophe that approaches but never overtakes me. It is the collision of free will and random occurrence.

He looks at Catalina, considers Georgia, with Beth's presence lingering on the edges, and asks himself which has more power over him—love or disaster—only to find he cannot say.

a moored pleasure boat
beneath a bridge

TORII KIYONAGA
(1784–1785)

::

The season is the beginning of summer.

After Yoshiwara burned to the ground in 1657, it was reopened three miles northeast of Edo Castle as Shin (new) Yoshiwara. Many visitors would travel to Shin Yoshiwara by boat, on the Sumida River, beginning the pleasures of the evening en route.

Nihonbashi (Japan Bridge) was the starting point for the roads leading out of the city.

Eventually it ended.

Georgia sent Nash, by way of Nash's friend who asks no questions, a variety of letters. Mostly articles, sometimes accompanied by a photograph.

When Georgia was in college her father began mailing her articles with little notes paper-clipped to them. Sometimes the notes read HowAreYouIAmFine; other times there would be a sentence or two that commented on the article sent. Something along the lines of "I was thinking about this last week. It did not seem possible" (a scientific discovery, for example). Or "I hope this doesn't keep you up at night" or "What about quarks?" or "Are you still thinking about architecture?"

These almost cryptic notes, mundane personal bulletins ("I leave for Istanbul next week"), and the miscellany of texts and articles finally added up to a quilt of correspondence. Full of bits of daily life and occasional insight without actually taking on the scope of a full-blooded exchange.

It was as if Georgia could know what her father was doing (the mundane, traveling to Istanbul), know what caught his eye or engaged his mind (lighthouses, butterfly migrations, chaos theory, dying religious movements), without knowing *him*. Unless, as she sometimes mused, that is precisely the way in which we do know one another: captured in the glimpses, embellished with the imagination.

Georgia always promised herself that she would be quite clear in her own letters, and that they would be letters, not questions, theories, or statements.

Then she grew up and began to understand the nature of her father's communication with her. He wanted to lead her to the world as a way of leading her to himself. Ruth Orkin, the photographer who published two volumes of pictures taken each day from the same window in her Manhattan apartment, said of her work, "I think that taking pictures must be my way of asking people to look at this—to look at that." Georgia was convinced that her father's scraps of information, articles, and notes were similar to snapshots.

Being her father's daughter, she too began writing to loved ones in his style. She learned that it was quite effortless to send a traditional letter to anyone. This was another early misunderstanding of her father's missives, which she once believed to be impersonal, indicative of a failure of affection or interest in her, and it was only when she began sending similar notes and articles that she knew how personal and precise they were.

And so it was with her letters to Nash.

::

THE LETTER SITS unread on Nash's desk. Inside the envelope is a single sheet of paper, outside is Nash's name above the address of his friend. The window is open, inviting the spring breeze to rustle about in his high aviary of a room. He wishes the wind would lift the envelope with the letter inside and blow it right off his desk and out of his life. He sighs, rests his chin on the palm of his hand. He is weighted down by the work of obligation, connected to the breakup with Georgia.

There was the tentative farewell, then the resolute good-bye, followed by the lingering, a guest unwilling (or unable) to take her leave. Endless lingering in which he is never allowed the distance required to miss her. He is denied the luxury of wanting her. He wants to miss her.

He wants every song on the radio to break his heart a little; he wants a particular fragrance to cause his throat to tighten with the threat of tears; he wants sadness and memory; he wants to visit someplace that recalls a vanished, great moment, leaving him to fight the urge to call, promising her the moon.

He wants Georgia to fade into silence so he can conjure her up in all her vibrancy.

None of this is fair, he knows, which is why he does not cut her off completely, saying, Please don't call me again. He owes her something in the failed attempt to make up for the thing he cannot give her.

::

HE CALLS OUT TO CATALINA that he is going to walk to the store, does she need anything? He buttons his dark blue cashmere overcoat. As he walks he remembers a painting he had seen in a Vancouver museum. It was an eighteenth-century family portrait, with the mother and the children and the dog arranged on their rather elaborate Greek Revival porch. The absent father's silhouette was painted on one of the pillars.

The note the artist left explained that the father was unavailable to sit for the picture and had gotten the idea for the silhouette from reading Pliny the Elder. Pliny the Elder wrote of a Corinthian maid who once traced the shadow of her departing lover on the wall.

Nash wonders what it would be like to be left with a shadow to love.

::

ONE WEEK PASSED. A friend of Nash's offered him the use of his sailboat, moored in the Marina of the San Francisco Bay. Catalina was attending a play with a friend, their daughter was away for the night, and Nash thought it might be pleasant to spend a warm spring evening with Georgia, in an attempt at friendship.

She had recently asked him if they could be friends, and he'd said he didn't think so because she didn't really want to be his friend.

"That isn't as cold as it sounds," he explained. "What I mean is that we've never been friends, exactly, and, well, given recent *events*, it might be a little hard." His tone tender, he said, "I just think with your streak of sweetness and your heart on your sleeve, you might not be up to it."

::

GEORGIA HAS BEEN FEELING off lately. Evidence of this was Nash calling, inviting her to supper on his friend's boat, sailing on the bay, and her almost saying no when she did want to see him. These days she was as unsteady as if she were already at sea, and wasn't sure she could manage that rolling shift of balance that leaves you a little green.

Who knew a six-week embryo could have such an all-encompassing effect on a grown woman? She was a million times bigger and stronger than the embryo, yet it was already pushing her life around. She has not mentioned the baby to Nash because she doesn't know how she feels about it (mostly she wishes it had never happened so she wouldn't have to decide anything), but there is another reason that even she cannot quite name.

In the end, she accepted his invitation and told herself it would be good, this first outing as friends.

::

NASH LOOKED GREAT as she stood on the other side of the locked gate, preventing her from venturing any farther down the dock toward the boats. He was jumping on and off the boat, taking things aboard. Her heart collapsed in on itself a little when she recognized the sweater he wore; she had borrowed it more than once. She used to think that it was the quality and cut of Nash's clothes that made her want to crawl into whatever he had recently removed, then realized that it was, more likely, the smell and warmth of Nash.

She thought of something she'd read about Gerald Murphy (patron to all those Famous American Writers in Paris), when he was reeling from the loss of his boys and began having terrible dreams from which he would awake and cry, "Will one's heart never touch bottom?"

⠶

THEY WERE GLIDING about the bay, passing day-cruise tour boats with PA systems so loud they could hear the badly recorded voices pointing out the various sites:

"Alcatraz. No one has ever successfully escaped."

"Angel Island. Like Ellis Island but different." This made them laugh. They heard the usual statistics about the Golden Gate Bridge: how long it took to build, how much it cost, what sort of material, manpower, loss of life, the logistics of spanning the distance between the city and Marin County (buffeting winds, wild seas, unpredictable earthquakes).

"Why don't they mention the increasing tolls?" said Georgia.

"Isn't that supposed to stop once the bridge is paid for?" said Nash, and they both laughed.

In the distance they saw the ferry, making its run between Larkspur Landing and the Ferry Building, with almost no one onboard.

⠶

THEY WERE NEARING the bridge. It was not their intention to pass under it, where the water is very different, depending on the side of the bridge you are on. On the bay side it is manageable, particularly tonight, when it is smooth and glassy; the open sea side is uncivilized and reckless.

When Georgia and Nash were walking across the bridge one breezy, sunny afternoon, they had seen a jumper. First, they noticed a small knot of pedestrians looking over the bay side of the bridge; this prompted them to stop and look over too. What they saw was a middle-aged black man, wearing a cap and holding on to one of the cables, swaying back and forth, his feet planted on the ledge below, ignoring the entreaties and commands of the would-be rescuer hanging toward him over the guardrail.

Georgia and Nash looked at the middle-aged jumper, then looked below, since they all shared the same view. Another crowd had gathered along the shore.

After twenty minutes, the jumper took one giant step backward (presumably to launch himself) while his would-be rescuer took advantage of the closer proximity by throwing his own body farther over the rail and grabbing the jumper. The jumper seemed too surprised to fight the man who now held him and hauled him over the rail to safety. As impressive as it was to see one full-grown man lift another, the incident was weirdly anticlimactic. All energy—the jumper and rescuer, the onlookers above and below—immediately dissipated and everyone moved on. It was only when it was done that Georgia realized how painfully clenched her jaw had been during the entire incident.

Later, Nash asked Georgia why the rescue felt like nothing, instead of as enormous as a man's life.

She shrugged her shoulders, slightly confused by his reaction, and said, "I guess because it is less thrilling to be saved."

THE EVENING WAS SETTLING upon them; it was hard to imagine a more perfect sunset. There was no fog, no clipped cold as the warmth of the day seamlessly led into the night. As Nash went below to assemble their supper, Georgia fought her (now) usual low-level nausea. She closed her eyes.

::

WHAT MADE GEORGIA give in to Nash almost four years ago was the day they were walking down Clement Street and she tripped, catching the toe of her shoe on one of the sidewalk's many imperfections, and fell. They had been strolling, side by side, with Nash telling her something. By the time he turned toward her, she was sprawled on the ground at his feet. As he said later, "One minute you were there, and then you disappeared."

As she said to Beth, "I fell and then I fell."

She felt no sense of embarrassment. As he reached down to lift her up, she had the perception that this event was natural and inevitable. The sidewalk was badly made, and she is not a clumsy girl. There was no awkwardness as Nash picked her off the cement, checked her for bruises, and brushed her off. She took this as an omen—the ease of these tiny events—signaling the beginning of the affair. It was familiar and slightly breathtaking.

Beth had other ideas when Georgia told her about Nash. She said, "You aren't paying attention."

"I am. I am," said Georgia. "It isn't as if I want to break up his happy home."

"Maybe. But where does all this really have to go?"

"Why does it have to go anywhere? Why can't two people just enjoy themselves for as long as it lasts?"

"I don't know *why*," said Beth. "I only know they can't."

"Who made you the expert?"

"Okay, think of it this way: The best thing that happens is you fall uncontrollably in love with each other, except that it devastates his girlfriend and hurts their kid. Or, you fall madly in love and he agrees to leave, and his girlfriend is destroyed, and just when you think the worst is over, they decide to work it out. Maybe he falls for you and you don't for him and he leaves his girlfriend, or he confesses and she leaves him, and he can't let go and becomes a stalker."

"A stalker? In that case I better warn the people at work since the innocent co-workers are always the first to go."

"You have Selective Love Deafness," said Beth, "which places you beyond the pale."

"Oh, come on, Beth. I wish I led such a dramatic life."

::

GEORGIA, on the boat, wrestling with her nagging nausea, turning over other things Beth had said. Something about how everything escalates, or drifts and vanishes, that things don't stay the same (not happiness, not misery), reminding us that we are made up of unstable elements. Reminders that we (and the world) are just water, water, and more water. Tears and brine and fluids.

Beth said, "Do you know what a tipping point is? It's that more of something isn't more, it's different. It's the same way with less: Less is also different. For example, once you are loved you cannot reasonably be loved less and have the relationship stay the same, because it changes everything; it isn't just less of something, it's different.

"K. C. Cole says that the tipping point is a very singular, sensitive moment"—"Like when I was friends with Nash, and then lovers?" interjected Georgia—"she says, for water to turn to ice it is only the decrease of one degree—one—and what was fluid and liquid is now a solid, fixed form."

Georgia struggled with tears. She imagined the embryo caught in the current of amniotic fluid.

There was a time when she accused Nash of wanting to live two lives, of wanting to live and breathe and love in tandem universes. The world of Catalina, and the world of Georgia, each with its distinct landscape and citizenry. That he wanted to be family man and a rogue, and that ultimately he would, out of this split existence, find his true self.

This longing of his, this doubling of a single life, made her respond with mistrust. If she believed that all he wanted was two lives, his greed would protect her from disappointment, but she thought that he was after another kind of life, something she had not quite worked out. It was as if he wanted pure sensation, or something outside of everything he knows. What he wanted Georgia intuited but could not yet name, and that was when she began to perceive the danger he presented to her heart. It was the threat of his unpredictability.

Even if she wasn't correct, this is what she thought.

"This is not fun anymore," he had complained to her once she started working out these ideas of Nash's life (though not telling Nash). "You make everything so difficult, so fraught."

"And you wouldn't want things difficult for you." There was an unpleasantness to her voice.

Nash sighed. "It's just that you don't seem very happy either."

His use of the word *either* made Georgia mute.

::

NASH BROUGHT HER SUPPER to her on the deck.

"Are you feeling okay?" he asked.

"I'm fine."

He commented on the beauty of the night. He looked wistful and fell silent. He poured her wine, filled her plate with foods that he knew she liked. He seemed on the verge of a tender confession, then turned away.

She was about to tell him about the baby when they saw how close they were to the bridge. "That won't do," said Nash as he got up to steer the boat back toward the bay.

The bridge.

Suddenly, it was as if someone had turned on all the lights and every shadow that had moved about her love affair with Nash dissolved. This wasn't the first time this evening they had come this close to the bridge, Nash turning them back before they went under; Nash having brought them so close, too close, to the open ocean to begin with: the approach, the risk, the retreat.

There was the jumper and Nash's dissatisfaction with the outcome, though she knows he would not have wanted to witness someone's death. There was the way he talked about his family and how much he loved them while loving her. He never said much about the encounter at Enrico's, but she had suspected something in it disappointed him, though she could not say what it was. She couldn't be certain, but there was something in Nash that wanted something, anything, to happen. That happiness wasn't big enough for him, and misery too much. He seemed to want something that would shake him apart. When *will* Catalina be home tonight?

They were heading back into the bay, eating dinner, Nash chatting happily with her. He didn't know it, but his easy way with her was seducing her again. Maybe he did know it. Maybe a dangerous friendship would be the only kind of friendship they could have. Well, if what she had always meant to him was a flight from contentment and safety, he was finally getting what he wanted; this baby, this one element with the power to change everything because more is different.

lunacy—unrolling letters

This print is part of a series, "One Hundred Aspects of the Moon," by the nineteenth-century artist Yoshitoshi. He made one hundred prints in which the moon appears, though the stories behind the pictures are in no way related. *Lunacy—unrolling letters* takes place in the seventh month, sometimes called "letter-spreading month," when people were encouraged to unroll and air their letters.

The girl in the picture has gone mad upon learning about the death of her lover. In her hand is a letter he had written to her, rolled and unrolled so often it shows signs of wear and damage.

Some words can be made out: *think, heart, first snow.*

As John Stevenson writes regarding this picture: "The letter seems to have a life of its own, wanting to be released. The girl holds on to it, unwilling to let it go." She is lost in a state called *monogurui*, thing-madness. She is fixated on the letter.

A L e t t e r a n d T h i n g - M a d n e s s

NASH LEFT GEORGIA's letter on his desk; Catalina found it. She was searching for something else in his office when she came upon the letter.

The first thing she noticed was the address on the front (she almost didn't pick it up), then thought it was odd that Nash had it and that it had been opened, until she saw Nash's name. It didn't look like an invitation, or a friendly note; it looked like what it was, somehow, a love letter. She hesitated. She was not given to suspicion, or challenging her life with Nash.

Then she picked it up. Then she read it. Then she carefully put it back.

This went on for days. Reading it and rereading it when Nash was out of the house. She tried to throw it out, only to retrieve it from the trash. She put it inside a desk drawer; she took it back out. She tried leaving it on the dining room table, thinking that when Nash came home she would act normally but he would see it, and she would see what he'd say. Then it occurred to her that he might whisk it away and not mention it.

He was the same sweet Nash, and she was coiling ever tighter. She was becoming obsessed with the letter, needing to know where it was at all times.

She had reached the point where she was distracted with their daughter and short-tempered with everyone else. Nash responded by being more considerate of her moods.

One day, she had gone to a French jewelry shop off Union Square that had ordered some of her pieces. The spring day was so mild that she decided to walk before she caught a cab home. As she walked, her mind wandered. Her thoughts, random at first, began to coalesce into a pattern. She had gone five blocks before she realized that she was reciting the letter, it had become so embedded in her mind.

This made her lose heart.

::

CATALINA'S FRIEND LEFT word at Stars, where they were to meet for dinner, that her car had broken down halfway to the city. Her message read, "I called the will call at the theater, so you can still pick up your ticket if you want to go. I'm so sorry."

Catalina finished her drink, and remembered that Nash was going out this evening too. A friend of his had lent him his sailboat for tonight, and Catalina had said she would love to go but she couldn't because of her friend and reservations at Stars and the play. Oh, well, with their daughter out of the house and Nash not home until later, she could have a nice quiet night.

When the valet brought her car around she didn't head for the house on Buena Vista Avenue; instead, she surprised herself and went in the direction of the Marina. It was still light enough out where she could see the sun, and the ghostlike moon hung in the sky at the same time.

Catalina saw Nash's car and got out. There was a figure jumping off a sailboat that she presumed was Nash, bending down and picking something off the dock. As Catalina approached she noticed a woman, about her age, early or mid-thirties, standing at the locked gate that led to the boats moored at the dock. Catalina held still, told herself that the man greeting the woman wasn't Nash, and that the woman wasn't the one who wrote the letter that Catalina had unwillingly, unhappily committed to memory. She thought about their daughter.

::

WHEN NASH GOT HOME that night, he was surprised to see that Catalina was already there (surely the play went longer). He walked into the house, refreshed from the sea air, thinking that things with Georgia would work out, that they could be friends. Without removing his coat, he stopped in the kitchen and drank orange juice from the carton.

As he passed through the dining room, he noticed Georgia's letter on the table, and the vertigo that overcame him was so violent he was forced to grab the back of a chair. He believed he was falling and must not hit the ground lest he shatter into a thousand pieces.

Catalina.

He jammed the letter in the pocket of his midnight blue cashmere overcoat and began up the stairs, thinking, I can't lose her I can't lose her. When he got to their room she was calmly walking between the bathroom, her closet, and dresser, pulling her clothes and toiletries from drawers and cabinets.

On the bed was a single open suitcase. Catalina was dropping things into it without any sense of organization.

"Catalina," he said.

She ignored him, and piled in more clothes. Now she moved faster and was sloppier, the pile of clothes growing higher and higher. Her breath had quickened. More clothes. The suitcase had long since been obscured by the vast pile of Catalina's belongings, unable to hold a fraction of what she kept laying on it, and still she glanced around for more of her things.

She stopped and began to sob as she considered the mess on the bed. Nash saw her slump to the floor, weeping into her arms as she lay there.

And so began the first step toward their hegira, which they embarked upon three days later; the same day that Elodie arrived in the cab, missing them by moments.

A Letter and a Priest

IN THE BOOK *The Confessions of Lady Nijo* (1271–1306), the memoir of a concubine to a retired emperor in Kyoto who ended her life as a Buddhist nun, it is written: "It was unthinkable to write a letter without a poem, and it was a gross breach of etiquette for a lover to neglect to send a morning-after poem as soon as he returned to his quarters."

This sentiment is echoed in *The Pillow Book of Sei Shonagon* (written around 991–1000), where it is written that a man must rush home to write a next-day letter to his lover, sent with a sprig of flowers or leaves. The letter might be twisted or knotted in a specific fashion. The girl then writes back. If no letter arrives from the man, he is saying that he wishes to end the affair.

Shonagon's book is made up of observations, anecdotes, and one hundred and sixty-four lists with a variety of topics. Under one heading, "Things One Is in a Hurry to See or Hear," she writes: "A letter from the man one loves."

::

LADY NIJO TELLS A STORY of when her retired emperor takes ill and she is sent to fetch a priest. The priest, Ariake, falls in love with her, with an affection that increases each time he sees her. His declarations of love are often infused with tears, which make her "withdraw in confused embarrassment."

Ariake sends her letters, though nothing touches her heart.

Then, during one visit, she impulsively tears off a piece of her head-band, writing upon it the single character for *dream*. Her reason for doing this, she says, is that his love for her seems to trouble him greatly.

At the encounter following the note left on the torn headband, he tosses her a "fragrant star anise from the altar." She picks it up and discovers that he has written a poem to her on one of its leaves, referring to her as My Dream. And so begins their love affair.

Vermeer's Women

TO SEE THE MAJORITY of Vermeer's paintings is to be a guest in the artist's home. It is a house full of women: wife, daughters, serving girls. And in this house of women are letters: letters being delivered, read, written, and sent.

As he guides you through his daily life on what feels, increas-ingly, like an observant, mysterious, furtive tour, you, too, see young women being handed letters by smiling housemaids; you, too, inter-rupt the women as they read, or write.

The expressions on the women's faces, in regard to the letters, are puzzled, anxious, and pleased. The face of a girl might turn in impatience when she is distracted from the letter in hand, as if to demand, What is it?

Vermeer, husband and father, glancing into room after room, what is it? what is it? what is it? echoing throughout.

The paintings:

1. A girl is engrossed in her letter. The maid takes a moment to relax and gaze out the window.
2. A girl has been playing music on a stringed instrument. She is interrupted by an amused maid, who hands her

an unopened letter. The maid speaks lightly, the girl
looks serious. What looks like a view through a doorway,
you realize, is actually a reflection in a mirror.

3. A pregnant woman in a sky blue dress concentrates on a
letter as she stands before a table and a blue chair. The
gold in her dress matches the gold on the wall map
behind her.

4. Another girl stands before an opened window hung
with a red curtain, reading a letter. Her face is
reflected in the glass.

5. Another maid hands a woman (dressed in ermine, gold
velvet, and pearls) a letter. The maid speaks. The
woman with the pearls in her hair, circling her throat,
hung from her ears, sets down her pen. Her fingertips
lightly touch her chin in concern (or curiosity).

6. In a final picture, a girl stands at the virginals, playing
music, her figure in profile but her face turned toward
the painter. She looks happy. The sunlight in the room
has banished all shadows of mystery. There on the wall
behind her is a painting of Cupid, little god of love.
He is nude, with one chubby hand resting on his bow,
and the other hand held high, waving to get someone's
attention. And in that waving hand is *a letter.*

Georgia's Letter to Nash

ELODIE WRITES IN HER NOTEBOOK: "The letter I found in the blue
cashmere overcoat is similar to a Japanese morning-after letter in
that it is poem. It concerns love. But it is not sent with the thought of
continuing an affair; it is a farewell.

It read:

Dear Nash,

ONE ART by ELIZABETH BISHOP

The art of losing isn't hard to master
so many things seem filled with the intent
to be lost that their loss is no disaster.

Lose something every day. Accept the fluster
of lost door keys, the hour badly spent.
The art of losing isn't hard to master.

Then practice losing farther, losing faster:
places, and names, and where it was you meant to
travel. None of these will bring any disaster.

I lost my mother's watch. And look! My last, or
next-to-last, of three loved houses went.
The art of losing isn't hard to master.

I lost two cities, lovely ones. And, vaster,
some realms I owned, two rivers, a continent.
I miss them, but it wasn't a disaster.

—Even losing you (the joking voice, a gesture
I love) I shan't have lied. It's evident
the art of losing's not hard to master
though it may look (write it!) like disaster.

> *Yours,*
> *Georgia*

The Story of *The Story of O*

THE STORY OF *The Story of O* is a modern French love story, that is, after a fashion. Dominique Aury (not her birth name, any more than Pauline Réage was) was a middle-aged woman who was experiencing the waning attention of her even older, married lover. Each of them was involved in publishing; he was well known and respected.

READING A LETTER BY KITAGAWA UTAMARO

She cast about, desperately searching for a way of seducing him back. She could not bear to lose him. As she said, "I wasn't young, I wasn't pretty so it was necessary to find other weapons. The physical side wasn't enough. The weapons, alas, were in the head."

Dominique Aury began a series of letters to her lover (not a manuscript, for they were addressed and mailed to him, with no copies kept), depicting the sexual adventures of her fictional alter ego, O. O, who obeys *her* lover blindly. O, who believes her subservience to him is her salvation. Clearly, Aury knew her lover's erotic interests, since O's experiences are not everyone's soufflé.

She said that what pulled her lover back to her was his excitement over the "relationship of the story to her [Aury's] own life." He returned to her (never having completely left), he published her letters as a novel, he returned to her, and stayed until the end of his life. He returned to her.

the book lover

KITAGAWA UTAMARO
(1789–1801)

::

*This print (The Book Lover) is from a series
called "The Eyeglasses of a Watchful Parent,"
made by Utamaro late in his life. His skill
(or desire) at portraying the beauty and nuance
of mood and personality in his "large head
women" reached a kind of limit. And out of this
frustration at the boundaries of picture making,
Utamaro began to write "explanations" of the
emotional and mental states of his models.*

*This series, coming near the end of an artistic
career, was a marriage of pictures and words.*

A CLARIFICATION ON Elodie's time as an *Another Wise Child* contestant. Her life, so far, has not in any way reflected her early promise. She is not surprised: She read somewhere that a genuine child prodigy is one who can "best adults" and not someone who is simply ahead of her age and can "best her peers." A true prodigy, Elodie guesses, is someone who blurs the distinctions of generations.

In any case, her braininess forced her apart from other kids; she was literally pulled from her usual class and placed in a special program in which she was asked, twice a week with two other kids, to go to an unused classroom and encouraged to do whatever she wanted. Though she could be inspired by her solitude at home, this situation did nothing to spark her mind, so she spent the first couple of sessions socializing with her project mates.

The program director told her she would have to begin work on something, and Elodie wanted to say, I didn't ask to be in here, you know, but she stayed quiet.

Her parents bought her very few books; Elodie became an avid library patron. Her parents decided to buy a set of *World Book Encyclopedias*, which they kept in her room; Elodie became an avid encyclopedia reader.

Now she was telling the program director that she would need paint and a raw egg next time. The director said she would provide it, but what was the egg for? Elodie explained she had read about tempera painting and wanted to try it. The egg was supposed to make the paint luminous.

She never *felt* above average, she did not even think in those terms. If asked she would've pointed to a handful of kids she knew, explaining how and why they were smarter, brighter, or more artistically accomplished than she.

This was not false modesty; she was too young to be falsely modest. She believed she was simply identifying the salient points of her world. And because of all this she was always waiting to be found out and told, they were very sorry, but they had made a mistake.

Then, *Another Wise Child* came along and she was on it and she gave up trying to figure it out.

::

HER COLLEGE CAREER was idiosyncratic and eccentric, and though her grades did not reflect anything noteworthy (they looked like the work of someone hovering between barely passing and expulsion), she still had her champions, those professors and teachers who told her she was smart.

She dragged her heels, got distracted from her required work by some other line of inquiry, some other, newly arrived interest, and finally, reluctantly, graduated. She was someone who knew something about any number of things (she was always curious about one thing or another), but it was a shallow knowledge.

When it was too late to rescue her college education, she came to understand something about herself, but by that time she was stuck with a series of jobs, like house-sitting, that did not require degrees.

Sometimes, privately and quietly, she regretted the way in which she had abandoned what she called the thinking part of her. Then she gave up on regret, let those ideas go dormant, and released the past.

ii.

ALL HER LIFE PEOPLE have wanted to tell Elodie things about themselves. Personal things. They often remark, "I can't believe I am saying this to you," because the length of time they have known Elodie doesn't seem to have any effect on their desire to confess to her. She does not invite them to spill their secrets.

They'll say it is because Elodie is friendly, or sensitive, or trust-worthy, or understanding; quite often, they really don't know if she is any of these things. It is as if they wish her to be what they need and that is what she becomes.

If asked, she could tell them why they confide in her: It is because she is willing to hear it. And, even if it is something she doesn't want to know, her curiosity still allows her to listen. It isn't simply listening that loosens people up; you must speak to them in return. To get to the core of what they want to say, Elodie knows, you must offer the illusion of conversation; it is with an exchange that the truth is told, not in the monologue, which is really the ideal place to leave almost anything unsaid.

::

THERE WAS SOMETHING of the voyeur in Elodie, in this regard. And closely following that trait was another one that related to the voyeur: She had a tendency to allow emotional scenes to wash through her quickly, as if, in the midst of everything, a tiny little part of herself stood back and observed the action. It was as if she was thinking, while on the floor with misery, So this is what it feels like.

She did not know if this tendency was encoded in her genes, or if she developed it as a way of staying aloof from any unhappiness in her life.

After she began writing the stories of the habitués of the Youki Singe Tea Room—friends and friends of friends—she understood how well this voyeur, this curious mind, this interest in human behavior and consequences, served her. And as to the part of her that remained uninvolved, she read about a writer who described a similar response to difficult situations as having "a sliver of ice in his heart." This shamed her and intrigued her.

iii.

SHE BEGAN HER HABIT of writing at the Youki Singe Tea Room because she did not feel comfortable leaving her work at home, since she was, in the most literal sense, homeless.

The bartender kept her work behind the bar, in an unused, unlocked safe. There was her notebook, in which she recorded the lives around her and her impressions of the world, in the tradition of a Japanese pillow book. Pillow books go back centuries and centuries in Japan as the forerunners of a Japanese genre known as "random notes." They are kept by the bed, where the owner can record the events of the day, observations and anecdotes. Love. Little bits of daily life.

She also had a sheaf of papers, written on stolen stationery and tied in a Japanese paper folder. They are a series of letters, all written to one person.

Can it be said that one form of writing is more personal than the other? The pillow book is read by Elodie, and no one else. Yet it is full of the lives of those around her, many of whom she cares about a great deal, if for no other reason than her life intersects with their lives, making them a part of one another.

The letters are meant for (and read by) someone other than Elodie, and are deeply intimate.

And both the pillow book and the letters might be read by others one day (there is no way to know what happens to written words)—are they personal or public? Sei Shonagon, the writer of *The Pillow Book of Sei Shonagon,* claimed that her book was meant for no one but her, yet evidence within the writing itself suggests a certain disingenuousness.

Does the work have meaning if it is read by more than a single person? The Japanese believe that a bowl should show the fingerprints of the potter, and that poets should incorporate one another's essence. In *The Universe and the Teacup*, K. C. Cole says that people don't have "sharp edges" that define us, that our breath and hair and skin mixes with others'; that "in a chemical sense we blend in with the people around us like spilled paint." That we cannot help connection. Elodie's unfinished work waits for her at the Youki Singe (completed work waits for no one).

iv.

THERE IS A MAN she met while house-sitting at a very ordinary flat with five cats of varying ages and culinary needs, making mealtimes quite the event. The litter box was the other reason she was hired. The man she met had nothing to do with the house-sit, but she had developed a habit of marking the moments in her life according to her various residences (this man forever associated with the five needy cats).

It is to this man she writes the letters that now lay in the open Japanese paper folder, the ribbon that ties it together undone.

Elodie is in love with this man.

And the letters she writes him form a story.

They are about a girl who has no possessions, no home, no regular job. She is cool and proud. She often has sex in order to have a place to stay, though she is not a prostitute. She is like a *tayu*, a courtesan of Edo Japan, with her elegant finery, musical gifts, artistic ambitions, perfectly calligraphed poems. Poetry and words are the foundation of romance. *Tayu* are idealized figures, treated more like royalty than like streetwalkers. They move with grace and rhythm, singing with the sweetness of a choir.

The girl in the story seduces men and women for their homes and possessions. She provides their fantasies while withholding herself (the one thing they end up fantasizing most about), until they would give up everything in order not to have to give her up.

In the end, she always leaves.

There are sexual acts, some deviant, some uncomfortable, nothing involving minors or pets or specific body effluents—the girl in the story has limits. It is unnecessary to go so far. She is an artist, not a whore.

In the last letter, the girl is bewitching her half brother, the one who received her inheritance as well as his own. She experiences something like a pallid affection for him while also harboring a dislike; he is, after all, *family.*

In the end, the girl leaves and, as always, the heart of each conquest belongs to her while she is utterly empty. She is the girl who has everything and nothing.

The letters in the Japanese folder have been read (sometimes by Elodie to her lover) and returned for more chapters. Elodie's lover looks forward to the adventures of the homeless girl.

Elodie is so in love with this man that her inner thigh bears a temporary tattoo of the ideograph *inochi* ("I love you longer than life; I love you more than life"). For all that is ephemeral in her life, she wants this tattoo made permanent, but not if he is not going to love her back. Not if it turns into a permanent reminder of aloneness.

⠿

ELODIE'S LOVER is older than her and her friends. Elodie is twenty-eight. He has two ex-wives (no children with the first, two with the second). A house in the Seacliff section of San Francisco, and one in the wine country. He attends first nights at the opera (symphony, rock shows, theater, art openings, magazine launches) and dines in good restaurants.

He publishes a slick magazine that covers all things Californian, so he also attends events in Los Angeles (movie premieres and parties).

And he tells her he is drawn to her because she is everything he is not: Unfettered. Fugitive. Able to indulge her whims. He is enamored of the kind of freedom she represents, a freedom he cannot have because it would cancel out other things in his life.

Of course, what he doesn't know and doesn't want to hear is how dangerous this life can be. All the things that can go wrong and are made more serious by the lack of a cushion, a safety net, a margin of error. And how the years can clip by without your realizing it, and how the unattached life is a young person's life; it is a way of living that does not age well.

But he doesn't want to know it. He likes his illusions about it, and so Elodie has had to become even more of what she already was.

He likes sleeping with her in her temporary homes. Says he enjoys the newness of it. For example, not knowing immediately where the bathroom is pleases him.

In exchange, he takes her traveling (not understanding that her life is already a long series of strange beds), buys her clothes, and one or two pieces of stunning jewelry, because he wants to ornament her beautiful body, he says.

He slips her cash. He is kind to her. He likes her ideas and does not seem to tire of her observations of the world and theories about its workings. She makes him laugh. They have a connection of heart and body. He says he loves her mind.

::

ELODIE'S PILLOW BOOK story is about the patrons of the Youki Singe, who are adrift in pleasure. They politely refuse careers, or property, or marriage, or children so as to allow their lives to remain weightless and wind-carried. They sidestep all things long-term, difficult, demanding, and profound. It is the floating world of old Japan; it is Dawn Powell's *Wicked Pavilion*, where the characters of the Café Julien live a life of waiting and the "ruthlessness of peace."

There is something else in Elodie's pillow book story as well. It is so small it can almost be missed: Each story holds the unexpressed, unmistakable wish for something more.

Through her love for the man, Elodie longed for permanence. She craved the everyday, the predictable. She thought about returning to the university and finishing something she'd halfheartedly started. She wanted a life of the mind, and the heart; she wanted gravity and meaning. A shared address. She did not want to give or receive a kind of flip, postmodern ironic unsentimental love; she did not want someone with whom she had An Understanding; she did not want things to last as long as they lasted (even if that is the reality of our lives). She knows nothing can be counted upon, but she wants to give herself over to whatever can be counted upon. She sees this same willingness in her friends, and their friends, who spend their time in the Youki Singe.

Take the story of Max and James, with James so sick, Max's devotion to James having arrived almost too late. It seemed that one day Max discovered how much he loved James, and the next day (figuratively speaking) James discovered his illness. Max promised never to leave him, although James could not return the sentiment. Max was undeterred at the idea of embracing the substance of love, though the physicality of it is as ephemeral as smoke.

She writes this desire into her characters.

v.

ELODIE BEGAN TO FEEL the man leaving her (without actually leaving her). He was distracted; she was losing his attention.

It was not her way to smother, possess, stalk, beg, cajole. No false promises fell from her lips. No threats, no acts of minor violence. Since she did not know what to do, she decided to wait it out and see what happened.

Then it was spring and she was house-sitting the airy house on Buena Vista Avenue—the house in which she most felt at home—and she found the letter that was a poem in the pocket of the blue cashmere overcoat, and was distressed that the house felt like it could be her house, because it meant that the letter could be *her* letter—and she wept.

::

WHEN SHE WAS A CHILD, smaller than the other children, she developed a love for story and a dexterity with words that gave adults the impression she was more mature than she was and spared her the occasional wrath of another child, since she could be clever. Even young, she could listen and play back with verve.

The man she loved, with his magazine (not literary), his own love of books and words (she was acquainted with his mind), might be won back with words. And so she began the letters of the faithless girl who had no home. She made no copies and sent him the originals, which he asked that she read aloud as they lounged in bed in the afternoons, and evenings. He was an enthusiastic listener, always eager for the next installment; still, she could not be sure of him.

vi.

IN ONE LETTER the girl has a formal dinner party with six couples. In the past six months she has known, sexually, all six husbands, has granted their sexual wishes. Tonight at the party she is collecting from each wife a single piece of expensive jewelry, as a kind of party game, she says, although the rules remain vague. The wives laugh nervously as they go along, relinquishing their jewels.

The girl slides a cuff of emeralds up her arm, hangs pure, soft gold and rubies from her ears, pins on pearl-and-diamond brooches, clasps two-tone blue sapphires around her throat. She resumes her place at the head of the table. The other women notice that she is the sole unescorted woman.

"Now," she says, "we will play a game called Auction. Actually, it has a more formal, descriptive title, How Much Is This Piece Worth?" She catches the eye of more than one husband when she says "piece." "It begins now."

The husbands shift uncomfortably, the wives smile a little: *Is she serious? Buy their own jewels back?* Well, they don't think so when, to their surprise, one of the husbands opens the floor. Naturally, they refrain from bidding against one another unless prodded by the girl, who says, "You can do a bit better, I think," turning to another husband to create a bidding war. The amounts increase. Everyone wants to go home with what he brought.

What the men recognize as blackmail, the wives begin to enjoy, clapping their hands, exclaiming, "Oh, we *get* it! This is some kind of fund-raiser!" These are people accustomed to theme balls, high-end raffles, thousand-dollar-a-plate dinners, fairs, celebrity baseball games and golf matches, adopting zoo animals—anything that entertains them. It is as if they cannot part with the cash without some kind of sly bribe.

The girl is reminded of the movie *My Man Godfrey*, in which the socialite's scavenger hunt includes the retrieval of a Forgotten Man. Well, thinks the girl, San Francisco is full of forgotten men. They fill the parks, sit on sidewalks, stand at entrances to banks and buildings and MUNI metro stations. This new administration seems to encourage an undisguised pride in wealth. A sense of ostentation that feels cold and hard and selective. Along with this newfound love of cash (and a refusal to hide the affection) is an indifference to feeling, as well as a subtle message that you are a rube if you succumb to caring. There is a lack of gratitude for good fortune, replaced by a not very attractive sense of entitlement.

When the auction has ended and everyone has been reunited with his or her bijoux (the wives keeping their jewels, the men keeping their secrets), the discomfort of the strange evening doesn't quite dissipate. No one remarks, for instance, Oh this was fun. No one says, We should do it again.

The girl waits until the last person has gone, counts her cash, and is pleased to find much more than she imagined. (She never would've betrayed the husbands.) Living as she does, it could keep her for a while.

But she takes it to her lover's house ("She has a lover?" the man asks. "In every sense of the word," Elodie answers) and bestows it on him.

::

ELODIE'S MAN LOVED the dinner party, saw the humor of the times in it. With each letter the character of the girl's lover was more prominent, and he liked that as well. The girl in the stories wants to give him everything, because his love gives her everything. Without him, she is the girl who has nothing and demands (and gets) everything. Elodie's man likes the themes of freedom and engagement. And what had begun as a longing to see the letters transformed into a wild anticipation to see Elodie. What he said, with a kind of fascinated, pleasurable wonder, was "You and I, we think alike."

Beauty fades. Elodie is young and girlish, but she is not a girl anymore. She will not mourn the impermanence of the physical, if she can find something that lasts. It is the deepening of love that she wants.

The body cannot remain new or unknown, but the mind can constantly change. Change, we are told, is the root of sexual interest, all you need is a little imagination.

vii.

ELODIE LIKES WRITING in the Youki Singe because it is a place with its own, dreamlike atmosphere. Not a bar, not a café, not a restaurant, with its authentic Japanese teahouse, and the kitsch mélange of French and Japanese, or what is perceived by the owner as French and Japanese. She likes that it is a clear manifestation of one person's vision. This gives it a pleasing authenticity, and energy that is uncorrupted by consensus; it is the sensation of being inside one person's thoughts.

For all its flaws, beauty, whimsy, and unabashed obsession, it is one person's masterpiece.

Elodie considers (granted on a different scale): Church's Olana; Sara Winchester's Mystery House; Gaudí's Park Guell; Hearst's Castle, the Taj Mahal, the ceiling of the Sistine Chapel. High and low, they share the same element, which is a reaching for the moon.

The Youki Singe is someone's dream. It allows her entry into her own dream and from that place she writes her letters of love.

TWO PILLOW BOOKS:

the pillow book of sei shonagon &
the pillow book of elodie parker

THE DANDY AND THE MAIDEN:
BEHIND THE SCREEN

::

This picture by Hishikawa Moronobu, done in the late seventeenth century, is one of the erotic genre of pictures called shunga, *or "spring pictures." The season and the act yield pleasures that cannot last for very long, and so must be enjoyed in the moment.*

This particular illustration is the first in an increasingly explicit series of twelve prints. Moronobu's erotic prints' backgrounds often depict "emotional-seasonal allusions associated with classical literature" (Guth), a sort of anchoring of that which can never be truly held.

SEI SHONAGON WAS BORN A LITTLE MORE THAN ONE THOUSAND
years ago, and during the last ten years of the tenth century she was a
lady-in-waiting to an empress. Very little is known about her: her
real name, if she was married, if she had a child, what happened to
her after she left service.

All that is known of her is her *Pillow Book*, and a brief entry in
the diary of Murasaki Shikibu, the author of *The Tale of Genji*. Lady
Murasaki wrote:

> Sei Shonagon has the most extraordinary air of self-
> satisfaction. Yet, if we stop to examine those Chinese writ-
> ings of hers that she so presumptuously scatters about the
> place, we find that they are full of imperfections. Someone
> who makes such an effort to be different from others is
> bound to fall in people's esteem, and I can only think that
> her future will be a hard one. She is a gifted woman, to be
> sure. Yet, if one gives free rein to one's emotions even
> under the most inappropriate circumstances, if one has to
> sample each interesting thing that comes along, people are
> bound to regard one as frivolous. And how can things turn
> out well for such a woman?

Shonagon wrote her pillow book over approximately ten years; it
is composed of anecdotes, opinions, observations, and one hundred
and sixty-four lists with headings like: "When I Make Myself Imagine" or "Distressing Things" or "Elegant Things" or "Outstandingly
Splendid Things."

This book of Shonagon's time at court, distilled into a collection of impressions, and a single paragraph from a contemporary who could think of nothing more to say about her than to wonder if anything worthwhile will come of her, is the sum total of her life.

A paragraph and a diary. Nothing important. A passing remark, and a private book, an evanescent form, that is meant to last as long as its writer. Sei Shonagon wrote, in her final entry:

> I set about filling the notebooks with odd facts, stories from the past, and all sorts of other things, often including the most trivial material. On the whole I concentrated on things and people that I found charming and splendid; my notes are full of poems and observations on trees and plants, birds and insects. I was sure that when people saw my book they would say, "It's even worse than I expected. Now one can tell what she is really like." After all, it is written entirely for my own amusement and I put things down exactly as they came to me.

In a thousand years another young woman will work Shonagon's pillow book into her own: "Things That Arouse a Fond Memory of the Past." "Rare Things." "Things That Lose by Being Painted." "Things That Cannot Be Compared." "Awkward Things."

And anyone can make of that what he will.

::

IT IS LATE SPRING. Elodie is not working today and is sitting with her pillow book—using Shonagon's titles, incorporating some of her words—and her Japanese folder, thick with letters on her stolen stationery, on a curb across the street from the Youki Singe Tea Room.

All the idiosyncratic furnishings and details have been cleared out and carted away: the monkeys, the Eiffel Towers, the snow globes, the obis, the cherry blossoms, the sign CITÉ FALGUIÈRE, the tearoom. It has finally been slated for demolition.

She writes:

Things That Arouse a Fond Memory of the Past

"LAST YEAR'S PAPER FAN. A night with a clear moon."
The Youki Singe Tea Room.
Love.

Rare Things

"A PIECE OF SILK so beautiful one cries in admiration."
A hot night in San Francisco.
A perfect apartment. Two people, who meet in a converted church and fall in love.

Things That Lose by Being Painted

"PINKS, CHERRY BLOSSOMS, yellow roses. Men or women who are praised in romances as being beautiful."
A girl with an empty flat with whom you are in love.

Things That Gain by Being Painted

A GIRL WITH WHOM YOU ARE IN LOVE.

Things That Have Lost Their Power

A MAROONED BOAT. The possibility of disaster. The love you thought would save you.

Things That Fall from the Sky

"SNOW."
A beautiful house on Lake Street.
Love.

Things That Are Distant Though Near

THE POSSIBILITY OF FORGIVENESS.
Love.

Things That Are Near Though Distant

HER DIAMOND BRACELET set like a constellation on the bedside table.
A crescent moon.
Love.

Things That Cannot Be Compared

"WHEN ONE HAS STOPPED LOVING SOMEBODY, one feels he has
become someone else, even though he is still the same person."
Love.

Awkward Things

A BROKEN PROMISE.
Love.

Poetic Subjects

THE POET SHINKEI (1406–1475) said, Unless a verse is by one
whose very being has been transfixed by the truth of impermanence

and change of this world, so that he is never forgetful of it in any cir-
cumstance, it cannot truly hold deep feeling.
Love.

::

ELODIE WATCHES TWO MEN as they peer in the windows of the
deserted Youki Singe. Where will everyone meet? How will they find
one another?

Things That Make the Heart Beat Faster

THE HEAT OF THE DAY. His face in the crowd.
Love.

AUTHOR'S NOTE

Many thanks to the authors listed here for the help and inspiration their work provided during the writing of this book:

Palm of the Hand Stories by Yasunari Kawabata; *The Pillow Book of Sei Shonagon*, trans. and ed. by Ivan Morris; *The Confessions of Lady Nijo*, trans. by Karen Brazell; *The Universe and the Tea Cup* by K. C. Cole; *The Japanese Tattoo* by Donald Richie and Ian Buruma; *Japanese Art* by Joan Stanley Baker; *Duchamp: A Biography* by Calvin Tomkins; *Yoshitoshi's 100 Aspects of the Moon* by John Stevenson; "The Unmasking of O" by John de St. Jorre, *New Yorker* (August 1, 1994); *The Diaries of Dawn Powell, 1931–1965*, by Dawn Powell; *The Wicked Pavilion* by Dawn Powell; *Selected Writings* by Elaine de Kooning; *Ukiyo-e: An Introduction to Japanese Woodblock Prints* by Tadashi Kobayashi; *Utamaro: Portraits from the Floating World* by Tadashi Kobayashi; *Art of Edo Japan* by Christine Guth.

I am grateful to the following museums, galleries, and libraries for allowing me to reproduce the pictures that have been so integral to the story:

The Tokyo National Museum; the British Museum; the Metropolitan Museum of Art; the Luhring Augustine Gallery; Keio University; Carolyn Staley Fine Japanese Prints; the Philadelphia Museum of Art. And I want to thank these people in particular: Stacy Bomento, Akiko Sumihiro, Kenji Ichiko, and the staff at Carolyn Staley.

Thank you, too, to Francesc Parcerisas, Director of the Institucio de les Lletres Catalanes in Barcelona, for awarding me a much appreciated writing grant. Thank you to Iolanda Pelegri, Beth Kuhnlein, and David Parcerisas (for the use of his study). And to Jaume ("not a woman") Subirana for the PEN lunches. And to Katherine Slusher and Jésus Vilallonga for the warmth of their friendship.

I want to mention that as a fiction writer I do, from time to time, bend the facts a little. In this story, which takes place in the early 1980s, I use a photograph of Yasumasa Morimura's that was made in 1988, as well as have my characters refer to K. C. Cole's book *The Universe and the Tea Cup*, which was written rather recently. In case anyone notices and wonders if I noticed, too.

A few more thanks-yous and I will call it a day. So thank you Simone Seydoux, Jan Novotny, Karen Karbo, Stéphanie Abou, Alexia Paul, Leslie Daniels, Benjamin Dreyer, Hee-Jean Kim, and Shelley Silva, who introduced me to the work of Dawn Powell. Also, to Sylvie Rabineau, Joy Harris, and Lee Boudreaux—the three hardest-working women in show business.

And, finally, all my love to John, who really does know how to show a girl a good time.

Suzuki Harunobi. *A Story of Love on the Veranda (Ensaki Mono-gatari)*. Publisher unknown, 1767–1768. Collection of the Tokyo National Museum.

Yoshitoshi. *Full Moon*. Nineteenth century. Courtesy of Carolyn Staley Fine Japanese Prints, Seattle, Washington.

Kitagawa Utamaro. *The Hour of the Ram* and *The Hour of the Dragon* (*Hitsuji no koku, 2:00 p.m.*; and *Tatsu no koku, 8:00 a.m.*). From the series "A Sundial of Maidens (*Musume hidokei*)." Published by Murataya Jirobe, ca. 1795. Tokyo National Museum.

Kitagawa Utamaro. *Hanaogi of the Ogiya; Hinazuru of the Chojiya; Hanazuma of the Hyogoya; Takigawa of the Ogiya* (*Hyogoya-uchi Hanazuma; Chojiya-uchi Hinazuru; Ogiya-uchi Hana, Takigawa*). From the series "A Collection of Beauties at the Height of Their Popularity (*Toji zensei bijin-zoroe*)." Published by Wakasaya Yoichi, ca. 1794. Tokyo National Museum.

Keisai Eisen. *Oiso Station*, from the series "Beauties Along the Tokaido (*Bijin Tokaido: Oiso eki*)." Published by Tsutaya, 1830–1844. Tokyo National Museum.

Kitagawa Utamaro. *Love Deeply Concealed*, from the series "Great Love Themes of Classical Poetry (*Kasen koi no bu: Fukaku shinobu koi*)." Published by Tsutaya Juzaburo, 1792–1793. Tokyo National Museum.

Yoshitoshi. *Lunacy—unrolling letters*, from the series "One Hundred Aspects of the Moon," Nineteenth century. Courtesy of Carolyn Staley Fine Japanese Prints, Seattle, Washington.

Kitagawa Utamaro. *Reading a Letter*, from the series "Utamaro's New Designs for the *Nishiki-e* Print (*Nishiki-ori Utamaro-gata shinmoyo: Fumiyomi*)." Published by Tsuruya Kinsuke, ca. 1801–1804. Copyright © The British Museum.

Kitagawa Utamaro. *The Book Lover*, from the series "The Eyeglasses of a Watchful Parent." Rare Books Room, Keio University Library, Tokyo.

Hishikawa Moronobu. *The Dandy and the Maiden: Behind the Screen (Wakashu to musume: Tsuitate no kage)*. Rare Books Room, Keio University Library. Tokyo.

WHITNEY OTTO is the bestselling author of *How to Make an American Quilt* (which was made into a feature film), *Now You See Her*, and *The Passion Dream Book*.

ABOUT THE TYPE

The text of this book was set in Filo-sofia. It was designed in 1996 by Zuzana Licko, who created it for digital typesetting as an interpretation of the sixteenth-century typeface Bodoni. Filosofia, an example of Licko's unusual font designs, has classical proportions with a strong vertical feeling, softened by rounded droplike serifs. Born in Bratislava, Czechoslovakia, Licko came to the United States in 1968. She is cofounder of *Emigre* magazine.